Rose of Glenkerry

A County Wicklow Mystery

by Robert T. McMaster

UNQUOMONK PRESS
Williamsburg, Massachusetts
U. S. A.

ROSE OF GLENKERRY

www.WicklowMysteries.com

Published by Unquomonk Press, 50 Briar Hill Road, Williamsburg, Massachusetts 01096 USA

ISBN 9781087966793

Dedicated to

Nancy Mosher McMaster

(1954 – 1990)

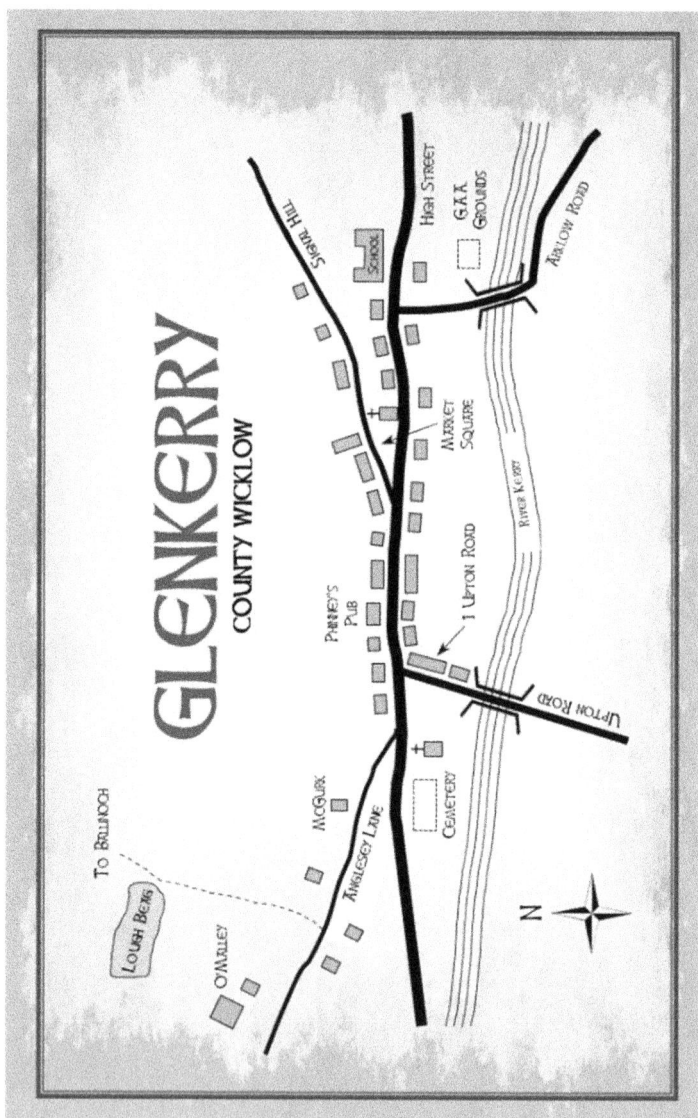

GLENKERRY

COUNTY WICKLOW

CONTENTS

I WILL WALK WITH MY LOVE

I once loved a boy, just a bold Irish boy
who would come and would go at my request;
and this bold Irish boy was my pride and my joy
and I built him a bow'r in my breast.

But this girl who has taken my bonny, bonny boy,
let her make of him all that she can;
and whether he loves me or loves me not,
I will walk with my love now and then.

Traditional Irish love poem

1

DUBLIN AND BEYOND

Cary McGurk stood outside a pub on O'Connell Street in Dublin at half six of a Saturday evening in early June. He'd been waiting nearly twenty minutes and a light rain was just beginning to fall. He stepped into the entryway out of the rain to check his mobile for messages. There were none.

Siobhan Sullivan had texted him that afternoon and invited him for a pint. He was knackered* and would rather be home in bed, but she had something to tell him–some news–some important news. Cary was weighing his options. Should he head home?

She's always late–give her a few more minutes, mate.

Just as he was about to give up and start for home, he heard a familiar voice.

'Cary.'

It was Siobhan waving as she made her way across the busy thoroughfare. When she reached him, she smiled as she always did, hugged him, which she sometimes did, and apologised, which she did when she was late, which she so often was.

Siobhan had come straight from her part-time job as receptionist at a small hotel a few blocks away, still in her work kit, a black skirt and white cotton blouse with a gold silk scarf wrapped around her neck.

'I got tied up at work. Last minute stuff.' She looked into his eyes apologetically. 'I'm so sorry.'

Cary shrugged it off. 'No worries. What else am I doin', anyway?'

Siobhan Sullivan was tall, brunette, with bright hazel eyes flecked with gold. She was American, although like so many Americans she had Irish roots–that is if you counted roots that were more than a century-and-a-half old. She had arrived in Dublin three years ago to attend Dublin City University. She and Cary met at a party at the home of a mutual friend that first year, then ran into one another again and again around the DCU campus until they felt like old friends.

Over the next two years they met often for drinks and light meals, went to concerts, and watched movies at his flat or hers, sometimes alone, sometimes with classmates. They were friends, friends who hung out, friends who enjoyed each other's company, but just friends. When they were together, they carefully avoided mention of one another's love lives. Neither it seemed wanted to know those kinds of details. Why, if they spent so much time together and enjoyed each other's company, had they remained just friends? It was a question Cary asked himself often.

That's just what it is, mate. Friends. Full stop.

Wherever she went, Siobhan was always the centre of attention. Men and women alike could not keep their eyes off her as she spoke, those flashing eyes, those lips that never stopped smiling, and that American accent that provided endless amusement to Irish ears, a delightful counterpoint to the voices of their countrymen and women.

Ask Siobhan what it was like being an American in Dublin and you were in for a real treat.

'Before I came to Dublin,' she told a group of uni friends one night at a popular campus watering hole, 'all I knew were those stupid stereotypes about the Irish–leprechauns, rainbows, pots of gold, yeh know? And I thought all the Irish ever ate was corn beef and cabbage, 24-7. Then I get here and I can't believe all the different foods–Indian, Laotian, Cape Verdean, Italian, Scandinavian, Estonian, Szechuan, Cantonese, Hunan. Do you know I heard that in Wexford Town there's a Mexican restaurant called Wex-Mex? How hilarious is that?' Everyone laughed.

But Siobhan could get some laughs at the expense of her Irish friends as well. 'One thing Ireland lacks is a good American style burger. They have no idea what a real burger on a bun is like. The first time I ordered a burger here, I asked for medium-rare. The waitperson acted like she'd never heard of such a thing before. She goes, "Well, like, it's already cooked, yeh know, in a big pan?" I thought to myself, Siobhan, this is not gonna end well. What I got was meat loaf.' Everyone roared.

Siobhan could be equally voluble regarding Irish notions of Americans. 'Cary here is always ordering Budweiser for me, like that's the only beer we Americans drink. And there was this little boy in a school in Phibsborough where I used to volunteer–when he heard I was American, what was the first thing he wanted to say to me? "Miss," he says with a long face, "I'm so sorry about Michael Jackson." Like Michael Jackson was a personal friend of mine.' Again everyone laughed long and loud.

But the tone this evening was entirely different. It was early yet and the place was quiet–the younger crowd, the boisterous and rowdy eighteen- and nineteen-year-olds, had not yet arrived. They found a small table by the window and Cary ordered two pints, a Guinness for himself and, of course, a Budweiser for Siobhan. Plus a platter of scampi fries.

He looked at Siobhan. In the muted light her face was lovely, her skin satiny and tan, her dangly gold earrings brought out the flecks in her eyes.

'Shiv, you look so nice all dressed up, you make my baggy Dockers and T-shirt seem a little bit outta place.'

Siobhan blushed, then flashed that smile. It was a beguiling smile, Cary had to admit to himself. But tonight her smile was exceptionally wide, her eyes had a particular sparkle, her face a certain glow. She was excited about something, he could tell.

'So, what's up?'

She looked into his eyes, those dark, deep-set, soulful, puppy eyes. And his hair, dark brown and wavy, usually on the long side since he refused to pay Dublin prices for a haircut. He definitely was not the typical college lad who wanted only to mimic all his male classmates–Cary's look was all his own. And there was no guise there, no pretence–Cary McGurk never pretended to be anything he wasn't.

Siobhan inhaled once, loudly, for emphasis. 'Car, I am so stoked–I couldn't wait to tell you.' She paused.

'Well, give it up then,' he said with a dimpled grin.

'I got a job. The *perfect* job, Car, the *absolute perfect* job.'

Cary smiled a broad smile. 'Shiv, that's grand. Is this the one in Cork with that wind energy company?'

Siobhan made a face like she'd tasted some bad cheese. 'Oh, no, thank God–I would've hated that.'

'What then, the one with the e-tailer in Belfast?'

She blushed. 'I can't believe I even applied for that–no, not that one either.'

'Right then, enough of the twenty questions–spill.'

She drew another deep breath. 'It's a little start-up company that designs software for web-based businesses, mostly user interfaces, but they're doing really creative things. You know, multichannel retailing, links to social media, voice activation, all kinds of slick animation. And they want me to work directly with customers, what they call a Client Service Specialist, to try to improve the user experience.' She paused, her jaw dropping. 'Can you imagine? It's like my dream job, Cary. It really is.'

'Wow, that is grand, Shiv–it's brilliant.'

Just then their pints arrived. And the scampi fries.

'Well, this calls for a toast,' said Cary. And they lifted their glasses and clinked them.

'*Sláinte*,' he said, 'to Siobhan Sullivan, Client Service Specialist– soon to be CFO or CEO of–what's it called?'

'Greater London Software Systems.'

Cary stopped sipping and set his glass on the table, his eyes riveted on hers.

'London? You mean London, as in England? Buckingham Palace–Carnaby Street–that London?'

'Yes, Cary, that London. Isn't it amazing?'

She could see a vague look in his eyes, as if he was trying to take in and process this news.

'I did all my interviewing on Zoom so I haven't even seen the place in person, but they took me on a video tour. It's really beautiful. My office will have this incredible view of the city. When I'm there, that is. They say I should be able to work from home two or three days a week. How awesome is that?'

He nodded, his eyes wide. It was awesome, for sure.

'Have some scampi fries?' offered Cary, pushing the plate toward her.

Siobhan declined, then took another sip of her Bud.

'And Cary, you are not gonna believe my salary.' His jaw dropped. It was way more than any job he'd ever aspired to–or even dreamed of, for that matter. And here she was, just about to graduate university.

'That is unbelievable, Shiv.'

'When the guy told me I had to ask him to repeat it. I mean, I could not believe it.'

Suddenly Cary's delight at his friend's good fortune presented its darker side, an unsightly underbelly of jealousy. He of course hid that, buried it, covered it with an especially wide smile and another pull on his Guinness.

Happy for her, right?

'Congratulations, mate. You deserve it, you totally do. I mean, look at how hard yeh've worked these last three years.'

Siobhan nodded and smiled but blushed. 'I'm sorry, I've been going on about me and this job. I'm just so buzzed. So, what's up with your job hunt? Any news?'

Cary shook his head. 'Not really. Yeh know, journalism's not exactly hot these days, especially print journalism. It's like the *worst possible time* to be looking for a newspaper job,' he said with a grimace. 'Except for advertising. If I'm willing to write advert copy, there are jobs, but they're crap jobs for crap pay. I'd be earnin' like a fraction–a tiny fraction of what you'll be getting.'

Siobhan reached across the table, touching the back of his hand briefly. 'Something will break for you, mate, I'm sure of it.'

Cary shrugged. Then Siobhan hesitated, biting her lip as if unsure of what she was about to say.

'Listen, Car, I've been thinking about something. How about if you come to London, too? We could find a two-bedroom flat. And I'd cover the rent until you got a job. Which you will so get in London.' Her face lit up. 'I mean, it's the business capital of the world, right?'

Cary was momentarily speechless, gazing out the window as he contemplated this idea—moving away from Ireland, his homeland, to one of the biggest cities in the world? And moving with Siobhan Sullivan? And sharing a flat with her? A flat that she was willing to pay for until he had a job—and even then how much could he afford to chip in once he had a job, that hypothetical crap job, whatever it turned out to be?

Siobhan could tell her friend was having a hard time grasping the idea.

'So, whatta you think, Car? Tick yes?' Her eyes were like saucers now, a shadow of doubt creeping across her face as she awaited his reaction.

Cary shook his head.

'I–I don't know, Shiv. That's a–a lot to digest, yeh know?'

Siobhan knew Cary well, and she knew that kind of digestion– cognitive processing she liked to call it–was slow for him.

No, not slow, downright glacial.

Even decisions that seemed small to her took him days, sometimes weeks. Like the time he bought that new rug for his flat. It was beige, no pattern, no design…

No anything to get hung up on, right?

And yet he spent nearly two weeks walking around that rug on his bedroom floor, keeping it clean in case he decided to return it. And even when he finally made the decision to keep the rug, he still brooded over it for the longest time, wondering aloud whether he'd made the right decision. No two ways about it, Cary McGurk was a faffer.

She said, 'Well, just think about it, okay? No pressure.'

'Does this mean you'll be leavin' right after grad?'

Siobhan nodded, her mouth drooping Buster Keaton style. 'Yeah, they want me to start A-S-A-P.'

An uncomfortable silence fell over the pair. They took several pulls on their pints before Siobhan broke the ice.

'Listen, Ciaran.'

Uh-oh, red flag, her calling you Ciaran–prepare yourself, mate.

'Now, don't think that, because we'd be living together, that–well–you know, there'd be expectations–it'd just be an arrangement of convenience between two friends. Right?'

Cary nodded. 'Oh yeah–yep–sure,' he said with a casual shrug.

Right–a course–what else?

After another round, Cary walked Siobhan to her flat just a few blocks away.

'Hey, some friends are coming by at nine,' said Siobhan. 'We'll probably go to Twenty's. Come along?'

Twenty's was a popular club near campus, and Cary knew it well enough. But he had learned to be wary of such invitations. Once when he first knew Siobhan, she had invited him to go to that club with 'friends.' As it turned out, he was the only bloke there. It felt like Girls' Night Out, the unspoken assumption being that he would fit right in. How emasculating was that? So he politely declined. He had laundry to do. And ironing.

You are probably the last guy in Dublin who does ironing, mate–and on a Saturday night?

As they parted, he promised he would think over the London proposition. And think it over he did, all the way home, and once at home then far into the night. He sat in front of the telly snacking on bacon fries and Club Orange, half-watching an old episode of 'Derry Girls' while contemplating his future. And then, in bed, still wide awake, he brooded.

He had to admit to himself that the London idea was tempting. Siobhan was right–the job situation would be much better for a journalist wannabe in London than in Dublin. It worried him, of course, the idea of pulling up stakes and moving away, out of Ireland, without a job. But, he reasoned, if it didn't work out, he could always come back, back to Ireland, back to Dublin.

And then there was the offer of a shared flat–that was hard to turn down. He had a sense that he and Siobhan would be good flatmates. They were compatible in so many ways, their interests, tastes in food, music, even sport. Somehow, she had developed a genuine passion for Gaelic football. They had watched several footie matches together and she had quickly become a devoted follower of the Dublin team known as the Dubs.

Who coulda predicted that?

One thing rankled him, though, like an earworm in his skull, or maybe lower. It was the thought of Siobhan Sullivan welcoming other blokes to their flat, stepping out with them, even bringing one back to spend the night, while he sat alone in his room like some pathetic lonely loser. True, they were just friends, he and Siobhan, but how would he feel about watching her social life, her love life, heat up before his very eyes? Of course, she must have thought the same about having him as a flatmate, but if she had, it apparently presented no obstacle for her.

We are, after all, just friends, right?

One more consideration–his parents. Patrick and Catherine McGurk lived in Glenkerry, a little town in County Wicklow, just twenty miles or so south of Dublin. His father had been owner and publisher of a small newspaper, *The Glenkerry Gazette*, for nearly thirty years. But like so many print publications, the *Gazette* had lost the battle with online news sources and social networking. The final issue went to press about five years ago. Since then Patrick had been working in the office of a brewery in Bray. Cary's mother, Catherine, once an operating room nurse in a Dublin hospital, gave up her job before the birth of their first child, Aiden, and never returned to work outside their home.

Aiden, now twenty-five, had moved to New Zealand after university, and there was little prospect of his returning to the Old Sod any time soon. But Patrick and Catherine still harboured the hope that their second child would one day come back to Glenkerry, or at least live close enough to visit his parents now and then.

Siobhan had travelled to Glenkerry with Cary for a weekend the previous summer, and not surprisingly, his parents were besotted with her. Ever since that weekend, his mother referred to her as that 'sweet little colleen,' regaling Cary with pleas for a return visit. And inevitably whenever he called or visited, she would probe him for news of Siobhan and what she imagined was an ever-deepening relationship. Which it was not. And Cary told her as much.

But does she listen?

So breaking the news of his move to London, if he decided to make the move, would be painful. In fact, as he weighed the decision, he began to see his parents' opposition as the biggest obstacle to overcome.

Cary shared a small, sparsely furnished two-bedroom flat in Glasnevin with another DCU student, Niall. The living room walls were decorated with posters of their favourite bands, Green Day, the Cranberries, the Saw Doctors. Cary's bedroom wall bore a photo of his DCU rugby team and two large posters, one a guide to 'Fishes of the Irish Sea,' the other a full-length portrait of Van Morrison with one of the Irish legend's most famous lines scrawled along the edge: 'Go up to the mountain, go up to the glen, where silence will touch you, and heartbreak will mend.'

On his bedside table stood a small watercolour on a wooden stand. It was a view of Glenkerry, a row of brightly-coloured houses set against a backdrop of emerald green pastures above, dark blue waters below, all in subtly shaded pastels. Inscribed in the lower right corner and visible only to the discerning eye among the rippling waves were the initials 'RO.'

Early the next morning, a Sunday, Cary stepped from his flat wearing a rugby shirt, sweatpants, and trainers, and went for a long run. It took him south a few k's to the Royal Canal, then east along the tow path for several more. Fishermen were seated on the banks, their lines hanging lazily in the quiet waters. Ducks and a few swans paddled silently along, briefly following him in hopes of a handout. After several more k's, he stopped and stood in the warm June sun, stretching his legs.

He was warming to the London idea, he admitted to himself, but he hated to present it to his parents as a fait accompli. He would have to talk to them first, before making any decision.

Maybe, he reasoned, his mother would see the move as a step forward in his relationship with Siobhan.

Which it is not. But maybe she'll see it that way.

As he started his return run his mobile vibrated, but he was in the running zone and decided to wait until he got home. Just a few blocks from his flat, he ran into Siobhan. Smiling, he pulled out his earbuds.

'I was just about to call round, mate,' she said.

'Yeah, I decided to have a run,' replied Cary, trying to catch his breath, 'along the canal.'

'Good day for it, eh? Not too warm, not too cool.'

Cary nodded, still huffing. After a few seconds, his breathing close to normal, he stood, hands on hips, flexing his leg muscles.

'Today's Whitsunday, Shiv–the seventh Sunday after Easter. A lotta people think this day is unlucky–they stay at home to avoid accidents and ward off evil spirits.'

'I suppose it's also a bad day to make big decisions?'

Cary chuckled. 'I haven't decided about London, Shiv, if that's what yeh're wonderin'.'

'Okay, I understand–it's big–real big–and you need time. No rush, Car.'

'Listen. I wanna do it–I really do. It would be scary, a little risky, but I need to learn to take risks now and then. I know I do.'

Siobhan was smiling.

'But…'

Her smile quickly faded. 'But what?'

'It's my olds. I hate to spring it on 'em just like that. I might have to make a trip to Glenkerry and talk to them face to face.'

Siobhan was disappointed, try though she might not to show it. Secretly she had her suspicions that this was just a delaying tactic, putting off a decision–more faffing.

'Maybe next weekend?' he asked warily.

Siobhan's forehead wrinkled. 'But my job starts in a fortnight. So we need to leave by next weekend, take the ferry to Holyhead, then rail to London. I Facetimed with my friend Ellen in Camden last night. She says we can stay with her while we look for a place of our own. But it's gotta be next weekend, Car.'

'Yeah, okay, yeh're right. I'll talk to Ma and Pa tonight. Sunday night's usually when I call 'em, anyway.'

Siobhan was relieved. 'That would be grand. And if they're okay with it, you're okay?'

Cary bit his lip, then nodded. 'I think so, Shiv.'

She hugged him, the way she did. 'I'm excited, mate, really excited. Call me, or text me, after you talk to your parents, okay?'

Cary nodded and smiled. 'Yep, will do.'

'Well then, guess I'll see you at grad.'

Graduation–in two days–God, everything's happening so fast, mate.

Back at his flat, Cary showered, then made himself tea, trying to be as quiet as possible for the sake of his flatmate who was snoring loudly from his bedroom only a few feet away. Niall was a business major in his second year at DCU. He was a big fellow, several inches taller than Cary, heavy set. When he snored, the walls of that little flat shook.

As Cary sat sipping his tea, he remembered the call he got while running. He stepped into the front hallway, picked up his mobile, and found a voicemail message from his mother.

It was graduation day at DCU. Siobhan was standing with a group of her business classmates, all in black robes and cream-coloured hoods, waiting for instructions to queue up for the ceremony. She was talking and laughing with her friends, all the while watching for some sign of Cary. The journalism majors were assembled a short distance away wearing white hoods; she recognised several of them from parties and other social events she had attended with Cary over the last few months. But he was not among them.

Finally, a steward spoke to the group, instructing them to queue up and prepare to march. As Siobhan took her place, she shot one last glance toward the journalism majors, hoping to see Cary. No sign of him. Just then her mobile vibrated. They had been warned to turn off mobiles during the ceremony, but when she saw who the call was from, she answered it.

'Where are you, Car? We're just starting to march.'

'I'm in Glenkerry.' His voice sounded weak.

'What? But you're gonna miss…'

'It's my da, Shiv. He died. Last night. In hospital. His heart.'

'Oh, Car, no.' She stepped out of the queue and walked away, hoping to find a quieter place.

'Ma called me, Sunday morning. She said he had a bad night so she dialled 9-9-9.'

'Siobhan, come on, we're marching,' rang out a voice that Cary could hear over the phone in the distance.

'Go, Shiv, get your parchment. Have a great day. Talk later.'

'Car–I am so sorry. Patrick was a good father, I know he was.'

Cary's voice cracked. 'Yeah, he was.'

'I'm comin' down to Glenkerry, straightaway after the ceremony. Okay?'

'Okay, Shiv.'

'See you soon, Car. All my love–to you and your ma.'

2

THE BRIGHT SIDE OF THE ROAD

Glenkerry is a town of barely 2000 residents in the southern part of County Wicklow. Wicklow has long been known as the Garden of Ireland, and if that is so, then Glenkerry is the perennial border of Wicklow, every cottage yard bristling with colour–daffodils, iris, and violets in spring, poppies, roses, and foxglove in summer, asters, astilbes, and chrysanthemums in autumn. The village itself consists of a few dozen buildings of granite or slate along the High Street housing little shops, a pharmacy, a tailor, a grocer, a fish store, and at least a half dozen small restaurants, many of them featuring exotic foods from faraway lands.

Spanned by a high stone bridge, the River Kerry runs through the village before winding its way toward the Irish Sea barely six miles distant. At very high tide each month you can tell the river is tidal from the sulphurous scent of briny seawater and decomposing sea detritus that hangs in the air.

Surrounding Glenkerry are pastures, mostly in sheep but some dairy cows and a few horses. And there are fields of barley and corn as well, each crop with its own signature colour and texture to the discerning eye. Narrow lanes lined with wild foxglove and fuchsia diverge from the main thoroughfare up the hillsides between the stonewalls, marking off the pastureland in a neat grid.

Anyone comparing Glenkerry today with a century-old photograph must be struck by how few changes are evident. Of course, there are some new houses along the main roads and several large school buildings of recent origin. The shops in the village now include an espresso stand, a day spa, and a computer shop. And farm vehicles still rumble up and down the roads–huge harvesters, combines, tractors pulling haywains–though nowadays such muscular vehicles must thread their way among Priuses, Volkswagens, Skodas, and Hyundais.

The funeral for Patrick McGurk was held at St. Brigid's Church in Glenkerry. It was well-attended. Patrick was remembered fondly here, as a boy, as a young man, but more recently as editor and publisher of *The Glenkerry Gazette*, the newspaper he started when he was just a few years out of university. Father Desmond gave the eulogy, reminding the congregation of the life of this man, his many qualities as a son, husband, father, friend, newspaperman, and Catholic.

After Mass Cary stood outside the church with his mother and several aunts and uncles, greeting people, thanking them, and reminding them of the afterparty that would take place at the family home on Anglesey Lane. Siobhan Sullivan was present but stood apart, not wanting to intrude on the family while they spoke to friends. When Catherine saw her all alone, she spoke to Cary: 'Son, ask Siobhan to come and stand with us, why don't you?'

Which he did and she took up a position next to him at the end of the queue, greeting people after the family and introducing herself as a friend of Cary's from Dublin.

Except for the summer after his first year when Cary lived at home and worked for a haulage company, it had been three years since he had spent much time in Glenkerry. So he found himself caught up at length with nearly everyone he saw, telling them about university, about Dublin, about the trials and tribulations of his DCU rugby team, and introducing them to Siobhan. There were his parents' friends, his father's business associates, and a few of Cary's old classmates from secondary school–John O'Neill, heading to med school, Sarah Healey, creche teacher soon to be married, and Delbert Samuels, now Garda Samuels.

At last the line of well-wishers dwindled down to just one, a young woman in a dark pleated skirt and white blouse standing alone and looking uneasy. It was Roisin O'Malley. She was slight, her face pale with many freckles, green eyes, and long red hair that glistened in the sunlight. She had never been one for broad, toothy smiles, recalled Cary, and today she was even more subdued than he remembered her. She stepped up to him, tilting her head as she spoke.

'Hello, Car,' she said softly. Tears welled up in her eyes.

Cary stood awkwardly for a moment. 'Rosie,' he said softly. Then he held out his arms and drew her to him.

'I'm sorry, Car, I am so sorry,' she said into his ear. Cary nodded as they separated. 'He was a good man, your da.' Again he nodded. 'Everyone should have a da like 'im.' She winced as she spoke those words, just barely keeping her composure.

At that moment Cary was far away, walking with that self-same lass along the River Kerry one summer's day five years earlier, admiring her softness, her shy, sweet way, all the time conscious of that air of melancholy that seemed to drape around her like a shroud.

Sweet memories, mate, sweet but sad.

Then he remembered Siobhan. 'Rosie, I'd like you to meet Siobhan, Siobhan Sullivan, a classmate from DCU. Shiv, this is Rosie O'Malley, an old friend from Glenkerry, and a classmate at *Coláiste Gaeilge,* our secondary school.'

Siobhan smiled, then reached out and shook Rosie's hand. 'Pleasure meeting you, Rosie. Thanks for coming today. It means a lot to Cary and his family.'

'Siobhan read Global Business at uni. And she's goin' to London next week to start a killer job.'

Rosie smiled. 'London, so. Congratulations, Siobhan.'

'Yeah, well, it's very exciting, but we'll see. It's an awfully big town, at least compared to Dublin.'

'But Siobhan grew up in Los Angeles,' added Cary, implying that she could handle London.

They all laughed. Siobhan blushed. 'Well, I don't know as growing up in LA necessarily prepares you for life in London. I may crash and burn.'

Cary shook his head. 'Siobhan is amazing, Rosie–she'll succeed wherever she ends up, count on it.'

'So, Rosie, where are you these days?' asked Siobhan.

Rosie shrugged modestly, raising both hands, palms up. 'Right where I always been–in Glenkerry.'

'You workin' now, Rosie?' asked Cary.

She shook her head. 'Not really a job. I'm takin' care of my da. He's been poorly for some time now. Won't see a doctor–quacks, 'e calls 'em.'

'Well, he's lucky to have you, I'd say,' replied Siobhan. She was about to ask about Rosie's mother but thought better of it.

'Well, I'll let you lot get going. Sounds like you'll be busy at 'ome.'

'Yeh're coming, right?' asked Cary. 'Good *craic*, Rosie, for sure. Maybe some old friends.'

'I don't know, depends on how my da's doin'. I'll try to get away for a while.'

As they walked to the car, Siobhan said, 'Rosie's sweet, eh?'

Cary nodded. 'Yeah, she is.'

'So, history–you two?'

'Well, at one time, yeah. But mostly just friends.'

'Did she go to uni?'

'Nah, the old man nixed it–said he needed her at home. A shame–she wanted to go to art school in Dublin–but that old buzzard wouldn't have it.'

'That's so sad.'

'She's like a caged bird in that house, I swear,' said Cary.

'What about her mother? I hesitated to ask.'

'Yeah, well, that's just as well. I'll tell you later.'

Caged bird–yep, that's Rosie, all right.

The McGurk home was a modern, one-storey house set on Anglesey Lane a short distance from the centre of Glenkerry, looking down on the village. It had many windows that afforded lovely views of green pastures and, in the distance, a glimpse of the River Kerry. Their neighbours had sheep, but the McGurk property was devoted to flower gardens, especially a rose garden at the back that was Catherine McGurk's particular pride and joy. They had recently installed a hot tub on the deck at the rear of the house and Catherine had just put in a flower bed around it so that you could have a soak while resting your eyes on lilies, foxglove, monkshood, and hollyhock.

When he and his mother returned from the church, Cary walked out into the pasture behind the house. He had fond memories of this place, especially in late spring and early summer when the gorse, eyebright, and pasture rose were in their glory and the skylark and meadow pipit were singing from the fenceposts. As a young lad he couldn't go outside in summer much because of his asthma. Back then, as soon as he stepped out the door, he'd begin wheezing and sneezing, then feel that tightening in his chest that was a warning. He'd retreat inside, take a few breaths on his inhaler, then lie on his bed reading or watching the telly. But miraculously those troubles subsided in his teens which was when he came to appreciate what it meant to be able to stroll a few minutes from his door, gaze across endless pastures, smell the sweet scents of summer, and listen to the birdsong. His favourite time was lambing season in March and April when the neighbour's ewes started popping. Within days of birth the new-borns could be seen bouncing around the pasture as if they came equipped with springs on their little hooves.

Good memories of an Irish boyhood, mate.

As he walked across the pasture toward his favourite spot, Cary realised that something was missing. It was a tree, an old, wizened hawthorn with gnarly bark. It had been bent low by an ice storm decades ago so that if he sat on a certain boulder the lower branches framed his view of Glenkerry. But where that tree had stood now there was only a stump, recently sawn clean at its base.

He stood for a moment thinking of that old tree, how much a part of the place it had always been to him, and now suddenly gone. He sat on the boulder looking out on the village, then buried his face in his hands and sobbed.

The caterers were busy setting up tables of food under a tent in the yard, mostly tiny sandwiches and finger food, sweets of all sorts, and lots of drink–lager, stout, wine, shandies, mixed drinks. A small combo of local musicians was seated in a circle, a fiddle, a tin whistle, an accordion, and a harp, warming up. When someone asked them when they rehearsed, the fiddler smiled: 'This is it, my friend.'

The band started out a little ragged, but gradually the music improved, or maybe it just seemed to improve with the quantity of alcohol consumed. As the afternoon wore on the tunes got livelier. Then the dancing began.

Siobhan had heard of Irish wakes. This wasn't technically a wake, this was an after-funeral party for the deceased, and despite the sadness of the occasion, she was enjoying every minute of it. She had changed from the long black dress she wore at the church to a short plaid skirt and a white blouse. One of the older single men, Chester Doyle, asked her to dance and Cary watched as the pair spun around, Siobhan's colourful skirt swirling up as she twirled. Then he looked beyond the dancers and spied Rosie O'Malley, standing appropriately enough in his mother's rose garden.

He took a shandy from the drinks table and brought it to her.

'Hey,' he said, 'glad you could make it.'

'I can't stay for long but I wanted to say hi again, maybe talk to your ma. She's such a sweet lady, I hate to see 'er sad.' Just then she looked out across the crowd and exclaimed, 'Oi.' It was Cary's mother, being swung about by old Billy Chandler. He had to be eighty if he was a day, but he could still dance a jig or a reel with the best of them.

'Well, she's doin' okay, as you can see,' noted Cary with a grin. 'But I'm sure there will be some dark days still for her,' he added, thinking ahead.

Yeah, mate, not just for her.

'Siobhan's nice, yeah?'

Cary nodded in agreement.

'How long you two been together?'

'Oh, well, we've been mates for three years, since we were first-years at DCU.'

'Mates, eh?'

'Yeah,' replied Cary. Their eyes met. 'Really, just mates. Good mates.'

'What's all this 'mates' business about? You two sound like a coupla Aussies.'

Cary chuckled. 'Yeah, well, so many of our friends at DCU were from Down Under, and they were all like "mate" this, "mate" that, "crikey," and "blimey." Pretty soon we were all talkin' like Aussies or Kiwis.'

Rosie chuckled. 'So what's next for Ciaran McGurk, B.A.?'

'Well, I'm meant to go to London with Siobhan, look for a job, ideally a newspaper job. We're leavin' in a few days.'

'Wow, that's exciting.'

'Yeah, exciting. Except for the fact that newspapers are the new dinosaurs, yeh know? Soon they'll be extinct–and so will would-be newspaper journalists–like me.'

'Oh, I bet yeh'll find your niche, Car. I'm sure of it.'

'Well thanks, Rosie, but I'm not so sure. And now, this...' He

paused, nodding toward the gathering for his father. 'It's been a bit
of a shock, yeh know? Took the wind outta my sails.'

'Yeah, a course,' replied Rosie. 'It's bound to set yeh back a bit,
eh? But you'll carry on.'

They both stood watching the festivities for several minutes in
silence. Then Cary took a breath and spoke softly.

'Hey, Ma tells me your mom left town. Where's she gone?'

A pallor spread across Rosie's face and her chin trembled. She
shook her head.

'Rosie, what is it?'

She turned away from the crowd to hide her tears.

'I know she's been unhappy for a long time. She finally decide
she'd had enough?'

Now Rosie was crying and she started walking away. 'I gotta
go,' she said through her tears. 'Tell your ma I'll call round in a few
days.'

'Wait, Rosie, lemme walk you 'ome, eh?' She stopped. 'Gimme
one sec.'

Cary found his mother and told her Rosie was in a bad way
and he should see her home. But he wouldn't be any time at all.
Then Cary and Rosie walked side-by-side without a word, up the
lane toward Anglesey Hill.

As they approached Rosie's house, they both knew that he
must go no farther–that his presence was not welcome, ever, not in
that house, not on that property–thus decreed Rosie's father, Harry
O'Malley, some five years earlier when he and Rosie were sixteen.

So much is unsaid between us, mate, you could write a book.

And that book started–and ended–right in this lane, not too
many years ago. They had been friends since toddlers, playing
together in his yard or hers. When they entered secondary school,

they rode the bus together from the village centre. And very gradually the relationship changed. They often strolled together and several times took long hikes along the Wicklow Way, Cary's father depositing them at one trailhead, then meeting them hours later at another miles away. Out there, high on the rugged Wicklow Mountains, they felt free to be themselves, free from Harry O'Malley's hostile leers, free from the fishbowl world of Glenkerry.

At the end of Fifth Year was the Debs, the big social event of the year, a formal dance–pretty girls in long gowns with serious hairdos, gawky lads in tuxedos with cummerbunds and boutonnieres in their lapels. Cary wanted to ask Rosie, but he was nervous, of course. Then one afternoon as they disembarked from the bus and walked together up the lane, he mustered his courage and spoke. He'd been rehearsing his line for days: Was she going to the Debs, he had asked. If you will ask me, she answered. Cary nodded, Rosie nodded, they joined hands, and the deed was done. Cary recalled how his pulse settled down then for the first time in days.

But it was not meant to be. As soon as Rosie's father got wind of the assignation, he put an end to it. Not with that boy, not with any boy, yeh hear me? Rosie was heartbroken. Her mother consoled her but refused to intervene on her behalf. And Rosie's disappointment turned to anger at her father. When she told Cary she couldn't attend, he too was disappointed and angry. Their meetings from then on had to be surreptitious. He went off to a sport camp that summer and when he returned, by some unspoken mutual agreement they reverted to the friend zone. But truth be told, it was only when Cary headed off to uni the following year that he found some measure of relief from the pain of that forced separation.

They stopped and stood in the lane. Finally, Rosie seemed prepared to talk.

'Ma left, about a month ago now. A couple days before I took the bus to Wicklow for a dentist appointment. When I got back to Glenkerry, she was standin' there on the footpath as I stepped off the bus. She told him she was goin' to the market, but she wanted to see me outta his sight. That's how scared she was.'

'She told me she was plannin' to leave soon. She didn't have to explain, I understood. I told her more than once she should go, but she stayed, mostly for me, and for Buddy. She told me she couldn't say when she was leavin' or where she was goin', that the less I knew the better. She didn't want Pa thinkin' I had anything to do with it.'

Rosie sat down on the grassy slope and buried her face in her hands. Finally, she looked up at Cary.

'But she promised me she'd keep in touch. She said she'd bought a mobile. Can you believe it? My ma–with a mobile phone? I swear she's the lowest-tech person in Ireland. Anyway, she promised she would text me and arrange to meet. And she gave me a phone, one of those, whataya call 'em, prepays? She told me to hide it away, so that Pa could never find it. She figured, if he did, he'd find out where she was and come after her.'

'She's really frightened of him, isn't she?'

Rosie nodded, biting her lip. None of this was exactly new to Cary. Even back in primary school, he knew that Rosie's home life was fraught. For a time her health took a bad turn, though he never knew any details. Then after the Debs debacle it was clear that she hated her father.

Back then Cary was young and naïve and never stopped to

consider the possible meaning of all that. They had both pretended all was, well, rosy. But he was older now, and wiser, and pretending was no longer an option. He knew too well what the word abuse meant, about the awful reality behind that word, how it shattered lives–and families. He reached out and took Rosie's arm. Their eyes met and locked. She knew what he was about to ask.

'Rosie, you gotta tell me, please.' He paused. 'Has that man– has he ever hurt you? In any way?'

Rosie's chin trembled. Then she shook her head slowly. 'No, Car, honestly, never. He's hit Ma, and he's been terribly cruel to her over the years. And he took a sick pleasure in walloping my brothers–which explains a lot about them and their troubles, yeah?'

She paused, gazing up at the hillside where sheep were grazing in the late day sun.

'But I was always his golden girl. Not that he was nice to me, or ever complimented me, or ever said he loved me even a little. But he never hurt me, not physically anyway. But, Car, it's been a month and I haven't heard from Ma. She said a couple weeks. But not a word.' Again her chin started to quiver. 'And I miss her, Car, and it's so lonely without her. And all I do is take care o' the man that mistreated her all those years. How sick is that?'

'Yeh're sure that prepay is well hidden?'

Rosie blushed. 'I put it in a box of tampons–figured it was safe there.'

Cary nodded and chuckled. 'Good one, Rosie.'

'But why hasn't she called or texted me?'

Cary was thinking and looking for ways to reassure his friend.

'There's lots of possible reasons, Rosie, I mean, maybe she's not settled yet and doesn't want to risk contacting you until she's sure of where she's gonna be living. Or–yeh know–maybe she got your number wrong? Or...' He knew he was grasping at straws now. 'Or maybe she left you a voice message–are yeh sure yeh've got the mailbox set up on that phone? She'll contact you in time, Rosie, of course she will.'

'Thanks, Car. I got nobody to talk to around here,' she said, gesturing toward her house. 'And no one else is supposed to know she's left.'

'Listen, why don't you call round tomorrow, yeah? In the mornin', maybe eleven or so? And bring that prepay. Not that I know all that much about them either, but maybe we can figure out if your voice mailbox is set up. Or maybe it's full of spam, yeh know? That happens a lot.'

'I hate to keep you away from your ma–and Siobhan.'

'No worries. I'm takin' Siobhan to Wicklow at half eight to catch the train to Dublin. Me and Ma got some things to tend to, but in the afternoon.'

'Thanks, Car.' She mustered a meagre smile, then turned and walked slowly up the lane, a sad replay of that day five years earlier when they parted after she told him she couldn't go to the Debs.

He watched her for a moment, then walked back down the hill as the chorus of 'Bright Side of the Road' drifted up from the celebration for the dearly departed.

The music had taken a softer, more sombre turn by the time Cary rejoined the festivities.

'Everything all right with Rosie?' asked his mother.

He shook his head. 'No, not really. I'll tell you about it later.

Wanna dance?' He took his mother's hands and they moved slowly to a sweet air.

'Thanks, love,' said Catherine when the song had ended. 'But don't forget...' Her eyes shifted toward Siobhan who was now standing alone, watching.

Cary went to the drinks table, retrieved another shandy, and brought it to Siobhan.

'Sorry I had to bail on yeh, Shiv. Rosie's not doin' too well.'

Siobhan nodded. In a few minutes, when a livelier tune was struck up, Cary held out his hand.

'Dance?'

Siobhan smiled and her face reddened just a bit. 'I'm a crap dancer, mate.'

'Oh, I don't know. You and Chester Doyle were cuttin' a pretty good carpet there.'

They both laughed. Then Cary put his hands around her waist, she put hers on his shoulders, and they moved ever so slightly to the music, no steps, no discernible rhythm–but neither cared.

'I know it's a sad day for you, Car, but this is so nice, you and your mom with all these friends around you, bucking you up.'

'Yeah, that's how this place is, Shiv. One big family. A strange family, maybe a bit dysfunctional...'

Siobhan gave out a loud guffaw.

'But mostly just real nice,' he added.

'I gotta tell you, mate, this is so different from the world I grew up in–the caring, the sincerity. It's nice to know there's a place like Glenkerry left on this sorry planet of ours.'

3

THE LADY VANISHES

The next morning Siobhan shared a teary goodbye with Catherine in the drive before Cary drove her to the rail station in Wicklow. It was early and the town was just beginning to come to life, shop doors opening, school buses rolling, fishing boats just returning at the harbour. They stood on the platform in the warm sun, waiting for the train.

'Thanks so much for comin' down, Siobhan. It means a lot, to me and to Ma,' he said, his eyes fixed on hers.

'No worries, mate. She's lucky to have you through all this, you know? Really lucky. But I wish you'd called me straightaway when your dad died. I could've come down sooner.'

'I didn't want you to miss grad, Shiv. You deserved that day.' The Dublin train was now approaching. 'Well, I guess I'll see you in London–imagine that?' he said with a smile.

'It'll be great, Car, it'll be deadly.' She gave him a quick hug, then added, 'and you'll find your dream job, I'm sure of it.'

She picked up her suitcase just as the train drew to a halt, boarded, then found a seat by a window on his side. She waved as the train pulled slowly away and in that instant Cary was seized with a curious sensation, perhaps a premonition, he wasn't sure. The windows of the train moving past reminded him of frames of a film, maybe even a film of his life. And the image of Siobhan's face was one of those frames–it approached, passed, and moved on. He stood on the platform for several minutes looking down the track as the train shrank into the distance, then disappeared. Suddenly he was feeling quite alone.

Lonely with her, mate, lonely without her.

Back home Cary found his mother talking on the telephone. She was speaking with Aiden. Cary stepped out into the yard and walked along the perennial bed, now bursting with colour. A few minutes later his mother joined him.

'It's beautiful, Ma. Yeh've put so much work into these gardens over the years, eh?'

'Yes, and Pa, too. Aiden says hello, by the way. And he wants to talk to you. But he couldn't just now. It's late there.'

She paused, admiring the handsome young lad standing before her. 'Car, come, sit down. I want to talk to you about your father's affairs.' They sat on a rustic wooden settee nestled in among the roses. The morning sun was just burning though the mist and a dove was cooing in the distance.

'He left everything to me, Car, your da did. That's the way we set it up: whoever passed first would leave everything to the other. But we each made a list of requests for the other to honour. And that includes the Upton Road property, the newspaper office and all.'

'Oh?'

'He wanted you to have it.'

This was a surprise to Cary. Patrick McGurk seldom tried to influence the life choices of his sons. Not that he didn't care, but he had faith in Aiden and Ciaran. They were smart, they were motivated, they were fully capable of finding their own way, he said more than once to Catherine. So he did not feel it necessary or wise to try pushing them one way or the other. He was naturally delighted when Cary decided to read journalism at university, but even then, he employed a hands-off approach. If his younger son decided to follow in his father's footsteps, that would be fine, but no pressure.

There had been a few times in the last three years when Cary sought out his father's advice, on course selection, on writing. Once they even had a conversation about Cary's love life, or lack of one. But it was initiated by Cary, and his dad wasn't able or willing to offer much in return. Maybe it was his humility that drove Patrick McGurk's reticence with his boys–perhaps he was simply not sure that he had much wisdom to impart. Sometimes Cary wished his dad had been more forthcoming, more involved in his life. But that just wasn't Patrick McGurk's way. If his son wanted his advice, he'd ask–that was his unspoken mantra, and it had become Cary's mantra as well, with his parents and with his mates. There were times in his young life when it served him well–other times, perhaps, not so much.

'Ma, I didn't realise you still owned that place. I thought you sold it a few years ago.'

'Well, we talked about it. Your da had some inquiries from estate agents anxious to list it. But he couldn't bring himself to let it go. It had–well–sentimental value. You know he ran the newspaper out of there for nearly three decades. So it had special meaning to him.'

'It's right in the centre of town. I'm surprised he never considered renting it–to a chipper or a Costcutter or something.'

'It needed work, dear, plumbing, wiring, even the foundation. It seemed so overwhelming, he never found the time to get it done. So that's the thing, you see. We want you to have it, Car, but you may not want to get into all that any more than your father did.'

'Yeah, probably not, Ma. But let's have a look, anyway.'

'Well, that's one thing for our list for later this afternoon. Stop in, have a look around.'

'Yeah, a course, let's do it.'

'But yeh're moving to London, and you and Siobhan, well, yeh've got plans of your own, no doubt.'

Cary shook his head. 'It's not like that, Ma, I keep tellin' you. We're just friends is all.'

'Okay. But don't let her slip through your fingers, love. Or you'll regret it for a long, long time. Do you understand what I'm saying?' No response. 'And wasn't it nice of her to come down for your dad's funeral Mass?'

'Yes, it was. She thinks the world of you, Ma. Speakin' of that, Rosie might come by a little later. She was sorry to rush off last evening, but she asked if she might call round today–maybe eleven or so?'

'Of course, poor thing. I suppose she's missin' her mother.'

'So you know?'

'Yes, Beatrice Foley told me, Devi Patel told her. I guess that good-for-nothing husband of hers is trying to keep it a secret, but there's no such thing in a town like this–full of curtain twitchers.'

Rosie O'Malley appeared at the McGurks' house shortly after eleven. Catherine greeted her at the door and the two sat in the parlour for a long while, mostly talking about Patrick. Cary was in the kitchen trying not to listen in, but he did hear Rosie say several times to his mother if she needed anything, to let her know.

As if that girl doesn't have enough on her mind without catering to a grieving neighbour.

It was almost noon when Rosie stepped into the yard and waved to Cary. He was clad in cut-off jeans and a T-shirt and working on the lawnmower. He looked up, smiled, then wiped the grease from his hands. They sat side-by-side on the wooden bench, now in the shade of several small birches. Rosie reached into the pocket of her dungarees and produced a mobile.

'So this is the prepay me ma gave me. I thought it was all set up to take messages. Can you tell?'

Cary fiddled with it for several minutes. 'Well, yeah, it looks as though it is. And yeh've got quite a few, but they look like adverts– life insurance, security alarms, online dating services.' He looked up at Rosie and winked. 'Just what you need, eh?'

Rosie smiled weakly.

'But I can't really tell if it's enabled for text messages.' At that he pulled out his own mobile. 'Watch, I'll send you a text.' They waited several minutes. 'Nope, nothing. I'm not really sure how this kind of phone works, especially for texts, but my message didn't go through.'

Rosie perked up. 'So maybe Ma's tried to send me a text?'

'Very possible. And she'll probably try again. How about if I keep it for a few days? It'll be safe here, and I'll ask Del to have a look at it.'

'He's a garda now, you know,' offered Rosie.

'Yeah, so he told me yesterday. But he's also a tech whiz, and he'll know how to set this up. I'll try to talk to him today. And a course I'll let you know as soon as I learn anything, or if you get any calls or texts. I can still call you on your regular mobile, right?'

With that Rosie departed and he watched her walking slowly up the hill. He would talk to Del Samuels, not only about mobile phones, but about the matter of reporting a missing person although he wasn't sure that the term accurately described Mary O'Malley. And perhaps he needed to ask, discreetly, about domestic abuse as well.

The Upton Road property, former home of *The Glenkerry Gazette,* Patrick McGurk, editor and publisher, was situated at the busy intersection of High Street and Upton Road, not far from the town's little market square. Like most of the buildings in the village, it was of limewashed stone but distinguished by cornerstones or quoins painted black. It was bounded by brightly coloured buildings, the tailor's a brilliant red on one side, the florist's a subtler peach on the other.

Catherine wasn't kidding when she said the Upton Road property needed work. It had lain empty now for nearly five years. Only a few odd pieces of office furniture testified to the building's past, and the rooms echoed as if offering a lonely greeting to the first visitors in months, maybe years. The paint on the walls was badly faded, some of the plaster cracked. Light fixtures hung from walls and ceilings on frayed flexes. The place had a distinct mildew odour as well, and Cary found himself sneezing almost as soon as he entered.

'Your da loved the *Gazette,* Car–it was simple, old-fashioned, like him. They had phones–land lines of course–and electric typewriters for the longest time. And then they finally got computers, long after everyone else had them. To him they were little more than gimmicks–it wasn't his way, you know?'

Cary nodded. 'Yeah, I remember him lookin' over my shoulder while I was doing homework on my laptop. He was amazed at what it could do, but he showed no interest in learning.'

'Well, at the brewery he finally learned to use a computer–he had to, to work on the books. But he groaned about it constantly.' They both chuckled.

They climbed the narrow stairway to the first floor, a small flat that had served for little more than storage space for most of the years that the newspaper was in operation. There was a sitting room, a kitchen, a tiny bedroom, and a loo.

'This is small but could be nice enough, with some work, don't you think?'

Cary nodded but could muster little enthusiasm.

'So what are you thinkin', son?' she asked at last. But she had a feeling she knew the answer. His posture, demeanour, and occasional sighs and groans spoke volumes.

'Well, I suppose the simplest thing to do would be to sell it, as is, wouldn't it, Ma? I'm sure the estate agents would come round like a swarm of bees as soon as they heard you were thinkin' of sellin'. It's a mess, but you know what they say: location, location, location.'

Catherine nodded but regret was etched on her face. 'You don't think, maybe a few years down the way, you might put it to use? Maybe move back to Glenkerry, live upstairs, rent out the ground floor?'

Cary knew where this was going. 'Ma, I know what yeh're

thinkin', and like I've said a thousand times, we're just friends.'

Why bother, mate? She won't listen.

'Yes, I understand, and no that was not what I was thinking–love nest and all.' She reached out and patted his cheek. 'Listen, Car, whatever you want is okay by me. Just think it over.'

Catherine knew she had to tread very lightly on subjects like girlfriends and marriage with her younger son. She still feared that what she regarded as very mild and occasional encouragements of Aiden had been one of the reasons he had left Ireland and travelled about as far away as one could travel, to New Zealand, or, as her husband dubbed it, 'the arse end of the world.'

The subject was dropped for the time. They walked the short distance up High Street to the Bank of Ireland where Catherine showed Cary her safe deposit box, explained about keys and access, and showed him the contents, mostly just documents–deeds, mortgage papers, copies of their wills, and the like.

Before returning home, Catherine explained that there was one more stop she wanted them to make–the cemetery. They walked silently among the weathered stones carved with crosses, cherubim, weeping yews and willows. Toward the back of the cemetery, they stood among several stones engraved with the name McGurk. One of marble had fewer lichens and mosses than the others. It bore two names.

'Those are your da's parents, Car–John and Irene McGurk. You probably don't remember them. They lived most of their married life in Arklow which as you know is where your da was born. They moved to Glenkerry late in life but came to feel that this was their home.'

'So what about dad, should we get a new monument for him?'

Catherine teared up, then sniffled. 'We never discussed it, yeh know? He wanted to be cremated and we never went beyond that in our plans. So we could have his ashes buried here. But I'm inclined to simply have his name added below his parents. What do you think?'

Cary nodded. 'I think that would be fine, Ma.'

'But we'll leave a space for me, too, eh?'

Cary put his arm around her. 'Quit talkin' like that, Ma. Yeh're not goin' anywhere for a long time, hear?'

'None of us knows, love, none of us can say. Have you heard the old Yiddish saying?' Cary shook his head. 'When we make plans, God laughs.'

Cary chuckled and nodded. 'Uh-huh–I like that.' He looked around at the older stones. 'Who are these other McGurks, Ma?'

'Oh, those are your great-grandparents, John and Margaret. And John's brother and sister–they died very young.'

Cary smiled. 'It's nice to think that the whole family is together, in a way.'

Catherine looked at her son, shaking her head. 'But they're not, Car, not by any means. So many were lost during the famines, no one had the time or the money to have headstones carved. And they say many of the famine victims were buried in mass graves.'

Cary nodded.

'And so many others emigrated, mostly to America and Canada. One story your da used to tell was of Hannah Hughes. She married Bernard McGurk and they had four children. He was convicted of theft in an English court–for stealing a single loaf of bread.' She shook her head in disbelief. 'Tryin' to feed his family, no doubt.'

'Bernard was sent to prison in Tasmania. That left Hannah with her four children at the height of the famines. So they emigrated. They had little more than the clothes on their backs when they arrived in Boston in October, 1849. But she made a home for them there and those children all grew up and lived long lives. The two boys fought in the American Civil War, so.'

'Gee, I suppose that means I have some distant cousins in America.'

'Without a doubt, son. And I'll bet they dream of comin' back to Ireland one day.'

Cary looked out at the rolling pastures beyond. 'Yeah, I bet they do, ma. Wouldn't it be somethin' to meet one of 'em some day?'

As they walked back to Catherine's car, Cary asked, 'So what about Pa's ashes? What should we do with them?'

'Well, Car, I had a thought.'

Finally, they drove the short distance back home. Catherine brewed a pot of tea as Cary stood looking at the copy of his father's will that she had removed from the safe deposit box. They sat at the kitchen table together, sipping their tea.

'What does Aiden think about all this? The Upton Road property, I mean. Have you told him?' asked Cary.

'No, I haven't yet. I had all of ten minutes with him on the phone last evening–it wasn't the time or the place. But Car, your father wanted you to have that property, if you wanted it. And we agreed that we'd make some kind of arrangement for your brother. Either the two of you could own it together, half and half, or we'd set up something for Aiden, perhaps an annuity, of equal value.'

Catherine paused, took a sip of her tea, then placed the cup down with a sigh. 'Ciaran,' she began. He stiffened.

Prepare yourself, mate.

'I know about Aiden, dear. That he's–that he's gay.'

Cary nodded. He could have made light of her statement and mocked her for being the last person in Glenkerry, maybe the last person in Ireland, to know. But he cared too much for his mother to treat her like that.

'Did he tell you himself, Ma?'

She shook her head. 'No. I may be an old-timer but I'm not completely doddy.'

'I never thought you were, Ma. So you figured it out yourself?'

'Well, he told me that he couldn't come to Pa's funeral because his friend Tom had Covid and he needed to look after him. And last night he said that he and Tom were hoping to buy a house in Auckland.' She bit her lip. 'But I already suspected, partly because he never talked about girlfriends, and because you never mentioned anything about his love life.'

'It's too bad he couldn't tell you himself, Ma.'

She nodded, tears running down her cheeks. 'It's really a shame, you know? Here we are in the twenty-first century and young people still have trouble telling their parents such things. And parents still have a hard time hearing and accepting them.'

'Ma, if it makes you feel any better, I was in denial about Aiden's, uh, preference for a long while myself. So it's not just your generation.'

She smiled. 'Well, in a way that makes me feel better, dear. It really does. But you know, three of my lady friends have family members who are gay or trans. You remember Jonah Fallon from *Coláiste*? His mother is Muriel Fallon from the church. Well, he's now Joanne Fallon. I figure if my friends can deal with such things and accept them, so can I.'

'For what it's worth, Ma, my friendship with Siobhan has nothing to do with my sexual preference. I find her attractive, very attractive, and I like her a lot. But she doesn't feel that way about me, and that's the way we stand. I'm a little nervous about our living arrangement in London because of that. So if we live together, it will only be for a while, till I can afford a place of my own. I like girls, Ma. It's just that they don't seem to like me back.'

Cary chuckled at this admission. But he could see a new sadness in his mother's face.

Here we go again.

'I know, Ma, "Siobhan–she's such a sweet colleen," right? Although I'm not sure an American girl qualifies as a colleen, does she? Well, she is sweet and pretty, et cetera, et cetera. But it's not going to happen. And I'm okay with that, heck I just turned twenty-one. I'm not withering on the vine...' He paused. 'Yet.'

They both began to laugh. Catherine stood up, leaned down and kissed the top of her son's head. 'Thanks for bein' so good to your mam, Car. I'm lucky to have you, especially now.'

That evening Aiden called again, this time to talk to Cary. When the call was finished, Cary spoke to his mother.

'Ma, I asked Aiden if we might Skype with him. Would eight o'clock Saturday evening be okay?'

'Oh, that'd be lovely, Car. What a good idea–while yeh're here.'

'Grand, I'll text him to confirm.' Cary hesitated for a moment, then he added, 'Ma? I asked him if Tom could join us, if he's feeling up to it. I hope that's okay.'

4

WHAT HAPPENED AT LOUGH BEAG?

Cary devoted much of the next day to yard work for his mother. But late in the afternoon he changed into jeans and a collared shirt and walked down the hill to the High Street. He stood outside Phinney's Pub for several minutes before he saw the familiar figure of his friend, Delbert Samuels, all six foot two of him, ambling down the street.

Del's skin was deep caramel, his face smooth as silk, with curly dark hair close-cropped and a smile that could light up the darkest night. His biceps bulged beneath a knitted jersey, reminding Cary that he always envied his friend's physique. He'd even asked him once about his workout routine, but Del said he had no workout routine, adding to Cary's dismay. When Cary asked his doctor why his own musculature was so paltry compared to his friends, the man went off on a ten-minute lecture on the dangers of anabolic steroids.

Gee, Doc, never thought o' that. Thanks, mate.

Del was one of Cary's best friends in Glenkerry. His family came to Dublin from Jamaica shortly after he was born, then moved to Glenkerry when his father got a job in a factory in Arklow. Del also attended *Coláiste Gaeilge*, one of the few black students in the school. Cary always got a hoot out of hearing Del speak Irish with a Jamaican accent. Del was an average student overall, but he received his Leaving Certificate, earning special recognition for his accomplishments in computers and technology. Then he joined *An Garda Síochána* which needed new trainees with expertise in technology.

'How's my lad?' asked Del, his voice sounding for all the world like James Earl Jones. Cary had to laugh as he recalled how Del would entertain his classmates with his spot-on impression of Darth Vader: 'Luke, I am your father.'

'Okay, Del, okay.' They smiled, shook hands, and entered. They sat at the bar and ordered pints.

'Thanks again for coming to my da's funeral, Del, and the afterparty.'

'No problem, Car. Your dad was a real good man. And you and me go way back, eh? How's your ma doin'?'

'Well, pretty good, considering. And your folks?'

'Yeah, they're okay,' replied Del.

'So tell me about your work. What's the life of a garda like these days?'

Del chuckled. 'Not too glamourous I'm afraid–lots a lookin' into a computer screen, to be honest. The guards used to complain about paperwork, yeah? Now it's screentime–filing reports, updating databases, doing searches. Once in a while I actually get out on the footpath and it feels good, yeh know, away from that *eerie glow*,' the last two words delivered with a mock sinister expression.

'You still seein' Margaret, Margaret I-Forget-What, from *Coláiste*?'

Del shook his head. 'Maggie Randall? She's in Cork, mate. Married. Has three kids aready.'

Cary's jaw dropped. They both laughed.

'Well, she always said she wanted kids. I *suppose* she's happy–I *hope* she is. Me, I'm seein' a little lady in Wicklow Town. But she's a garda, too, so we have to keep it on the down-low, as they say.'

'Ahh,' replied Cary with a knowing smile and a nod.

'So, not a word, right mate?'

'Your secret's safe. Although, if I ever need a favour, I may have to hold it over yeh.'

Del chuckled. 'And that American lass, Siobhan? She's quite a catch, I'd say.'

'Yeah, well, she's not on *my* line, I can tell yeh. We're just friends. Soon to be roomies in London.'

Del's eyes popped out in amazement. 'How the hell does that work?'

Cary nodded. 'Darned if I know. I'll keep you posted, okay?'

'Oh, mate,' replied Del, his eyes now dancing. 'If you tell me the two a you are havin' pillow fights in your knickers, I'm gonna recommend some serious hormone therapy for you, yeh hear?'

They both laughed. Cary was reminded of why Del was so well liked in *Coláiste*. He had the best sense of humour of anyone in their class, and he used it skilfully. He sometimes teased his classmates, but no one objected, especially when accompanied by that deep chortle in his chest and those animated facial expressions.

'Listen, Del, I got a tech question for you if you don't mind puttin' on that hat for a minute.'

Del took a long pull from his pint. 'Anytime, mate. Just so long as I don't have to write up a report.'

Cary smiled, then pulled out the prepay phone. 'You remember Rose O'Malley–Rosie–right?'

Del nodded. 'Sure, another one of your old sweethearts, as I recall.'

'Once upon a time, maybe, until the ole man shut us down.'

'Her mother left, I understand.'

'Oh, so the gardaí know about that, eh?'

'Well, not officially, but we have eyes and ears, and it's part of our job to keep 'em open.'

'Well, this is strictly off the record, yeah? Rosie doesn't want it gettin' back to him. Her ma told her a few days before she left. And she gave Rosie this prepay, promisin' to be in touch. But a month's gone by without a word, and Rosie's worried. What I'm not sure of is if this thing is set up for texts, yeh know?'

Del took the phone, switched it on, and examined it.

'No password, that makes it easy. Ah, yeah, well, a lot of these prepays come with no data. And without data there's no texting. Let's see.' He swiped the screen a dozen times or more in rapid succession. 'Yeah, okay, it can send and receive texts. Ah-hah, there's one from you here. I won't read it, mate, might be too hot to handle. A little sexting with your old crush, mebbe?'

'No, it's nothing like that. She brought the phone to me yesterday to see if I could figure it out. I sent that message as a test. But it didn't seem to show up on her phone.'

'Well, maybe it was delayed. That sometimes happens, who knows why? But this thing is text-enabled and it looks like she's got data, not a lot, but some. But, mate, her voice mailbox is full, so it's not accepting new messages. If she's had this for a while, it's probably mostly spam. I could delete it all, but maybe it would be better to let her go through those messages herself before she deletes them.'

'Good to know,' replied Cary. 'So her ma might a tried to leave her a message, but the voice mailbox was full. Which means maybe she'll try again.'

'Rosie could always call her ma,' offered Del.

'Yeah, except she didn't leave her digits. So all Rosie can do is wait.'

'I feel sorry for her, Car. That old man of hers is bad news. But she's old enough, right? What is she, at least nineteen, maybe twenty? She could just walk away.'

'Yeah, she could, but he's not well and she's takin' care of him. Buddy's up in Dalkey, and, Jimmy, well, we both know where he is.'

Cary and Del exchanged knowing glances. Jimmy O'Malley was at Arbour Hill, the prison in Dublin, serving time for a drugs offense. He was one of Glenkerry's saddest stories, and yet hardly anyone felt any sympathy for him and rarely spoke of him. 'Less said, soonest mended' seemed to apply.

'That girl's the prettiest thing in Glenkerry, Car. Maybe you and her…'

'Listen, Del, don't be troublin' yourself about my love life, eh? Whatta you think I got a ma for?'

They both laughed over that line, nodded in agreement, then finished their pints together. As Cary walked back up the hill, he was thinking of his former classmate and how good it was to reconnect with him. And somehow yesterday's bout with loneliness seemed to fade from view.

Siobhan called at eight o'clock sharp that evening. As she spoke Cary could hear a loud clanging in the background. 'What the heck is that, Shiv?'

'I'm standing in front of Westminster Abbey, Car. Can you tell?'

'What?'

'That's Big Ben striking the hour. Just in case you didn't believe I was really here.'

'Okay, Shiv, I believe you. I had my doubts, but yeh've convinced me.'

'So how are you? How's your ma?'

'Yeah, we're both okay. She's sad, yeh know, but she's also determined to carry on. What else can she do?'

'Tell her I'm thinking of her, won't you? And I'm not just saying that, Car, I really am. I feel bad, being here in the Big Smoke having a once-in-a-lifetime adventure while you and your ma are going through all that.'

'Don't worry, we're doin' all right. And later we're Skyping with Aiden–and Tom.'

'Wow, really? That's big, Car. That's really big.'

'Yeah, well, I'll tell you all about it when I get to London.'

'You still flying over tomorrow?'

'Yeah, and Ma wants to drive me all the way to the airport. But I'm gonna try to convince her to just drop me at the station in Wicklow. I can be at the terminal in about ninety minutes, easy. My flight gets into Heathrow at about five your time.'

'Okay, well, I will be there to greet you, Car, and we can take the tube to Camden. Listen, I found a place, a flat, a two-bedroom. It's in a small block of flats in Chelsea which is perfect for me. I hope you'll like it. I posted some shots on my Facebook page–have a look, okay?'

'Yeah, sure. But don't worry about me, Shiv–if you like it, I'm sure it will be fine with me.'

'You should have the front bedroom, Car. It looks out on the street. You'll appreciate the view more than I will. I'll be happy with the one at the rear. It has a view of the alley, although it'll probably be quieter, so if you'd prefer...'

'It's your call, Shiv, really. I'll be fine either way.'

They talked on for quite a time, about jobs, and furniture, and friends back in Dublin. Then the conversation circled back to bedrooms. Cary suspected all this discussion about the two bedrooms was Siobhan's way of making a point: they were strictly on a friendship basis.

Message received, Shiv, loud and clear.

But suddenly, the next morning, Cary's travel plans had to change. Rosie appeared at his front door looking distressed.

'I'm sorry to bother you, Car, but I'm scared, I'm really scared.' Her chin was quivering.

'Come on through, Rosie.'

She hesitated. So Cary stepped out onto the front veranda in his bare feet dressed in a T-shirt and pyjama bottoms. They stood there, face to face.

'Heman Murphy, you know 'im?' she began.

'Yeah, well, a bit. I know where his farm is anyway, up beyond

Anglesey. Has a small herd of dairy cows?'

She nodded. 'He called round this mornin', wanted to talk to me da. Pa hasn't been too good the last few days but he was glad to see Heman and managed to get outta bed and they sat in the front room talkin'. I made them coffee, then I went outside. Pa hates it when he thinks I'm spyin' on him, so I gave them lots a space. Anyway, they talked for a long time. Finally, Heman got ready to leave and he came lookin' for me in the barn. He said he just heard about Ma leavin' and thought maybe we oughta know somethin'.'

Rose bit her lip and looked as though she was about to cry. Cary reached out, offering a hug, but she backed away, both hands raised as if to fend him off. 'I'm okay, Car, I'm okay.'

'What did Mr Murphy say, Rosie?'

'He saw Ma that morning, Car, the day she left. It was real early, just after sunup, and he was mending fences out on the back side of his acreage, by Lough Beag, you know where I mean? Where we used to walk?'

Cary nodded.

Yeah, I remember Lough Beag, mate, I sure do.

'He said he was followin' the fence row down toward the lough when he saw Ma. She was standin' on the dam, he said, lookin' out across the water. That dam is high, Car, remember? And it's dangerous–there's lots of loose stones.'

Cary was trying to take in all he was hearing, to process it, to think of the possible implications.

'Heman was surprised and wondered what she was doin' out there so early in the mornin' and so far from home. She was never a big walker, yeh know? And Car, he thought he heard her sobbing.'

Again, Rosie's composure started to crack. But Cary resisted the urge to try to hug her. 'What did he do, Rose?'

'He said he called out to her and when she heard his voice, she acted like nothin' was wrong. He talked to her for a few minutes and she seemed all right. She said she was just gettin' some exercise. He decided maybe he hadn't really heard her sobbing after all, maybe it was just the water goin' over the dam or something. He offered to walk her back home but she declined. So he went on his way and didn't think any more of it till yesterday when someone told him Ma had left. Then he started to worry.'

'Did he tell all this to your da?'

Rosie shook her head. 'He was plannin' to, that's why he called. But when he saw how poorly Pa was, he thought better of it. Then he decided he ought to tell me. And Car, after he left, just thinkin' about it, I got sick to my stomach–I boked.'

Finally, she broke down and sobbed. Cary stepped up and put one arm around her shoulders.

'Oh, Car, I can't help but think, maybe Ma never got any further than the lough.'

When she had regained some of her composure she looked into Cary's eyes. 'My ma's been unhappy for so long with that man. Now I wish I had tried to convince her to go earlier. Maybe even while I was still in school. We coulda gone together, yeh know? Instead of her sneakin' off all alone in the middle of the night.'

Just then Catherine came around the side of the house and saw them.

'Rosie? What's the matter, dear?'

Catherine had expected Cary to go to Mass with her, but he

declined. A few hours later he was standing on the shore of Lough Beag, a small lake just a few miles north of Glenkerry surrounded by a dense forest of spruce and larch. It was one of those times in his life when he felt as though he was standing apart from himself, from his life, hovering high above, watching events unfold like in an old-time newsreel. He wished he didn't have to be here, to witness what was happening. But he couldn't walk away. Not for Rosie's sake nor for her mother's.

Lough Beag had always been a place of wonder to him. Once part of a vast demesne owned by an aristocratic English family, it was now a public trust. The lough had been a frequent fishing trip destination for Cary with his father and brother, then later with his friends. In secondary school that same lough was legendary as a place where teenagers gathered and carried on far away from the peering, judging eyes of adults. He and Rosie had walked there a few times, just the two of them, skimmed rocks, even kissed once, although it was a brief and furtive kiss for fear that unknown eyes might be watching.

One summer evening they had an unforgettable encounter out there with a nightjar, a rare sighting. They first heard its song, a rapid chitter like a buzzsaw in the forest. It was Rosie who spotted it on a fencepost, looking like a clump of lichens. As they approached the bird opened its enormous craw, perhaps as a warning. He recalled with a smile how Rosie tried to mimic that rasping call with her tongue against the roof of her mouth.

But now this place of wonder had suddenly been transformed into a scene of dread. A garda in a wet suit and scuba kit was about to dive into the dark waters, perhaps to recover the earthly remains of Mary O'Malley. At the same time another officer with a search dog was circling the lough on the chance of picking up some scent, perhaps an article of clothing, anything that might offer a clue to what took place here four weeks earlier.

'Shiv, I gotta change my travel plans,' he had begun in a phone call a few hours before his scheduled flight from Dublin to London. 'It's about Rosie's ma, Mary O'Malley? A neighbour talked to Rosie yesterday. He saw Mary early on the morning that she disappeared. At a place called Lough Beag, about a mile north of the village. It's really isolated. He said she was standing on the dam crying. Rosie's terrified. She thinks maybe her ma fell into the lough.' He paused. 'Or jumped.'

'Oh, Car, that poor thing. Of course,' replied Siobhan. She listened to Cary for a moment. 'Yeah, well, you have to. She needs you. Yeah, no, I understand.'

Whatever the gardaí found, Cary promised his friend he would be in London soon, maybe four or five days, a week max. If the worst happened, he was thinking, he'd want to be there for Rosie through whatever arrangements were made for her mother, and maybe a few days more. Maybe Rosie's aunts from Roscommon would come and stay with her for a time. And there was her brother, Buddy, and her father. It broke his heart, thinking of how alone Rosie must be feeling about now.

Garda Samuels had driven to the McGurk home as soon as Cary called. He talked to Rosie and Cary, taking down the information on a notepad. It was the first time Cary saw his old schoolmate in action and he was impressed. His voice was soft, his words reassuring to Rosie, but at the same time he was efficient and well-organised in his questioning and note-taking.

'Don't worry, Rosie, leave it to us, okay? You just take care a yourself and your da. We'll open a missing persons incident. And my Super, Garda Lewis, he knows your da. I think he said they went to school together in Dublin. He'll probably be the one to talk to 'im.'

Del's gaze shifted briefly to Cary, then back to Rosie. 'But why don't you start by telling me everything, okay? When you last saw yer ma, what her state of mind was, and so on?'

Rosie recounted her conversation with her mother on the footpath in Glenkerry, the day she stepped off the bus from Wicklow Town. She told him about her mother's plan to leave. And her promise to be in touch.

'And she gave you that prepay, right? Cary showed it to me the other day.'

Rosie nodded.

'And you haven't heard from her since she left, right?'

Rosie nodded. 'But Car said the voice mailbox was full of junk. He cleaned it out for me on Thursday.'

Del turned to Cary. 'Still no calls?'

'Nope,' replied Cary with a shake of his head.

'Or texts?'

Again Cary shook his head. Del watched Rosie's eyes tearing up.

'So your ma gave you no hint of where she planned to go, is that right?'

Rosie nodded. 'I think she thought it would be best if I knew as little as possible until she was gone, because a 'im, my da.'

'And she didn't give you her mobile number?'

Rosie shook her head. 'I shoulda asked. But I didn't.'

Del looked into her eyes. 'And your da, she didn't give him a number where she could be reached?'

Rosie winced. 'She was afraid a 'im. We all were–are.'

'Why didn't you report your ma's disappearance sooner? I

know, mate, I understand, but I have to ask. My Super will want to know.'

'Pa said she left of her own accord. And she'll be back, he keeps sayin'. And anyway he didn't want the gardaí snooping around, is what he said. He figured he'd be blamed, they'd say he mistreated her.'

'Rosie, *did* your da mistreat your ma?'

Both Del and Cary were watching her intently. She was twisting a plait of her red hair in the fingers of one hand distractedly. Finally, she nodded, then bit her lip and looked away.

'Did you ever see him hit her?'

More hair-twisting. Then she shook her head. 'No. But I saw bruises on her face and arms a couple times. Once she said she fell in the garden and hit her head on a rock. But I didn't believe it.'

'So your ma never said that he hit her?'

'No, not to me. She was ashamed. That's what I think. Embarrassed.'

'Okay. I understand. One more thing, Rosie. Did your da ever mistreat you?'

She quickly shook her head. 'Uh-uh. But he could be mean, especially when he'd been drinkin'–verbally, that is, to me and my brothers.'

Del slipped his notepad and pen into his vest pocket.

'Okay, Rosie. Thank you for all this. I'll talk to Buddy. I have his address and mobile number. As to Jimmy, well, someone will go to see him in the next few days.'

Del climbed into his car and drove off while Rosie and Cary stood in the front yard.

'He's a good man, Del, eh?' said Cary.

Rosie nodded.

'I'll go up to the lough in a while. And I'll call you as soon as–if there's any news, okay?'

She nodded and got up to leave.

'Lemme spin you 'ome,' said Cary.

She smiled a bit but shook her head. 'I c'n walk, ta.'

He watched as Rosie walked up the lane. His heart was breaking for her, for what she was going through. It was the uncertainty that was most painful. Knowing what happened, even if it proved to be the worst, was better than not knowing, than never knowing, than being at the mercy of her imagination.

Cary sat anxiously on a boulder overlooking the lough, watching the diver's bubbles churn the water along the near shore, then continue along the farther side. At the same time he could see the yellow vests of the garda and his dog, a hyperactive border collie, snuffling along the shore. Rosie had pulled a jumper out of her mother's closet and given it to the garda to present to the dog. Four weeks was probably too long to expect any scent would remain, they said, but they were willing to give it a try.

He was thinking about those days he spent here as a boy, of how exciting it was, to be not too far from home yet so isolated. The shallows of this small lake teemed with life, water striders zipping along the surface, water boatmen scudding about just below among the yellow and white waterlilies, arrowhead, and yellow loosestrife growing in the shallows. He remembered a day when he stood on this very spot watching a kingfisher in its looping flight along the shore. It perched on low tree limbs, then swooped down over the water in search of fish. Every so often he heard a splash as the bird dove for its prey, then flew away, often with a minnow or stickleback in its beak. It had fascinated him and moved him, that little bird. He even wrote a poem about the kingfisher once, about patience, persistence, and precision.

After several hours the diver emerged from the water near the dam. He spoke to another garda who approached Cary.

'Mr McGurk, sir?'

Cary stiffened, feeling a queasiness in his gut, then rose.

'Garda?'

'The diver found nothing, sir, not a thing in the way of human remains.' Just then his radio crackled and he stepped away for a short conversation. In a few minutes he returned.

'The dog found something other side of the dam there. An article of clothing, a hoodie, a thin plastic hoodie. No scent, at least nothing strong enough to get a reaction from the animal. So he can't say if it was Mrs O'Malley's. But we'll show it to the family, see what they say, if they recognise it.'

Cary nodded. 'Any clue as to what might've happened to her? Blood or anything?'

'No, sir, nothing.'

An hour later Del revisited the McGurk home and spoke to Rosie. She had already heard from Cary but there needed to be further discussion. No, the diver found nothing, no remains, no items of clothing other than an old pair of boots that probably had been in the mud several years.

As to the hoodie. 'It's hers,' began Rosie. 'She wore it on cool days when she worked in her garden, or if it was raining.'

So Mary O'Malley had visited Lough Beag, as the neighbour had reported. But there was no evidence to suggest she had met her death, not in the lough anyway.

'My Super wants me to talk to your father, Rosie. He needs to know where our investigation stands, of course. And I have some questions to ask him.'

'Oh, yeah, a course. Well, he's probably asleep. How about if I go first and let him know yeh're coming? Can you give me a few minutes, yeh know, to be sure he's–presentable?'

Harry O'Malley had lived in Glenkerry all his life. In fact he had lived in that very house since a lad. His parents raised sheep and had a few cows. But his father also worked for a company in Arklow for many years. Harry left school when he turned sixteen and worked for a time for an automobile dealership in Wicklow, eventually rising to salesman for the company.

But Harry's principal livelihood soon became real estate. With several associates he began purchasing land around the county and reselling it. He had some very successful deals for a time, although some of the transactions raised questions with local authorities, questions of legality and propriety. One property that he sold proved to be less than half the acreage he had claimed and a lawsuit ensued. Another deal was based on a questionable deed and the sale eventually was cancelled. In several instances he and a colleague purchased a large acreage, subdivided it, and sold off house lots.

Harry met Mary Malone through a mutual friend in Wexford. She moved in with him in the mid-nineties and their first child,

James, was born in 1997, followed by Rosie in 2002 and Brendan in 2004. As Harry's real estate fortunes soured, his drinking became a major occupation.

Harry was seated in the parlour, dressed but unshaven, his hair tousled, when Rosie showed Del in.

'Mr O'Malley, sir, I'm Garda Samuels, Del Samuels. I'm an old school chum of Rosie and Buddy.'

'Yeah, I remember yeh. What can I do for yeh?'

'Well, sir, we're gonna open a missing persons incident for your wife, Mary O'Malley. I understand she's been gone for over a month?'

Harry grunted but looked away out the front window.

'I am sure this is very difficult for you, sir. But I want to assure you that the gardaí are doing everything we can to locate Mrs O'Malley.'

Again Harry grunted. 'Waste a time.'

'Uh-huh. Why do you say that, sir?'

Harry took a deep breath. 'My wife'll come home when she's ready. No need to go searchin' for 'er.'

'Well, sir, we were alerted to the matter when a local citizen reported seein' her early one morning in May up at Lough Beag. He thought she was upset, cryin', sir.'

Now Harry turned to the garda. 'Who saw her?'

'Uh, well, it was Mr Murphy.'

'Heman? Well, he never mentioned it to me.'

'He told your daughter, sir. And she contacted the gardaí. Rosie was worried that her ma might have had an accident out there, of some sort.'

'An accident?' For the first time Harry seemed concerned.

In his training Del had learned a good deal about interviewing victims, witnesses, family members, and potential perpetrators in connection with investigations of all sorts. He'd had several occasions to watch one of his superiors in action and could appreciate that this was a very subtle craft involving not only the interviewer's voice but body language, phrasing, and facial expressions. Equally subtle were the reactions of the subject, the words spoken, the tone of voice, the tiniest of visual cues–a blink, a tic, a slight moistening of the eyes.

'Yes, sir. We had a diver in the lough this morning. He didn't find anything, sir.' Del watched carefully for the old man's reaction. Harry nodded–he appeared to be relieved at that news.

'But they did find an article of clothing that Rosie has identified as belonging to her mother. A hoodie, sir. So we're anxious to find her, sir, as I am sure you are.'

'Like I said, she'll be back.'

'Well, sir, hopefully she will be. But we are of course continuing our investigation. I wondered, sir, if you had any idea where she might have gone?'

Harry shook his head. 'Nope.'

'Did she tell you anything of her plans before she left?'

'Nope.'

'Any hints at all of where she was intending to go?'

'Nope.' Harry was getting impatient. 'Listen, garda, can we wrap this up? I got things ta do.'

'Certainly, sir, I'll be on my way.' Del stood up and stepped toward the door, then turned back to Harry.

'One more question, Mr O'Malley. Why did your wife leave, sir? Do you have any ideas?' Again Del was watching the old man's face closely. He thought he detected a slight softening of his expression, the tiniest glint in his eyes.

But just then Harry turned away shaking his head. 'Nope.'

A few minutes later Harry made his way into the yard where Rosie was hanging some sheets on the line.

'Why'd you have ta go to the gardaí?'

'Because I'm worried about Ma.'

'Yeah, well, as I recall you didn't seem too surprised when she left, eh? And anyway, as I tol' you, she left a her own accord. And she'll come back when she's ready.'

Rosie tossed a few clothespins into the basket at her feet, then stood facing her father squarely.

'Yeah, so you tol' me. But I don't believe it. I don't think she is comin' back, Pa, ever. And we both know why.' With that she picked up the laundry basket and stalked back into the house.

Glendalough

5

WHERE'ER SHE WALKS

The next morning Cary called Del and asked if he could stop by the garda station. A few minutes later he appeared, and they sat at Del's desk in the middle of a room with three other desks.

'So when do you get your own office, mate?'

Del chuckled. 'When I'm promoted to sergeant, maybe–or thirty years a service–whichever comes first.' He threw back his head and laughed.

'So how did your interview of Mr O'Malley go?'

Del winced. 'Not too helpful is all I can say. He insists his wife left of her own accord and that she'll return when she's ready. But he couldn't name anyone she might be staying with. He's not exactly one a them "new age sensitive guys," yeh know? But I do think he misses her. And he says he 'as no idea why she left.'

'And I'm guessing he denied ever hitting her, or his sons?'

'Well, I decided not to go there just yet. If he thought he was under suspicion, he'd probably clam up entirely. As long as we don't have a formal complaint against him and nobody in the household is presently at risk, I'm thinkin' we ought to wait on that. Detective Superintendent Lewis agrees.'

'So what next, Del?' asked Cary.

'My Super wants to start the process of posting a missing person alert for Mrs O'Malley. That happens in Dublin, then it's circulated to every garda station in the Republic and in the North as well. But before we do that we're supposed to make contact with family members and friends. Rosie promised to call me with a list of names–I'll get on it straightaway as soon as I hear from 'er.'

Cary nodded. Then Del continued. 'And a K-9 team is planning to do a wider survey of the Lough Beag area for any kind of evidence–including remains. On the possibility that she never got far from the lough. Or that she was just wandering out there with no particular destination.'

Their eyes met as they imagined the woman lost in those trackless wild lands north and west of the lough, perhaps falling and succumbing to hypothermia.

Del broke the silence. 'But assuming the lough was just a stop on her escape route, the next question is where was she headed from there?'

'I was thinking about that,' said Cary. 'At first I thought Lough Beag was an odd place for her to be. But then I started thinkin', if she was trying to get away from Glenkerry without being seen, then following that footpath to the lough makes sense. She probably figured she wasn't likely to see anyone out there at that hour–although, as it turned out, she did.'

'So where could she have been headed from there, Car?'

'That lane runs down from the hill to the dam. But it continues beyond the far end of the dam. I remember my da had an old ordnance survey map that showed it goin' all the way through to Ballinoch. I walked it once, just to see where it came out. It meets the county road just west of the village, maybe a couple miles from the lough. I'm guessing some fishermen still use it to get into the lough from that side.'

Del's eyes lit up. 'Do you suppose Ballinoch was her destination? Maybe she had arranged to meet someone there, figuring no one would know her. Or–let's see, the bus stops there several times a day. Maybe she planned to get the bus from Ballinoch, either north toward Dublin, or south to Wexford.'

'That makes sense,' replied Cary. 'It's not a route where she would be likely to see anyone from Glenkerry. Do you suppose we could circulate her picture with the bus drivers, see if any of them remember her? A lot of times on routes like that the drivers get to know the regulars, yeah?'

'Regulars, sure, I can see that. But a one-time passenger over a month ago? That's a long shot, I'd say,' offered Del. 'Still, it might be worth a try.'

Cary was thinking. 'I could contact Bus Éireann, maybe drive up to Bray, or Dublin?'

'Thanks, mate,' replied Del, 'but you better leave that stuff to the gardaí.'

Cary nodded. 'What about CCTV?' he asked. 'Any chance she might show up on archive footage somewhere?'

'Yep, I'll look into that, too,' replied Del. 'In the meantime why don't you help Rosie to draw up that list of family and friends of her ma's? You know, get her thinkin' about folk her ma may have been in touch with–family members, of course, but also clubs, civic groups, church groups, old friends, that sorta thing. Rosie's head might be overloaded about now, I mean with worry and fear. You could help her to think.'

That I can do, mate.

A few hours later Rosie and Cary sat in Catherine's garden. They were compiling a list of possible contacts, just as Del had suggested. It included all the categories the garda had mentioned, plus some places in Ireland where she had lived before she married Harry, including Wexford, Ross, Athlone, and Roscommon. But Del was right, Rosie was showing the strain of all this. Finally, Cary suggested she go home and have a nap.

Shortly after she departed, Cary received a call from Del.

'Hey, Car. Is Rosie with you?'

'Nope–she just went home.'

'Listen, I don't want her to hear anything until I have more information.'

'Hear anything?'

'Yeah. See, we just got a notice from a morgue in Dublin. An unidentified body. A white female, fifty or so, just brought in a while ago. Found in a cheap hotel in the city.'

'Oh, God. You don't think…'

'It's too early to tell, Car. But we have to follow up on this. The missing person alert hasn't gone out yet, but I sent them a scan of Mrs O'Malley, that photo Rosie gave us?'

Cary groaned.

'Yeah, I know. They said they couldn't be sure. There's been, well, decomposition.'

Again Cary groaned.

'Anyway, I got a question for Rosie. But I thought maybe you could ask her. Don't make a big deal, yeh know? Just tell her we're completing the description of her mother for the missing person alert and need to know if her ma has any birthmarks or tattoos. Okay? Just routine.'

Cary called Rosie and explained. Then he called Del back. 'No, Del, she says her ma had no birthmarks. And as to tattoos, she said "You gotta be kiddin'. My ma with a tramp stamp?" ' Cary and Del laughed.

'Yeah, I figured.'

'Why, Del, what's up?'

Del hesitated. 'Give me a few minutes, all right? I'll call you back.'

And in just a few minutes Del did call back.

'Sorry to be so mysterious, lad. But I didn't want Rosie to get upset. That lady in the morgue, she has a snake tattoo on her right shoulder.'

Cary exhaled. 'So it's not Mary O'Malley.'

'Sorry to alarm you, man. Maybe don't tell Rosie about this, yeah?'

'Right.'

'One more thing, Car. How well do you know Buddy?'

'Well, we were mates in grammar school. He seemed a pretty happy-go-lucky kid in those days. But I didn't see much of him at all after that–for a time he attended a secondary school in Arklow. But he left home soon after he turned sixteen and I haven't seen him for, I don't know, three years, maybe?'

'Has he had much contact with Rosie, or his father?'

'From what Rosie has said, I'd say not much. I think he wanted to stay as far away from the old man as possible, yeh know?'

'Thanks, Car. I'm headin' up to Dalkey to try and talk with 'im. Just wanted to have a sense of the guy, yeah?'

'Okay, Del, thanks. And hey, I'm gonna be outta cell range for a while tomorrow. I'm goin' up to Glendalough with my ma. But if there's anything important, any news, leave me a voicemail. We'll be home by tea for sure.'

That evening Cary sent an email to Rosie to let her know that he and his mother would be in Glendalough for most of the next day. He also told her of the Ballinoch scenario he and Del had come up with and asked her if her mother had any friends or connections in that village.

6

GLENDALOUGH–WHERE HEARTBREAK WILL MEND

'Paddy McGurk, may yeh rest in peace, love.' With those words, Catherine McGurk raised the urn and tipped it. The ashes of Patrick Louis McGurk, her husband of almost thirty years, sailed away on the winds of Wicklow, the place he loved. Her eyes glistened, then closed as she offered up a silent prayer.

Cary stood at her side, his thoughts drifting off to one of those marathon treks he and Rosie made along this same route. He remembered how they lay on their backs, looking up at the sky, watching awestruck as a merlin soared not far above their heads, and a hang glider soared far above the merlin–two drifters off to see the world. He and Rosie were just friends then. He secretly harboured hopes of a closer relationship, but somehow as he drew closer, she retreated. He took that as a sign, her way of saying let's stay friends.

Yeah, a course, what else?

When Catherine at last opened her eyes and lifted her head to Cary, he smiled, kissed her on the forehead, and hugged her. They had climbed the Spinc Trail in historic Glendalough, just a few miles from Glenkerry. Below them lay the lough of Glendalough, the midday sun reflecting off its now calm waters. At the far end of the lough was the ancient monastery and its iconic round tower, beyond that the rolling pasturelands of County Wicklow, and in the far distance, like a shimmering ribbon on the horizon, the Irish Sea. On a very clear day, you could even see the mountains of Wales from this vantage.

'He loved this place, didn't he, Ma?'

'Oh, he did, Car, sure he did. He and I climbed this path every year back when we were young and spry.' She paused. 'A course, we were stronger walkers in them days, weren't we? We'd climb to the very top. In fact, you know, he proposed to me right up there.' She gestured toward the summit, still a long way ahead of them. 'I a course said yes. And as we walked down, we talked about the future–work, home, children. It all started to take shape right here. It was wonderful, a day I'll never forget.' She began to sob.

'But you two had a good innings, Ma, right, you and Da?'

'We did, lad, we did. I was very lucky. So many of my friends fell for a boy, got themselves up the spout, then spent many, many years in unhappy marriages. It pains me to say it, Car, but most of them ended badly.'

She paused, looking down at the dark waters far below, remembering. 'But your da wasn't a drinker, or a philanderer, or a layabout. He worked hard, he took good care of you and Aiden, and he was frugal–maybe to a fault, I suppose.'

'And he loved his Katie, didn't 'e?'

'Yeah, he did. And I loved him dearly as well.' Her gaze

shifted out over the lough toward a distant summit. Then she turned to her son. 'And, yeh know, Car, he loved his work, too. And that's important, I think. So many men toil their lives away at jobs they hate, and it sours 'em, it damages 'em, their families, often their marriages. But Paddy loved that paper, he did. He couldn't wait to get to the office most days and get the next issue ready for press.'

'And you, Ma, did you love your work?'

'Oh, aye. It was satisfying and mostly heart-warming, yeh know, to see broken bodies repaired, shattered lives put back together. There was of course some sadness as well. Like tellin' a family that their loved one didn't make it, that 'e died in theatre. But at least we had the satisfaction of knowin' we'd done all we could for the patient.'

'Why did you never go back to work, after me and Aiden–eh, Aiden and I–were old enough?'

'I dunno, love. I guess I just wanted to keep a home that you boys and your da could come back to each night and find your ma there to greet you. Old-fashioned, I know, but that's what was most important to me.'

'I'm glad you did that for us, Ma. But sad in a way to think you gave up your career for us.'

She shook her head. 'No regrets, son, really.' She knitted her brow, as if to reassure him. 'But Car, whatever you do next, wherever yeh end up, I want yeh to be happy, so? Whether it's in London or Dublin or Auckland or Timbuctoo–just be sure it's a place where you feel good about your work, about your life. Don't go just for the brass, yeh hear me? Or the prestige.'

Cary nodded.

'Now that lass a yers, she's such a dear, she is. But I hope she's not one of those who has to be always climbin' the ladder of success, leavin' behind everything–everyone she loves.'

Cary smiled. 'Not my lass, Ma. But yeh're right in a way, Siobhan's driven, she's set herself on a path to success. But she's also got a heart of corn, as they say.'

'And yeh're tellin' me this Irish lad isn't a part of that heart o' corn?'

'No, Ma, it's not like that.' He sighed. 'Will I never stop havin' to remind you?' he asked melodramatically. Then he laughed.

'Okay, son, if *yeh're* not pinin' over her, I suppose *I* shouldn't be. But I worry about yeh, especially now without yer da.'

They resumed their hike, Cary now recalling several of his longer excursions with Rosie.

'For a time, as I recall, you two were inseparable. But something happened between you. I never knew exactly what. And you were very sensitive back then, so I hesitated to ask questions.'

Cary laughed. 'Unlike now, eh? Well, yes, we were. I always liked Rosie, you know. Goin' way back. But she was really sick for a time. She was out of school for months at one point. And when she came back, she seemed healthy enough. But she was different. She kinda, I don't know, backed off. You know, when yeh're fifteen or sixteen, you want to, well, move forward. But somethin' was holdin' her back. And I thought she just didn't feel the same about me anymore. Then I asked her to the Debs that year. She said yes, but her dad said no. That kinda ended it.'

Catherine shook her head. 'Her ma and I were never really close, but once or twice she said things that made me think that Rosie's health situation was precarious. I feared for her for a time, I really did.'

'She's a bit of an enigma, Ma, to me, yeh know? Always has been. And I still care about her, I do. But just as mates.' He glanced apologetically at his mother, knowing that she would be distressed at that last word.

On their return ramble, they walked through the ruins of the Glendalough Monastic Site–St. Kevin's Church, the cathedral, the round tower. It was one of Wicklow's, one of Ireland's holiest sites, founded over 1500 years ago. A place where men lived and worked their faith.

As they stood looking at St. Kevin's Cross, Catherine dared to raise what she suspected was a sensitive issue with her son.

'Car, 'ave you not been goin' to Mass these days, above in Dublin?'

Cary groaned. 'No, Ma, I haven't. Not in two years, anyway.'

She stopped and turned to him. 'Why ever not?'

'Well, to be honest, I guess I'd have to say I lost my faith.'

'Cary, dear, God loves you, so. Surely you believe that.'

'I didn't say I lost my faith in God.'

She looked perplexed.

'It's the Church, Ma. I lost my faith in the Church.'

'Well, Car, I suppose I understand. But the priests, the nuns, the bishops, the Pope, they're only human.'

'That's just it, Ma. They always claimed to be more, to be men and women of God. Pure. Spiritual. Above earthly concerns.' Cary was speaking now from the heart and Catherine listened carefully, her eyes fixed on her son as he spoke.

'They betrayed us, Ma. And truth be told, they betrayed Jesus

Christ and the Heavenly Father. Judases, every one of 'em. If there is a hell, they'll burn there, Ma, for their sins, I believe that.'

She looked her son squarely in the eye. 'I know, Car. It's inexcusable.'

'When I think of how they hid the abuse of little ones all those years–and the way the Magdalenes treated those mothers and their bairns–I don't see how anyone can trust the Catholic Church now, or ever.' He was referring to an order of nuns that took in unwed mothers, wrested their babies from them, then set them to work for their sins, often never to be reunited with their children.

Catherine was shocked at the depth of emotion her son was revealing. He was standing, gripping the branch of a small sessile oak as if for support, his hand shaking like a leaf. What she saw suddenly worried her.

'Car, what's the matter, dear? Is there somethin' yeh're not tellin' me? Did somethin' happen–to you?'

'No, Ma. But my flatmate, Niall? You and Da met him once.'

She nodded.

'He has a little brother. Fourteen years old. Tried to hang himself in their barn one night a few years ago.'

Catherine gasped. 'Oh, dear God.' She looked into her son's eyes fearfully.

'Yes, Ma. Exactly what yeh're thinkin'. Their pastor. Not just once or twice, but a bunch o' times. The lad couldn't admit it, and he couldn't confess it, all he could do was tie a noose around his neck and jump off a bale a hay.'

Catherine's face was now twisted in pain. 'That poor child, I had no idea, son.'

'So you see why I can barely bring myself to step into a church these days? I almost got sick the other day at Da's funeral. I had to take a pill to settle my stomach just before we left for the funeral, that's how bad it was. So I'm sorry, but I'm soured on the Church, now and forevermore.'

She nodded to say she understood.

'But Ma, I been goin' to a Buddhist temple in Dublin for a while now. And a couple of Friends' meetings with Siobhan. Her parents are very conservative—Bible-thumpers she calls 'em. She says it would kill them if they knew she was associating with Quakers. That's one of the reasons she came to uni in Dublin, to get away from that, as far away as possible.'

Cary and his mother walked around the Monastic Site in silence, wandering among old gravestones, looking up at the 100-foot round tower. On their way back to the parking lot, Cary had a reflection on Glendalough.

'When I think about it, I wonder if maybe St. Kevin had the right idea with his monastery up here. Far away from civilisation, alone, a place where nothing and nobody could come between him and his God.'

In the car on the way back to Glenkerry, Catherine had one more thing she wanted her son to know about her faith.

'Your Pa and I felt terrible, too, when all that business about clergy abuse came out. You know, it started to come to light in the eighties and nineties, a little at a time. At first we were sceptical of some of those accusations, but in time we realised they were true and it was devastating to us as citizens of this country and as Catholics.'

'And we felt just like you that we had been betrayed by our own leaders, our own priests and bishops. Even popes. We started attending meetings of a group in Arklow, they call themselves *An Dílis*, the Faithful. Faithful as in true to our faith, not to the terrible perversion of the Church that has taken place. True to our faith *in spite* of the Church. It was just starting back then and the bishop warned people against being involved.' She chuckled. 'But you know? We figured if the bishop was opposed to it that was the best possible endorsement of what we were doing.'

'I've heard of that, *An Dílis*, Ma. They've become really big.'

'Yes, dear, they have. Because we realise that the Church has almost destroyed itself in Ireland, all because of those revelations. And even now they're so slow to accept responsibility. They seem more interested in preserving their wealth than reconciling with the victims and their families.'

'You know, Car, Ireland once had the highest church attendance of all Catholic countries. But church attendance in Ireland has fallen by half in the last twenty years. And most of us who still attend Mass regularly are the older generation. I read that fewer than one in five young people between fifteen and thirty attend Mass regularly today.'

Cary nodded.

'We can get angry at those priests and those bishops, of course. But yeh know, we really have no one to blame but ourselves, for being blind, for defending those people for so long. And for not believing all those children, those women, those victims.'

'Well, Francis seems to be a different kind of pope. Maybe he'll turn things around, yeah?' asked Cary.

Catherine shook her head. 'I wish I could believe that, Car. And he is a breath of fresh air in some ways, it is true. But he's the leader of a church that has strayed so far from its foundation. I'm not sure he can save it from self-destruction.'

'Yeh know, Ma, when Niall first told me about his brother, I fell into an awful state for several weeks. I don't think I've ever been as depressed. I could barely get out of bed. But I was lucky to have him as a flatmate. 'Cause I could see him carryin' on, knowin' how devastated he and his family were. And I finally realised that if he could find a way forward, so could I.'

'Oh, dear, I'm so sorry you had to go through that. You shoulda told us.'

'Well, I came home one weekend when I was just beginning to feel better. And I went for a hike up to Glendalough, tryin' to heal. You know that famous line of Van Morrison: "Go up to the mountain, go up to the glen, where silence will touch you, and heartbreak will mend." It helped me. It took on a whole new meaning for me after that.'

That evening Rosie called around to Cary and Catherine's house. She and Cary sat out in the garden talking about her mother, trying to think of additional names of people she might have been in touch with. She had some good friends in Glenkerry, several in the church, that Rosie agreed she should talk to. And they talked further about Mary's sisters in Roscommon, Rosie's aunts, Marguerite and Elizabeth, and Marguerite's four children, Rosie's cousins.

'I know you hate to worry them, Rosie,' said Cary, 'but they need to know about your ma. And they might have an idea where she's at.'

'But I can't imagine if they knew where she was, that they wouldn't tell me.'

'Well, who knows? Maybe your ma told them you knew, to discourage 'em from contacting you until she's ready. But you oughta reach out, yeah? And they'll help you contact those cousins, for sure.'

When all their ideas had been exhausted, they sat in the cool evening air listening to the crickets chirp. Somewhere out in the pasture a skylark was singing its evening song.

'So, how was your trek at Glendalough with your ma?'

'Oh, it was grand. I do love those mountains, and the views. It's good for the soul, bein' up there.'

'And your da's ashes?'

'Yep, we returned 'im to the place he loved.' Cary bit his lip. 'It's hard, lettin' go, yeh know?'

Finally, Rosie bade Cary and his mother good evening.

'*Slán agat,*' she said.

'*Slán leat* to you, love,' replied Catherine.

After Rosie was gone, Catherine said, 'How's she doin'?'

'Oh, yeh know. But I think I've convinced her to call her aunts up in Roscommon.'

'She's lucky to have you as a friend, Car.'

'I wish there was more I could do, I really do.'

Mid-morning the following day, when she was certain her father was asleep, Rosie placed a call.

'Aunt Marguerite? Hi, it's Rosie O'Malley.'

Rosie listened to the familiar voice of her aunt in Roscommon.

'Oh, I'm okay, ta. But I'm worried–about Ma. She left my da, maybe you heard?'

No, replied Marguerite, she had not heard. But she was not surprised. She knew her younger sister was unhappy in her marriage. She had hints that there was abuse. And in their occasional telephone conversations Maggie had even suggested gently that Mary might consider leaving him.

'I'm so sorry, dear, for you and your brothers. How are you gettin' on, then?'

'I'm worried, Auntie. Ma left in early May. Yeah. She wouldn't say where she was goin', but she promised me she would be in touch once she was settled.' Rosie's voice began to crack. 'But I haven't heard from 'er. I'm awful worried, Auntie.'

'Oh, dear. And she of course has no mobile.'

'Actually, she bought one, just before she left. And she said she'd call me. But here it is the middle of June and still not a word.' Rosie decided not to mention the Lough Beag business for fear of alarming her mother's sister. 'I was hopin' you or Aunt Elizabeth might a heard from her.' Elizabeth was the eldest of the three sisters, now in her late sixties.

'Well, no, I'm afraid not, dear. The last we heard was around Easter when Mary wrote us a note. I've still got it, a very pretty Easter card. But not a hint of her leaving.'

'What about Elizabeth?'

'Oh, well, if she had heard she would have told me, dear.' The two sisters lived together in a small stone cottage outside of Roscommon. Marguerite had been married to Cornelius Finley who died nearly a decade ago. Elizabeth had never married.

'I don't suppose any of yours would have heard from her?' Marguerite had four children, all now young adults.

'I can't imagine Mary would have talked to any of them, really. She doesn't know them all that well, and they're all in Dublin or thereabouts, except for Charlie and his wife.'

'Could I speak with Auntie Elizabeth? Is she at hand?'

'Uh, no, dear, she isn't in at the moment. But I'll be sure to tell her you called.'

'Could you ask her to give me a call, Auntie? I'd love to talk to her.'

'Uh, well, of course, I'll do that. But–well, I'll see if I can get her to call yeh.'

Rosie rang off but sat for some time thinking about her conversation with her Aunt Marguerite. There was something a bit evasive about her manner that seemed unlike her. Maybe she was trying to avoid some topic–or hiding something. Rosie wasn't sure, but she had the distinct feeling something was amiss in Roscommon.

Down the lane at the McGurk home, Catherine spoke to Cary as he sat at the kitchen table gazing into his laptop.

'Sorry to interrupt you, Car.'

'No problem, Ma. I'm just lookin' for jobs, yeh know? Around London.'

'You can do that on the internet, can yeh?'

Cary nodded. 'What's up?'

'I spoke with Gloria Hennessy this morning at her office. You know who I mean, the estate agent?'

'Oh, yeah, sure. I remember her. Billy was in my class at *Coláiste*. Played football, quite the athlete as I recall.'

'Yes, right, and now at Trinity. Anyway, Gloria's a real go-getter when it comes to her business. She doesn't fool around with little cottages, you know? Only the most desirable properties.'

'Yeah, so I've heard.'

'Well, she's very excited about the Upton Road property. Naturally, why wouldn't she be? It's prime property according to her.'

'Oh, what did she have to say?'

'She's smart, Car, got a good head for business. She's always looking ahead, watching trends, thinking down the road, you know what I mean?'

Cary nodded. 'Just like everyone else these days. But good on her if she can do it successfully.'

'She says Glenkerry is changing, which we know. Lots of folks from Dublin moving down here, buying or building nice places. Many of them are working from home, especially since the pandemic. And she says not only have they fired up the housing market, but also the commercial real estate situation. She listed a half dozen new businesses that have opened in the town centre or are coming soon. And it's because those businesses see the new, well-to-do homeowners as potential customers.'

'Yeah, I can see that. I noticed on our way from Wicklow the day you picked me up two or three new housing developments. Posh places, too, not little country cottages.'

'That's right. Glenkerry is becoming a commercial centre for half a dozen little villages and townlands. Yeh know, Ballinoch, Dunbraugh, Kloughnarra, Whidfield, and all. Some don't have much in the way of businesses, no chippers, no convenience stores– not even a pub. Imagine that?'

They both laughed.

'I'll bet Gloria Hennessy thinks you should put the Upton Road property on the market straightaway.'

'Well, she recommends selling it, yes. She could list it for rent, of course, but she'd rather get the big commission on a sale, naturally. Either way, she suggests spending a little on the place first. Cleaning, painting, some minor electrical repairs. Just to improve its appearance, she says.'

"Kerb appeal,' replied Cary. Again they both laughed.

'She says it would be a small investment that would easily pay for itself. And my goodness, she was talking about an asking price...' Catherine paused, staring into her son's eyes in amazement. 'Well, I could not believe my ears, Car, I was astounded.' She told him the figure.

'Well, I don't know much about property values, Ma. I haven't ever been in a position to buy or sell anything bigger than my electric bass and amp. But it sounds like an awful lot of money–for that place.'

'She says the market is hot right now, but of course she's lookin' ahead. And she's nervous about the pandemic–and Brexit–and the border–and the EU. She says things could change for the worse at any moment. That this might be a good time to sell.'

They were sitting in the kitchen. Cary stood up, opened the refrigerator, and stared into its depths.

'One other thing, Car. Gloria's the chair of Save Glenkerry, you know about them, right? They sponsor roadside and river clean-ups, Glenkerry's Green Town programme, those kinds of things.' Cary nodded. 'She's called a special meeting for tomorrow morning, at half eight at Phinney's. Yeh're invited, Car. I think you'd be interested.'

Cary nodded. 'Okay,' he replied absently.

He was still staring into the refrigerator.

'What are you lookin' for, Car?'

'Oh, nothing, really. You know, Ma, I'm on a seafood diet: whatever I see, I eat.' Again mother and son laughed together.

'Well, help yourself, dear. I hope that lass Siobhan realises how much you eat.'

'Well, we'll probably not be having meals together or sharing food so much, Shiv and me. Just flatmates, you know, comin' and goin'.' He poured himself some orange juice and opened a package of biscuits.

'So, what do you think?'

'About what, Ma?' he asked as he munched on a custard cream.

'Try to focus, Car,' she replied, a note of frustration in her voice. 'Upton Road, of course.' She shook her head but was smiling all the while.

'Sorry, Ma, I'm just distracted is all.'

'About London and Siobhan?'

'Well, a little, but mostly about Rosie–and her mother.' He paused. 'Ma, how are you set right now, financially, I mean? It's none of my business, but just in general? What I'm gettin' at is, could you afford to spend a lot of money on that place before putting it on the market, that is, *if* you put it on the market?'

'I think I could, Car. You can look at our bank statements and our other holdings, if you want.'

Cary shook his head. 'No, no. It's your money and your business, Ma. And, honestly, I have a hard time keepin' my own chequin' account balanced.' He shook his head. 'Pa would hate it if he knew, but I don't even bother to balance my chequebook anymore. And these days it's all digital, all online.'

'Well, yes, I can afford it, Car, I believe I can. And I'm perfectly willing to make the outlay. But I want to know what your thoughts are on that property before I get into this any further. So before you leave for London, dear, please tell me how yeh're leaning: should we sell, rent, or what?'

Cary sighed.

'Think on it, dear. Just think on it, okay?'

Cary agreed to think on it. But it was a big decision, and, as he admitted to himself, even small decisions sometimes stressed him out.

Like that rug–in my flat–possibly a mistake.

Just then his mobile rang. It was Siobhan. She'd be wanting an update on Rosie's mother. And his new travel plans.

But at the same moment there was a knock at the front door. He could see through the window that it was Rosie.

His mother, Siobhan, and now Rosie–all wanting answers. Suddenly Cary was feeling besieged. He wasn't prone to panic attacks, but he could feel his muscles tense and his stomach churn.

'Ma, can you get the door and chat up Rosie, just for a few minutes, okay?'

Me, I'll just step into the loo for a moment, have myself a wee little nervous breakdown.

7

BALLINOCH TO DUBLIN

Cary went for a run the next morning, down Anglesey Lane to High Street, then into Upton Road, across the bridge and along the river. After several k's he turned around and retraced his route. When he was back on Anglesey Lane, he saw Rosie approaching in denim dungarees and a T-shirt, shopping bag in hand. He stopped and pulled out his earbuds, letting them hang from his shirt pocket.

'Hey, Rose. Goin' to the shops?' he inquired breathlessly.

She nodded. 'How was your run?'

He was panting hard still, leaning forward with hands on his knees. 'Good, yeah. Pretty good.'

Rosie reached for one of his earbuds. He tried to deflect her, but too late. She held it to her ear.

'You gotta be kiddin' me. Really? Taylor Swift? What are you, thirteen?'

Cary looked embarrassed. 'Well, I had a huge crush on her when I was about that age, and I still like to run to her. I got over thirty of her songs on my MP3 player.'

'Oi, do your friends at uni know about this?'

He shook his head, smiling sheepishly. 'Nah, it's my little secret. They probably think I'm listenin' to Metallica or Guns N' Roses.' They both laughed.

'Ciaran McGurk, you are a man of many mysteries,' she said with a twinkle in her eye. 'Oh my God, Taylor Swift.'

Then she got serious. She'd had a call from Del and was headed to the garda station.

'Come along?' she asked. And they walked together to the station.

Del was anxious to give them an update.

'Did Cary tell you his latest theory, Rosie? That maybe yer ma was headin' to Ballinoch when Heman Murphy saw her up at Lough Beag that morning? It makes sense when yeh think about it– she probably figured she wouldn't be recognised there. Plus there's the bus that stops there. Fortunately there's a CCTV camera in the centre of the village. It's not at the bus stop but, assuming your ma came down the road from the west intendin' to catch the bus, I figured she woulda had to pass along in view of the camera.'

He led them to his desk and his computer terminal. 'Heman Murphy saw her 'bout seven that morning at Lough Beag. I figure it would've taken her at least an hour to walk from there out to the county road and into Ballinoch. So I watched the CCTV footage from eight o'clock on. The northbound bus stops every hour in Ballinoch, at quarter past the hour. The southbound bus comes through around the half hour.'

Rosie was looking anxious and biting her lip. 'Did you see

her?'

'Well, that's why I wanted you here. I've got the video file on my terminal. I saw three women of about your ma's age and size who seemed to be alone and headed in the direction of the bus stop over the next hour or so, one at 7:50, one at 7:55, and one at 8:01. Have a look. It's grainy and there's some glare from the sun but see what you can tell.'

Rosie sat nervously at the computer with Del and Cary looking over her shoulders as the CCTV video played, starting just before 7:50 am. Soon a figure entered the picture walking along the far footpath. It appeared to be a young woman with a quick pace.

Rosie shook her head. 'Even though I can't really see her face very well, the way she walks, that's not my ma. Too fast, and too straight, yeh know?'

'Okay, so, here comes number two.'

Another figure appeared, this one on the near footpath. The angle was steep and the face was not clear. Again Rosie shook her head. 'Her hairline, it's wrong. She has a part, see? Not anything like my ma's.'

Del exhaled. 'Okay. Good. One more.' Number three appeared, crossing the street right in front of the camera. Again a woman, but dark skinned and wearing what looked like a sari.

Rosie shook her head. 'Nope, definitely not my ma, unless she was wearing a disguise.' She looked up at Del. 'That's it?'

He nodded. 'Well, we can skip ahead to 8:30, but I didn't see anyone coming from that direction, man, woman, or child. And I looked at the 9:00 and 9:30–no joy there either.'

The CCTV footage was still playing and Cary was looking at it intently. No one was walking on the street or either footpath. 'Wait, Del–can you pause the video?' said Cary.

Del stopped the video. The grainy still image showed someone sitting on a bench in front of a shop across the street from the camera. The face was obscured by a shadow from an awning. 'Look at that satchel, next to that person, Rosie. See the shape, and the handle?'

'That could be Ma's,' said Rosie. 'She used it mostly for shopping at the market. It was just that shape and had that long handle to make it easy to carry by her side. Can you zoom in on it, Del?'

Del magnified the image, focusing on the satchel. 'Yup, see, it's got that stripe design on the side,' said Rosie. 'That's it, that's my ma's–or it sure looks like 'ers.'

'Okay, well, let's see what happens to her. If she planned to catch the bus, she should get up soon and walk in that direction.' At about 8:10 the figure stood up, lifted the satchel, and emerged briefly from the shade of the awning.

'That's Ma.'

Just then a large lorry pulled up to the kerb, blocking the view. 'That's why I missed her,' said Del. 'She walked behind that tipper. That's grand, Rosie. We can guess from the time that your ma was planning on taking the bus north, maybe to Enniskerry, or Bray, or Dublin. So I'll contact Bus Éireann and see if they can tell me who the driver was.'

Before they left, Rosie asked about Del's meeting with her brother Buddy.

'Yeah, I spent some time with Buddy yesterday in Dalkey. He's workin' at a garage. He didn't know anything about your mom's plans before she left and he hasn't heard from her since. But like you he knew his mother was unhappy in her marriage. So it wasn't a surprise to 'im when she left. Oh, and I asked about other friends or family. He mentioned a cousin of your ma's who went to the US some years ago.' Del referred to his notes. 'Eileen Malone.'

'Oh, yeah,' replied Rosie. 'I forgot all about Eileen. Yeah, she lives in Virginia as I recall. I'm sure I don't have an address or telephone number for her, but I'll look through my mother's papers and see what I can find.'

'Brilliant. Okay then.'

By the next day Del was able to report on his further efforts to track the route of Mary O'Malley some five weeks earlier. Bus Éireann identified the driver of the bus that she likely boarded in Ballinoch that morning. He lived in Bray which was where he started and finished his shift every day. Del had scanned a photograph of Mary that Rosie had provided and sent it to the driver in the faint hope that he might remember her. Not surprisingly, he did not. But if she had disembarked alone, especially at an isolated stop, the driver felt he might have remembered her. He suggested that perhaps she got off at Bray, or possibly continued on to Dublin. In both places she would have been one of a number of passengers leaving the bus, and less likely to catch his eye.

Del had managed to obtain CCTV footage from the station in Bray and from three stops in Dublin for the hour or so after Mary's bus would have arrived on 7 May. He spent several hours watching the films but saw no women that looked at all like Mary. Nevertheless, he would ask Rosie to watch them if she was willing.

Later that day Rosie returned to the Glenkerry garda station. She took a seat at the same computer terminal as a few days earlier.

'Well, the driver didn't remember your ma,' explained Del. 'But he seemed to think if she was on that bus, she probably disembarked either in Bray or in Dublin. I've looked at the CCTV footage for Bray and for several stops in Dublin and I don't see your ma. You're welcome to watch them yourself, Rosie, if you like. Take all the time you need.'

Rosie spent over an hour watching the CCTV footage of Bray and Dublin but saw no one that looked like her mother. When she was finished, she turned to Del, shaking her head and looking discouraged.

'Now that bus route ends at Heuston Station, Rosie,' explained Del. 'It's a big station and I've looked at some footage from there, but the ticketing area, waiting room, and platforms are very crowded. I don't see much chance of spotting your ma, even if she got off the bus there.'

'But if she did, maybe she caught a train?'

'Yeh, it's possible. Trains run from Heuston to the west and southwest–to Cork, Limerick, Galway.'

'Kinda like lookin' for a needle in a haystack, yeah?' said Rosie.

Del nodded. 'One more possibility is that she transferred to one of the shuttle buses from Dublin to the airport. Do you know if she has a passport?'

Rosie shook her head. 'I don't think she does. But I can't imagine my ma leavin' Ireland, I just can't.'

8

SAVE GLENKERRY

A crowd of a dozen or so Glenkerry residents gathered one morning at Phinney's Pub. No, they weren't starting the day with pints of lager. Phinney's had opened especially for the occasion, offering tea, coffee, and a few biscuits, compliments of the establishment. Gloria Hennessy rose to address the group. She was an imposing figure, tall, broad-shouldered, with bright blue eyes, rosy cheeks, and a beehive of blonde hair held in place with a tortoiseshell comb.

'Morning and bless you all for turning out so early. First, I want to thank Liam and Johnny for allowing us in before their usual opening time. If a garda comes to the door, we'll all just have to crawl under the tables, won't we?'

Everyone chuckled.

'I imagine by now you all are aware of the reason for this meeting of Save Glenkerry. We haven't seen much action since the river clean-up last spring which, by all accounts, was a big success. I missed it and I am sorry for that–but in my defence I had important business to attend to that week–on a beach–in Florida.'

Again everyone laughed.

'But what we're here to discuss today is serious, as I'm sure you will all agree. It's a matter that could have grave consequences for our town and our local businesses in particular.'

She cleared her throat as she consulted her notes.

'All right, then. As you know, a company called Emerald Isle Enterprises Limited has filed a proposal with the County Wicklow Planning Board. And it's a project that has us all very concerned. I have no direct knowledge of this firm, but I'm led to understand that their parent company is based in China.'

A groan went up from the crowd.

'What they are proposing is a shopping centre, a 100,000-square metre complex down on the river road, on some land belonging to Harry O'Malley.'

Clucks, more groans, shaking heads.

'It would house dozens of shops, some small, some very large, plus restaurants, a twelve-screen movie theatre complex, with parking for over a thousand automobiles.'

Again there were groans at the prospect.

'Now I am an estate agent, as you all know. And perhaps you might assume that anyone who makes their living in real estate would look upon such a project favourably. Well, not this realtor, I can tell you that.'

Cheers went up all around.

'The developers are calling this monstrosity Glenkerry Mall. They're patterning it after those huge shopping malls you see everywhere in the States. Why, parts of Florida are nothing but one mall after another as far as the eye can see.'

More groans.

'They of course are suggesting that this will be beneficial to this town, that it will bring in all sorts of new businesses, jobs, housing, and money.'

There were guffaws and sighs of disgust and disbelief.

'But I think we all know what this would really mean for Glenkerry. Our little shops would be unable to compete and would be forced out of business. Our roads would be clogged with cars, lorries, and delivery vans.'

One resident spoke up. 'Yeah, and those places bring crime, too, I hear–pickpockets, drugs dealers, scam artists.'

Gloria nodded. 'I fear that if this project goes ahead, Glenkerry, the gem of South Wicklow, will be lost, destroyed by the single-minded greed of those investors, whether they hail from Dublin, New York, or Beijing.'

'Now Paddy McGurk, may God rest his soul, had attended several meetings in Wicklow where this proposal was discussed. Thankfully, his wife, Katie McGurk, is here today to speak about those meetings. Katie?'

Catherine rose. 'Thank you, Gloria, and thanks to all a you for coming out this morning. As Gloria said, my husband was following this business for some months before he passed. And I attended one of those meetings with him and have some notes of his from several others. To his astonishment and mine, the Wicklow County Planning Board has been encouraging the developers in this project. Which is as I say astonishing as this is really unprecedented in Glenkerry and in County Wicklow.'

Just then Cary entered and took a seat at the rear. Catherine smiled at him, then continued.

'Such huge commercial developments can be found in our cities, Dublin and Cork, for example, but nowhere in this county, perhaps nowhere in the Republic, can you find such a big development in a rural setting. That's because we treasure our rural landscape and the character of our historic village centres. They are, after all, what makes Ireland different than many other places. And we want it to stay that way, I suspect you would agree.'

The crowd cheered and Katie smiled.

'Now I'll sit down and let Gloria talk again. I believe she has a proposal for Save Glenkerry in this matter.'

'Thank you, Katie, thank you so much. We all loved your Paddy, we did, and we miss him, as we know do you and your boys. But his spirit lives on, doesn't it?'

And everyone cheered while Catherine and Cary exchanged smiles.

'Several of us have been compiling a list of action ideas for your consideration. It includes petitions, rallies, vigils, letter-writing, fund-raising, and publicity. Now that's a lot to think about, I know, and especially as we have only about three weeks until the proposal will be voted on.'

Groans rose from the crowd and heads were shaking in concern.

'So before we leave this morning, I'm hoping we can form subcommittees to get working on those actions, and perhaps others as well. But I do believe our first concern, our highest priority today, must be publicity. Without it, all our other efforts could be for naught.'

Gloria took a deep breath, then looked toward Cary and smiled. 'Now, we have with us this morning a recent graduate of

Dublin City University where he majored in *journalism*.' Her eyes grew wide as she said 'journalism,' as if to emphasise it. 'I am of course referring to this handsome young lad on my right, one of Glenkerry's own, Ciaran McGurk.'

Cheers went up and Cary blushed.

'Now Cary, I know this is a bit unfair, and if you feel press-ganged, I apologise, but…'

Everyone laughed.

'But what I would like to ask, if everyone agrees, is that you, young man, son of the esteemed long-time editor and publisher of the *Glenkerry Gazette,* and a fine journalist in your own right, if you would be willing to produce a special issue of the *Gazette,* the first in half a decade I might add, for the purpose of bringing this matter to the attention of our fellow townspeople.'

Cheers and applause rose from the assemblage. When it subsided, all eyes were on Cary. He looked from Gloria to his mother, then to some of the familiar faces gathered around.

'Well,' he began, 'I suspect that if I say 'no' I'll never get out of Phinney's alive, yeah?' Everyone laughed. 'And while I've done some writing, I've never published a newspaper, so I'd be learnin' as I go along. But I believe in your cause here, and I'd like to help. So if yeh're willing to entrust this to me, well, I don't suppose I c'n say no.'

Another round of cheers and applause.

'I do plan to move to London soon, but I will do my best to get the paper to the printer before I leave.'

'Bless you, son, for that,' replied Gloria. 'We all look forward to working with you.'

The meeting then turned to the establishment of subcommittees to tackle the rest of the list of actions presented by

Gloria.

'I felt ambushed, Ma,' Cary complained to his mother back home. 'You coulda prepared me, yeh know?'

'I'm sorry, son, but I was worried that if you knew what Gloria was up to, you might not attend. She can be very persuasive, she can, and I thought if you heard her speak about that awful project and saw the enthusiasm of the other committee members, you'd be willing to help.'

Cary shrugged his shoulders. 'Well, Ma, you were right. A course, I feel a bit like I'm steppin' on a hornet's nest. Rosie's dad owns that land. And once he knows I'm involved, I'll be on his enemies list. But then, I'm already on that list, aren't I? Probably at the top.'

'Car, believe me, yeh're in good company. Practically everyone in this town is on that list.'

Okay, mate, one more thing on your plate, better get a move on.

Cary spent the rest of the morning sketching out a layout for the paper. In the afternoon he made several telephone calls including one to a printer in Arklow who had worked with his father, the other to Gloria to ask for her input, promising to have a mock-up for her to see in a day or two.

Next he turned to content. Gloria had given him some material on the project, several newspaper stories, plus a copy of the proposal itself. After reading everything he had on the subject, he began draughting several short pieces about the project, the approval process, and some comments from concerned citizens and sympathetic council members.

In the afternoon he walked into the village and stopped at the garda station to talk to Del. Garda Samuels was out but was expected shortly, he was told, so he waited in the entryway until he saw his friend pull up, get out of his car, and enter.

'Hey, mate. What's up?' asked Del with a smile.

'I wondered if there was any news about Mrs O'Malley.'

'Haven't you heard? Rosie got a text–last evening.'

'Huh?'

'Yeah. She called me first thing this mornin' and I just ran up there to have a look. She didn't tell you?'

Cary shook his head. 'Uh-uh. I gave her back the phone cause she asked for it, said she'd secure it with a password and hide it away from the old man.'

'Yeah, well, this text wasn't to that prepay, mate. It was to her regular mobile.'

'So? Where is her ma?'

'She didn't say. Here–see for yourself.' The garda pulled Rosie's phone out of his pocket, tapped and swiped a couple times, then held it for Cary to read the text message:

> *Rosie. Im okay Your not to wory. Someday Ill tell you my reeson for leaving. Nothing to do with you, your brothers or pa. No need to call garda All my love, Ma*

Cary took the phone in his hand and stared at the message, then looked up at Del with a dubious expression.

'Probably not from Mary O'Malley, right?' said Del.

Cary nodded. 'For one thing, before she left Mary told Rosie she'd call her. She even gave her a prepay just for the purpose. So why call Rosie's regular mobile? Plus the message–she says nothing about where she is, which she would know was important to her daughter.'

'Yeah,' said Del, 'although, maybe she was still worried about Harry intercepting the message, yeh know?' Cary nodded. 'But there's something else that I wonder about–the spelling. Actually the misspellings. See what I mean?'

Cary looked closely at the message, then at Del.

'Those misspelled words,' observed Del. 'Sure, they could be just regular texting errors, yeh know? Slip of the thumb. But they really look like mistakes made by someone who can't spell very well, right? 'Your'–'wory'–'reeson'.'

Cary agreed. 'Mary O'Malley was well-educated, Del. Rosie told me she studied to be an English teacher for a while. It'd be surprising if someone in training to be an English teacher would make mistakes like those.'

'Yup, exactly,' agreed Del.

'What about the caller ID?' asked Cary.

'Yeah, well, that was blocked. The message was sent anonymously. See at the top? If the digits or the name of the caller were meant to be displayed it would be right there. But we can still find out where the call originated and from what phone. We do that all the time with mast data. I'll get on it straightaway.'

'Let me know, huh? Then I can talk to Rosie.'

Del hesitated, looking uneasy. 'Listen, Car. Maybe you oughta get that straight from Rosie, eh? I know yeh're concerned, and I know you two are mates, but I don't want to get in the middle.'

'What, did she say something, Del, something about me?'

'Talk to the girl, mate. That's all I'm sayin'.'

Cary left and walked up the hill toward his mother's house, thinking. He didn't feel free to go to the O'Malley home. Just then he saw Rosie walking down the lane as she did every morning heading to the shops.

'Rosie, I just saw Del. He says you heard from your ma.'

'Well, I got a text, yeah.'

Cary wanted to ask why she hadn't told him herself. But he wasn't sure he should ask the question. He didn't want her to feel obligated to answer.

And maybe I don't want to know the answer, mate.

'Well, that's brilliant, Rose. You gonna go to see 'er?'

'We'll see.'

'But she's okay?'

'Guess so.'

'Sound—I'm really relieved. Listen, if there's anything else I can do...'

He waited for a reply but heard none.

'I mean, like, feel free. I'll be here for yeh, Rosie, you know that.'

She stood looking off across the pastures toward the river, hands on her hips, still not speaking.

'Right. Well, I'll be around, is all I'm saying.'

He started to walk away. 'Car?' she finally said.

He turned. 'Yeah, what?'

'Aren't you supposed to be off to London? Doesn't Siobhan expect you?'

'Well, eventually, yeah. But she understands...'

'You should go, Car, to London. I'll be okay.'

He was beginning to see what this was all about.

'Rosie, I'm not—we're not—Siobhan and me...'

'Car, I don't want to be one of those girls who keeps a bloke from his girl. I don't wanna do that, not to you, not to her. So go–please.'

'Okay, Rosie. I hear you–I'll back off. But it's not like that with she and I–er, her and me–it really isn't.'

'So thank you, Car, thank you for everything.' Her voice was unsteady. She started to turn away.

Maybe it was meant as a sincere expression of gratitude, but what Cary heard was more like 'Get your beaker outta my business.'

Still he had one more question that he felt compelled to ask.

'Rosie, in that text, did your ma tell you where she was? Or talk about you gettin' together?' He of course knew the answer.

'I gotta bounce,' was all she would say, then she walked away.

The sense of relief Cary had felt when Del told him about the text had been short-lived. He was already worried anew for his friend but beginning to feel his presence was no longer welcome.

Listen to her, mate–your work is done here–get on that plane.

The next morning Catherine woke Cary from a sound sleep. 'Car, Car. Wake up, son.'

'Eh?' He'd been feeling low the previous evening, hung out at Phinney's too long, had too many pints plus a whiskey shot or two, and now was paying the price. His head was pounding and it hurt to even open his eyes the least bit.

'A convoy of garda patrol cars just went up the lane. I'm worried about Rosie, Car. Maybe they've had some bad news.'

He sat up, swivelled about, then set his feet on the cold floor.

'When?'

'Just now. Two minutes ago. Can't you go on up and see to Rosie? I'm awfully worried for her, Car.'

Cary nodded. 'Yup, I'm on it, Ma.'

Yes, of course, he would go, but he wasn't sure he'd be welcomed by the garda, by Rosie's father, or, for that matter, by Rosie.

He pulled on sweatpants, trainers, and his DCU rugby shirt, then stepped out the door and walked up the lane. As he approached the house, a procession of three yellow and blue garda patrol cars pulled out of the O'Malley drive and sped past him. In the back seat of one he could just make out Rosie's father, looking haggard and ashen.

Cary walked uneasily up the drive, not knowing what to expect, but then he saw Rosie standing in the yard in a knee-length night shirt and leggings. When she saw him she started to cry. For a moment he thought she might turn and retreat into the house to avoid him. But instead she ran to him, sobbing, and wrapped her arms around him, burying her head in his shoulder. Her hair was a mass of tangles, and yet somehow it smelled like fresh strawberries.

'It's gonna be okay, mate,' he said, wishing he could believe it. 'Come on inside. I'll fix yeh a cuppa.'

In the kitchen Cary fumbled around preparing a pot of Bewley's. Rosie disappeared upstairs but soon reappeared in jeans and a loose jersey, her hair now under control. They sat at the kitchen table sipping their tea.

'I'm sorry about yesterday, Car. I was a little harsh, I know. I just hate keeping you from London. And not just from Siobhan, but from that world, and the job a your dreams.'

Cary shook his head.

'But here I am, cryin' on yer shoulder again.'

'No worries, Rosie, come on. Tell me. What's goin' on with your da?'

'They've taken him in for questioning, 'for assistance with their inquiry' as Del said. They think Pa sent that text, using an old phone of Buddy's, pretending to be my ma. Del said it was sent anonymously. God knows what my brother needed to send anonymous texts for. I'm guessing my da didn't even know that the phone was set up for anonymous texting. But anyway, it was pretty obvious that the text wasn't from my ma, anyone could tell that. So Del says they're gonna have to question him about Ma.'

'Rosie, you mean to say they suspect your father had something to do with your mom's disappearance?'

She nodded. 'Well, in that text, he seems to be tryin' to cover up something, doesn't he?'

Their eyes met and Rosie knew what Cary was thinking.

'No, Car, I don't believe it. I don't think he had anything to do with her–her disappearance, if that's what yeh're wonderin'.' She shook her head in disgust. 'Except for the way he treated her for the last twenty-five plus years. But she was plannin' to leave, and I'm pretty sure she left of her own accord. I think he sent that text so I wouldn't worry about Ma. And maybe so I'd call off the gardaí. He's probably afraid they'll charge him with domestic abuse.'

'Well, you told them that, right?'

She nodded. 'But I'm supposed to go to the station later and make a formal statement. So maybe they'll just question him for a time, then release him. He's not fit to be in a holding cell, even for one night.'

Cary nodded in agreement.

'But they also say he could be charged with hindering a gardaí investigation, by sending that text to me. I don't care much for the man, Car, but I hate the thought of him goin' to jail, even if he has committed a crime. And I'm not sure he has.'

'Can I make a suggestion, Rosie? And if you want to say no, I'll back off, totally, I promise. But just hear what I have to say?'

She nodded.

'Let's take a drive up to Roscommon and talk to your aunts in person. See what they really know. You said your Aunt Marguerite sounded a little strange on the phone. Maybe if you talk to her face to face you can figure out what's goin' on, eh?'

'What about London? Won't this delay you again?'

Cary sighed. He looked away out the window as he spoke, not wanting Rosie to see his face and become suspicious of what he was about to say.

'Listen, I called Siobhan last night and told her I'd decided not to go to London. Not for a time anyway. I got too much to do right here. My ma is all wound up about the old newspaper office on Upton Road, and she needs my help around the house. Plus I promised I'd help out Save Glenkerry for a week or two on a special edition of the *Gazette*.'

Okay, okay, enough. Don't lay it on too thick, mate.

Their eyes met. Maybe Rosie suspected he was overstating the situation. On the other hand, maybe she just needed him–his help, that is–too much to say no.

'So, road trip?' he asked. 'Roscommon?'

She nodded ever so slightly.

'Is that a 'yes'?'

Rosie smiled, her first smile of the morning. 'Yes, Car.'

He seized the opportunity of this change in her spirits to enlist Rosie's help with a little photography and artwork for the special edition. 'If you have the time, Rose.' She agreed to help, on condition of anonymity–her father, after all, owned the land that was in question. And he stood to gain a lot if the mall won approval.

A few hours later Rosie received a call from Del. They were releasing her father, but they were sending him by ambulance to the hospital in Wicklow for routine tests first. He surely would have resisted that if he had the strength, thought Rosie–he must have been very weak. So maybe the hospital was the best place for him right now.

Del called Cary and told him the news of Harry O'Malley's release to the hospital. 'I still think he's tellin' the truth that he knows nothing about his wife's disappearance. And I believe he sent that text to Rosie hoping it would reassure her, and maybe to try to keep the gardaí out of it.'

Cary asked again about the possibility of charging Harry O'Malley with domestic abuse. 'One thing at a time is how I see it. We need to find his wife. Then, if they want to press charges, well, we'll cross that bridge, yeah?'

Cary and Siobhan had agreed to Skype that evening. It had been nine days since her departure and Cary was reassured at the sight of her smiling face and those sparkling eyes on his laptop screen.

'Hey, mate,' she began, 'long time, yeah?'

Cary chuckled. 'Yeah, for sure.'

'How are you doing? Everything okay, Car? I hadn't heard from you in a few days and I was beginning to wonder.'

'Yeah, no, everything's fine here. Busy, but in a good way, I think. So how's the flat?'

'Great. Would you like a tour?'

'Yeah, please, show me around.'

Siobhan chuckled. 'Well, there's not much to see yet. Ellen loaned me a few pieces of furniture, yeh know, until we get some of our own.' She swivelled her laptop around so she could show him the flat. 'This is the sitting room slash living room whatever. It's pretty empty, as you can see. Those boxes are my stuff from Dublin, they just came by freight today.' She spun the camera around. 'And this is the kitchen. See? A sink, a stove, a tiny fridge. And our kitchen table, a gift from Ellen. It's where we'll eat. There's no dining room.'

'Maybe we can call it the kitchen slash dining room,' joked Cary. They both laughed. The counter was covered with what looked like bags of takeout, several days' worth.

'So, have you done much cookin', Shiv?'

She chuckled. 'Uh, no. That, mate, will be your department.'

Cary laughed. 'Yeah, well, battered hot dogs and corned beef from a can are pretty much my culinary limit, remember?'

'And that will be fine with me, Car.' Then she carried the laptop across the room and through an adjoining door. 'This is your bedroom. Check out the view.' He could just make out a rain-soaked street through the window. She spun the laptop around. 'Your bed can go here—when you have one.'

In a moment Cary was looking at another tiny room. 'And this is my bedroom.' He could see a mattress on the floor and a cardboard carton for a bedstand, with clothes piled high on both.

'And here's the loo, Car.' Now he was peering into a tiny bathroom with a tub. 'No shower, but check out this neat old tub with claw feet.'

'Whew, that is something. But, eh, Shiv, it looks like the loo opens off a your bedroom?'

'Yup, it does.'

'Oh, uh-huh.'

'No biggy, right?' she answered.

'So, when I get up in the middle of the night, I'll have to walk through your bedroom to get to the loo, is that it?'

'Yeah—no problem.'

Then she placed the laptop on the bed and sat down in front of it. As she did that there was a moment when he could see her full length. She was dressed only in her knickers and a skimpy top.

'Whoa, Shiv, put some clothes on, eh? Or turn the laptop.'

She chuckled. 'Sorry, Car. I was just getting undressed when you called. But, hey, we're gonna be roomies anyway. Right?'

Suddenly Cary was panicking. He could almost feel his blood pressure spiking.

New topic, mate, and fast.

'Hey, you won't believe what's goin' on in Glenkerry.' Then he told her about the mall proposal and how he had been shanghaied into producing a special edition of the *Glenkerry Gazette*. 'I said yes, Shiv, I kinda had to, yeh know? But I told them right up front I'd be leavin' soon as the paper goes to press.'

'It sounds like a good project for Glenkerry's sake, mate—and maybe good for your CV, too, yeh know? Tell them that if they ever want to see what Ireland would look like in the hands of those developers, they should spend some time in southern California. Malls by the thousands, one right after the other. It would be a shame to let that happen to Glenkerry. So how's Rosie? Any news on her mom?'

Cary told her about the phony text message sent by her father and CCTV footage from Ballinoch.

'I feel terrible for her, Car,' responded Siobhan. 'I can't imagine what that must be like. All that worry about her mother, and now her father in the hospital.'

'So how's the new job goin'?' asked Cary. 'You haven't said much in your texts and emails. I even looked at your Facebook page and I didn't see anything about it.'

Her voice betrayed a bit of disappointment. 'It's okay, Cary, but it's not quite what I had hoped. Too many meetings, too much negotiating with clients, not enough hands-on, yeh know? I wish they'd just give me a project, any project, and let me go with it.'

'What about the people you work with? Good *craic*?'

'*Craic*? They don't know the meaning of the word. They're all too busy and frankly I'm surprised at how little staff interaction there is. It's kind of cold, to be honest.'

'Gee, I'm sorry, Shiv. But maybe it'll get better. Yeh've just been there, what, a week?'

'Yeah, well, it seems like much longer. You are comin', right? Soon?'

'Oh, for sure. The *Gazette* special edition goes to press in just a few days. As soon as it's out the door, so am I, Shiv. I'll be flyin' out Saturday, Sunday at the latest.'

Cary was waiting for a reply but there was a long pause as Siobhan looked away from the camera. Finally, she turned and looked at him. There was, he thought, a hint of sadness in those beautiful eyes as she spoke: 'It'll be great seein' you, Car. I miss you.'

Wow, did you hear her right, mate?

'Me too, Shiv. Well, I gotta go. Talk soon, yeah?'

'Yeah, talk soon.'

Now that was a strange conversation, he was thinking. Siobhan Sullivan, hard-driving, career-oriented Siobhan, was lonely. And missing her mate. An image flashed through his mind, of PJs and pillow fights, or whatever.

She's just a little homesick, is all. For Ireland, most likely. Who wouldn't be?

And then that earworm was back, gnawing into his brain.

Sharing a flat with Siobhan Sullivan—what were you thinking, mate?

The following day Gloria Hennessy called on Catherine and Cary.

'Okay,' began Cary as they stood over the kitchen table looking at a mock-up of the planned special issue of the *Glenkerry Gazette*. 'So we start with a single sheet like this, standard newspaper stock. We print it on both sides, then fold it twice, like this and this. It's called a folio. It's about as simple and inexpensive as you can get.'

'Simple and inexpensive—I like it, Cary,' said Gloria.

'On the front page will be your letter with a photo of you, Mrs Hennessy. Then a summary of the mall proposal. Rosie O'Malley has promised to take the photos for us, so long as we don't use her name anywhere.'

Gloria understood. 'Uh-huh. Got it.'

'She's already taken one of the site with sheep grazing around those yellow stakes. That ought to grab people's attention.'

'Ooh, excellent, Cary,' replied Gloria.

'Inside we'll have one page of just words of support from citizens and from several sympathetic council members like the one you mentioned, Kevin Leahy? The other page could have a detailed map of the project and a bullet list—yeh know, size, dimensions, number of shops, numbers of cars in the carpark, etc. Maybe a few photos of a big city shopping centre.'

'Perfect, Cary, absolutely perfect.'

Then she turned to Catherine. 'This young man came along just at the right time, Katie. We need him in Glenkerry. Maybe you can convince him to stay?'

Catherine shrugged. 'Eh, well, the thing is, he's got plans.'

'I understand.'

Gloria turned back to Cary. 'Well, thank you again for all this. Our big kick-off rally is Friday. If this could be in print by then it would be ideal. If it's possible.'

'I will do my best, Mrs Hennessy.'

She chuckled. 'Glo–please call me Glo.'

Cary laughed. 'Okay, Glo. By the way, how's Bill doin' these days?'

'Oh, he's up at Trinity, on the rugby team. And he was a Schols winner in economics.'

'Wow, well, tell him I said hi. He might not remember me, but tell him hi for me, yeah?'

That evening Catherine said, 'When you asked Gloria to say hello to Bill, you said he might not remember you. Why on earth would you think that? Weren't you two in the same class at *Coláiste?*'

'Oh, well, Bill was a star. And I was invisible.'

Catherine sighed. 'Oh, Car…'

'No, Ma, in a good way, I mean.'

Invisible works for you, mate.

Dublin

9

ABOVE IN DUBLIN

Cary was sitting at a table in Phinney's Pub two days later. He had ordered a latte and was sipping it as he watched the door. Several older men were seated together at the bar, hunched over their pints while engaged in a conversation with Liam Phinney. Soon a tall, stout man entered. He was bald with a round, florid face and a ready smile.

'Mr Leahy, sir?' said Cary, rising to greet the man.

'Kevin, call me Kevin, lad. Everyone does.'

'I'm Ciaran McGurk.'

'How do, sir. I knew your dad. Fine fellow, him. Very sorry to hear of his passing.'

'Thank you, sir–eh, Kevin.'

'And your ma, Katie, lovely lass. How's she doin'?'

'She's okay and asked to be remembered to yeh. Can I order yeh something, Kevin?'

He sat and nodded. 'I could murder a pint, lad–thank yeh.'

Kevin Leahy was a member of the Wicklow County Council representing Glenkerry and the surrounding villages. He was well known to all and could often be seen jawing with folks on the High Street on a sunny day. He had a loud, booming voice well suited to speaking before crowds.

'So, I understand Gloria Hennessy has got you workin' on that mall business, eh?'

'Yes sir, I'm trying to put together a special issue of the *Gazette* for the occasion. Get the word out, build support–or rather, opposition.'

Kevin laughed. 'Yep, right. Glo's a fireball, ain't she now? And she usually gets what she's after–including my brother-in-law.' Then he let out a particularly loud throaty laugh, leaned in and spoke softly: 'She can 'ave 'im, is what I say.' Again a deep laugh.

Cary chuckled. 'Yeah, well, she suggested I speak with you about the project–yeh know, get some ideas for the newspaper.'

For the next half hour Cary spoke with Kevin, all the while taking notes on a pad of lined paper. The man had some good insights into the project, the town, and county government as well as some valuable suggestions on what to emphasise in the special edition.

'Now, about the County Council, you have to go into that meeting well prepared. Understand?' Cary nodded. Kevin continued. 'You have to look real hard at the filings, especially the environmental data, is my advice, Cary. Get an expert to look 'em over. A lot of numbers, graphs, and maps can look impressive, but the devil is in the detail, as they say, eh? Water is always the trickiest issue, surface water, groundwater, runoff, all that. But you know all about that stuff, eh?'

Cary gulped. 'Yeah, sure. But I'm not gonna be able to do any more than get out the newspaper. I'm headin' off to London this weekend.'

Kevin's face dropped. 'Oh, I see.' He seemed discomfited by this information. 'Well, I imagine Glo will have this all in hand. Be sure to tell her, there's lots of groundwork that needs doin'. Lots.'

He shook his head and frowned. 'I gotta tell yeh, lad, there are some council members, more than a few I'd say, who think the project would be good for this town and for the county. They'll make this thing seem like manna from heaven. And anyone who challenges it will have to be ready, have their ducks in a row, as they say. Know what I mean?'

Again Cary nodded and Kevin went on. 'And that company, Emerald Isle Enterprises, someone needs to look into them, find out what you can about 'em. There's bound to be some skeletons in their closets, eh?'

Finally, Kevin took a deep breath. He was looking intensely at Cary, as if sizing him up. 'They need you, lad, we all do.'

He took one more long pull from his pint, then brightened up. 'Well, I've another appointment in Rathnew I gotta be off to.'

They both stood and shook hands as Cary thanked the man. 'See yeh round, Cary,' said Kevin with a wave. On his way to the door he looked around the pub to see if there were others he could gladhand before departing. But it was still just the two oldsters nursing their pints at the bar.

Cary sat alone for a few moments looking down at his notes while finishing his pint. Suddenly he was aware of someone standing over him, glowering. It was one of the men from the bar, Heman Murphy. He was a skinny, wizened old man with a shock of grey hair on the top of his head. The scowl on his face left no doubt of what was on his mind.

'Yeh're the McGurk kid, eh?' he said disdainfully.

'Yes, sir. That's right,' replied Cary cheerfully while extending his right hand. But the old man wasn't having any pleasantries.

'Yeah, I figured. Just outta college, eh? Come back home to make some kind a name fer yehself, I s'pose.'

Cary flushed. 'Eh, I don't know about that, Mr Murphy.'

'Well, if yeh're a smart college lad, then you'll take some advice from someone that knows a few things about this world.'

'Uh-huh.'

'Don't go stickin' yer nose in business you know nothin' about. Like that mall project.'

'Oh?'

'Be a shame to make a lot of enemies in this little town, yeh know?'

'So, yeh're in favour of the project,' replied Cary, trying to change the tone of the discourse. 'Sit down, won't you? Tell me what's on your mind, sir. Can I get you a pint?'

The man shook his head. 'What's on my mind is know-it-alls like you. So butt out. Right?'

Cary was about to say something like, 'I'm sorry you feel that way,' but Heman Murphy had said his piece. He brushed past Cary and out the door.

On his walk home, Cary was thinking about what Kevin Leahy had said, worrying about the proposal and wondering if he should be doing more than publishing the special edition of the *Gazette*. As he passed Gloria's office, he saw her at her desk. He stepped in to bring her up to date.

'I told my mother I was probably gonna make a lot of enemies over this project. Well, Heman Murphy just cornered me at Phinney's. He actually threatened me, Glo.' Cary grinned. 'A course, he's about seventy and waddles like a duck—but still.' At that Gloria let out a raucous laugh, her entire body shaking.

Then Cary summarised his conversation with Kevin Leahy. Gloria listened intently.

'Kevin knows this county and the workings of the Council as well as anyone,' she explained. 'He's on our side, Cary. If we're smart, we'll pay attention to everything he says.'

Cary relayed Kevin's thoughts on the environmental data, looking into the firm, and being prepared on the night of the public session. 'He seemed to think I was doing all that.'

Gloria winced. 'I have to be honest, Cary. I am worried about this business, very worried. One of my colleague realtors from Wicklow Town knows several of the council members. She says a subcommittee travelled to Cork City last week to see a similar project of Emerald Isle Enterprises and came back singing their praises. They told some of their fellow councillors it was a very clean, well-managed facility—and that the economic projections for it were proving accurate. And the Cork City officials told them how impressed they were with the firm, how it addressed environmental concerns, presenting data to allay their worries about runoff and possible groundwater contamination. They said they were genuinely responsive to the concerns of the city and its citizenry. It sounds like the momentum has swung against us on the Monster Mall. I fear we're going to lose, Cary, I truly do.'

She looked at Cary grim-faced. 'I know you've got plans, but we could sure use your help on this. It's more your area of expertise than us old folks.'

Cary winced. 'I'll do what I can, Glo, but I'm runnin' outta time.'

'I know, so whatever you can do, we'll appreciate it. No pressure.' Then she smiled a sheepish smile. 'You know, we're lucky Kevin's willing to help us on this. I got, well, involved with his sister's husband, Jack Haley. No big deal, yeh know, just a one-night stand–what you young folks call a hook-up.'

Cary blushed. 'Well, I gotta get going.'

'I'm sorry, Cary, am I embarrassing you?'

'No, not at all. See yeh.' And he was out the door in a hurry.

Too much information, mate.

Cary spent the rest of the afternoon putting the finishing touches on the special edition of the *Gazette*. He made revisions to several of the articles, then asked his mother to proofread them. He also spent a good deal of time on his laptop adjusting the layout, paying particular attention to Rosie's photographs and the arrangement of the text around the images. He was especially pleased with the masthead that Rosie had created and worked hard to adjust its position and size on the page. He printed out the entire paper as best he could on regular-sized paper, then brought it to Gloria for her approval. Finally, just before supper, he sent it off to the printer in Arklow, breathing a sigh of relief as he did so.

Over tea Cary told his mother of his meeting with Kevin Leahy, his encounter with Heman Murphy, and his conversation with Gloria Hennessy. He confessed that he was overextended.

'I promised Gloria that I'd get the special edition to the printer, and I have done. But now it sounds like she wants me to follow up on Kevin Leahy's suggestions. That'd be a lot of work, Ma. Hours of research, tracking down people, in Dublin, in Cork, yeah? And I think she's hoping I'll speak at the public meeting. I'm supposed to be in London by then, yeh know?'

'Well, Car, I understand. Yeh've got obligations. Siobhan is expecting you. And you want to start job hunting in London, a course. So maybe you should just tell her you've done all you can.'

Then Catherine paused, a worried expression on her face. She grimaced.

'What, Ma? What's the matter?'

'Car, this mall project is big. And I fear it will change this town, and it breaks my heart thinkin' of it, especially for your dad's sake– he loved this place, yeh know? I just don't know what else we c'n do.'

Cary lay in bed for a long while, trying to get some much-needed sleep. But the words of Kevin Leahy kept running through his head–that and the pleas from Gloria and his mother. Finally, he gave up on sleep.

Not gonna happen, mate.

He sat up in bed and opened his tablet. He started searching for information on Emerald Isle Enterprises, the company's history, past projects, names and affiliations of its owners, board members, and staff. He was surprised at how little information he found on the firm. One of the few links he did come across was a newspaper story about that commercial development in Cork City. It described a shopping centre about the size of the one proposed for Glenkerry. The reporter had interviewed a member of the Cork Planning Department who was familiar with the project. That individual spoke favourably of the project and of Emerald Isle

Enterprises.

Although he was getting bleary-eyed staring into the screen, he wanted to see if he could access the Cork proposal and the environmental analysis that was submitted with it. But neither seemed to be available online. That might require a telephone call or even an in-person visit to Cork. He was exhausted just thinking about it. It was nearly midnight when at last he fell off to sleep, his tablet lying on the bed next to him.

'You were up late, Car,' his mother observed the next morning.

'Yeah, I couldn't stop thinking about the Glenkerry Mall. And I was surfing around trying to find more information on that company, Emerald Isle. I spent hours and I have very little to show for it.'

'Maybe you should ask someone who's familiar with those kinds of matters. You know, an environmental scientist, or a writer? How about one of your tutors at DCU? You said you had some excellent professors there. Would any of them know anything about this?'

Cary looked at his mother and nodded. 'I bet they would–that's just what I should do. I have to go back to Dublin anyway to get the rest of my things out of the flat. Thanks, Ma.'

Minutes later he was composing an email to Professor Charles Jurgenson, one of his DCU tutors, asking if he could have a few minutes of his time the next day in his office. He briefly described the mall proposal, including the name of the firm involved and their recent project in Cork City.

Then he called Rosie. 'Hey, how are you doing?'

'Oh, I'm all right, Car, but nervous about Ma, yeh know? The CCTV from Dublin and Bray seemed to be a dead end. Del's talkin' about lookin' at her bank accounts and credit cards, but I don't know where that stands right now.' She sighed. 'How about you? Any progress on the *Gazette*?'

'Done, Rosie. Sent it off to the printer yesterday afternoon.'

'Well, congratulations, Car. That was a lotta work, eh?'

'Yeah, but thanks to you for all your help, the photos, the masthead. I just hope it will help defeat the Monster Mall. I'm worried about that, Rosie, and I can tell my ma and Gloria are, too.'

Then he described the meeting with Kevin Leahy and the conversation with Gloria. 'She's hopin' I can do lots more research, maybe even speak at the meeting in Wicklow. That makes me nervous, just thinking of it.'

'Whatta yeh thinkin', then?' asked Rosie.

'Call me daft, Rosie, but I'm gonna go for it. I'm headed to Dublin tomorrow, to clean out my flat, and then to meet with one of my journalism tutors—see if he has any ideas on the mall and what I can do about it.'

'Car, I think that's grand. I'll bet your ma is happy, yeah?'

'Well, it was her idea, talking to my old tutor. So, yeah, she's happy.'

'And your da, yeh know he's behind you, too—in spirit.'

Cary chuckled. 'I was thinkin' about that. I guess he is. Yeh know, he hardly ever tried to urge me one way or the other as far as school and career are concerned. But now, I can almost feel him pushin' me ahead on this mall thing.'

Barely twenty-four hours later he was on the road to Dublin.

It had been only three weeks since Cary left Dublin, but it seemed much longer. He left abruptly on Whitsunday when he got the call from his mother about his father's medical crisis. There was still an ache in his chest as he recalled that day, of riding the train south from Dublin, of not knowing what he would find. He'd long since decided that prayer was a waste of time, but on that day he had prayed silently, tearfully, as the coastal scenery of Dalkey, Bray, and Greystones whizzed past. He wasn't ready to lose his father.

He had expected to return to Dublin just a few days later to clear out his belongings from his flat before departing for London. Then his father died, his plans for London changed, and now, barely three weeks later, he was heading back to Dublin to do what he'd promised Niall he would do several times before, remove his belongings that were stowed temporarily in a hall closet.

Fortunately, those belongings consisted mostly of some clothing, his sound system, and his flatscreen TV. And then there were a few items of sentimental value including his Van Morrison poster, that group photo of his rugby team, and the little watercolour of Glenkerry painted by Rosie for him when he left for uni three years earlier.

Niall was not at home when Cary let himself into the flat. He made quick work of loading most of his belongings from the hall closet into the boot of his mother's Hyundai. His bed frame took more doing as he had to tie it down to the roof of the car. And somehow with the aid of a kindly neighbour he was able to stuff the mattress into the rear seat of the car. He had already decided to make the return trip on back roads where he could drive more slowly lest the load on the roof suddenly shift, break loose, and fly away. Plus, he reasoned, he was less likely to be stopped by a garda patrol car on those quiet country lanes.

When the car was fully packed, he walked the short distance to campus and found his way to the building that housed the journalism faculty. As he walked across the campus where he had spent so much time the three previous years, the realisation struck him: he had already left his uni days behind. Ahead lay his career, his adult life.

You've turned a corner, mate, you've set out on the sea of life–smack into a bloody fog bank.

Professor Jurgenson greeted him at his office at two o'clock sharp, offering his condolences on the death of his father. He was interested to learn of his former student's career plans and his move to London. But as to the project in Glenkerry and the firm involved, Emerald Isle Enterprises, the professor was not very helpful.

'I can't say that the company name rings a bell. My work has mostly been here in Dublin and in Belfast. I have never had anything to do with Cork City. But that project you mentioned in your email, Emerald Isle Shops, I have heard of it. Somewhere I have a pdf that I'll send you. It's a story from a Cork newspaper about how the objections to that project proved unfounded. Oh, and can you tell me the names of any of those staff people? Maybe one of them will be familiar.'

Cary immediately pulled out a bundle of papers from a folder in his lap.

'Yes, I have several names here–a project manager, an environmental specialist, and an environmental lawyer.' He jotted down the names for his tutor. 'I think there were several other names that I don't have here, but I'm sure I can find them back home, or reach someone who has them. I'll text them to you as soon as I get home.'

Professor Jurgenson also promised to talk to a colleague in the Dublin Planning Department to see if she had any insights into Emerald Isle or that list of people.

'I wish I could do more for you, Ciaran. It sounds like a project that could set a dangerous precedent for rural development, not just in Wicklow but nationally. I hope your group is successful in stopping it.' Then he paused. 'But you know, win or lose, this project could be really good for you. Gain you some valuable experience in environmental journalism–maybe open some doors for you. You never know where something like this might lead.'

Cary thanked him and promised to get those names to him by the end of the day.

For his return to Glenkerry, Cary chose the scenic route, the old military road from Rathfarnham to Laragh, through some of the wildest country in all of eastern Ireland. The narrow mountain road wound along the spine of the Wicklow Mountains, rising to 1600 feet near Killakee, dropping into the lush valley of Glencree, then rising once more over Kippure Mountain before descending towards Glendalough. The needle-like silhouette of Great Sugar Loaf stood like a sentinel above the lowlands to the east while the hulking mass of Lugnaquilla rose imperiously to the south. This was the other Wicklow, a wild, windswept land, entirely unlike the gently rolling pasturelands to the east. Cary loved to revisit these ethereal heights from time to time–they pleased his eye and his soul. But the pleasure he derived today from that rugged mountain scenery had to do battle with a sinking feeling in his chest, a gnawing worry that the Monster Mall was now an inevitability.

His mother had a hearty supper waiting for him, lamb shank and fresh garden peas. He ate, but quickly.

'Why the rush, dear?' asked his mother.

'I'm worried, Ma, about the mall. I was hoping Professor Jurgenson would be able to help me more. So I'm gonna work on my laptop for a while. But I'm not too optimistic.'

That evening he resumed his search on the web, looking for anything he could find regarding those two companies. Much of what he did find were the company's own press releases and public relations hype, although there were some newspaper stories as well. But once again he was surprised to find no stories beyond the last eighteen months or so, nothing prior to the Cork development about which he had heard and read so much.

He called Gloria who was able to provide him with additional names and titles of representatives of Emerald Isle Enterprises named in the proposal submitted to the Wicklow County Council. He texted Professor Jurgenson with those names, then returned to his web search, growing less optimistic by the minute.

It was nearly ten when his phone buzzed.

'Professor Jurgenson–hi.'

The professor apologised for calling so late.

'No, that's okay. I'm still working.'

'I been busy with a birthday party for my ten-year-old daughter.' He groaned. 'If I have to listen to one more Taylor Swift song, Ciaran, I think I'll go mad.' They both laughed.

'But she's asleep now and I was able to focus on your questions for a few minutes. I found something that might be helpful. The Companies Registration Office in Dublin maintains a database of all firms registered to do business in Ireland. You can search on the name of a company but also on the principals, board members,

CEO, senior staff members, and major investors. And you can learn a lot about a firm's history, financial condition, organisation, office locations, that sort. I'll send you a link. You might find it useful.'

'Oh, well, yeah, that's what I need. Because I'm coming up dry on that company. It seems odd.'

'Well, here's something that might interest you. It seems Emerald Isle Enterprises is a relatively new company, at least in name.'

'In name?'

'Yes. But nearly all the principals were in another firm, Ireland Visions, Limited. They were based in Dublin. As I said, I'm not familiar with Emerald Isle Enterprises, but I do know a bit about Ireland Visions, Ciaran, and I think you'll be very interested.'

The professor went on to tell Cary about a proposal submitted by Ireland Visions to the Dublin City Planning Department about seven years earlier. They sought approval for a commercial development to be located close to the banks of the River Liffey. There were questions about the possible vulnerability of the river to surface runoff from the proposed carpark including leakage or spillage of petrol, oil, antifreeze, and other petroleum products from parked vehicles.

'Look at the Tarmac in any carpark,' explained Professor Jurgensen, 'and you can find plenty of evidence of such materials, sometimes even puddles of it. Ireland Visions hired a consulting firm called Hydrotech to do the water analysis. Their office is in Kingswood, just outside of Dublin.'

'I was following the project, planning to write a story on it for one of the Dublin dailies. Then suddenly the proposal was withdrawn. I was surprised–Ireland Visions had invested a lot of money in the project already including purchasing most of the land. At the time I asked a couple of my contacts in the Planning Department about it, but no one had any explanation.'

'That is odd. And they never resubmitted it?'

'No, never. But I just looked them up on that CRO database. It seems that Ireland Visions went out of business just a few months after they withdrew that Dublin proposal.'

'Really. And that was seven years ago?'

'Yep. But here's where it gets interesting, Ciaran. All the principals of Ireland Visions are now affiliated with Emerald Isle Enterprises.'

Cary was perplexed. 'So Ireland Visions gave up that big project in Dublin, went out of business, then reopened under a new name?'

'Exactly.'

'But why would they do that, Professor? Isn't that a little suspicious? Like they were trying to cover up something having to do with Ireland Visions?'

'Very possibly. Here's what I suggest you do. Start with the Planning Department. Unfortunately, the head of the department at that time passed away a year or two ago. But I do know a couple of staff members who are still in that office. Maybe one of them could pull that file for you. I'll send you their names and contact information in the morning.'

'Wow, professor, this is really helpful.'

'Good, I'm glad, Ciaran. And honestly, I think this is worth pursuing. You may find that Ireland Visions and their new identity, Emerald Isle Enterprises, have something to hide.'

'Well, thank you so much. I'll watch for your message tomorrow and I'll follow up soon.'

With that Professor Jurgenson rang off. Cary sat at his desk thinking.

The following morning, as promised, Professor Jurgenson emailed Cary two names of staff members in the Dublin City Planning Department, urging him to use his name when contacting them. He also provided him with the name of the Project Manager at Hydrotech who was involved in the surface water runoff study.

The first name in the Dublin Planning Department was the Assistant Director who he quickly learned was on maternity leave. The second name was a clerk in the same office. He had heard from Professor Jurgenson and was expecting Cary's call.

'I have that file right in front of me. It's mostly letters and documents submitted by Ireland Visions. And there's a copy of their complete proposal, dated June 2015. It's a public document so I can share it with you—how about if I send you a pdf?'

'Yes,' replied Cary, 'that would be brilliant. Does it include a report from Hydrotech on water quality?'

'Uh, let's see. Yes, that's attached—as an addendum.'

'That is grand. Thank you so much. I don't suppose there's anything in the file about the withdrawal of the proposal—any letter or explanation?'

The clerk could find nothing to that effect. Cary thanked him and rang off, then tried to reach the Hydrotech person, a Carl Swinton. He got his voicemail and left a message asking him to return his call.

Later in the day Cary received a return call from Mr Swinton. When Cary described the project and mentioned Ireland Visions, the man remembered the matter.

'Eh, yes, sir, a bit of a sticky wicket as I recall. We did an analysis and submitted our findings to Ireland Visions. We had concerns about the impacts of the project on the river, on water quality. We said as much right up front in our report. I can send you a copy.'

'Is that why the project was abandoned?'

'Eh, well, not exactly.' He hesitated. 'What's your name again?'

Cary repeated his name.

'Yeah, well, Mr McGurk, there was a bit of a problem with their submission to the Dublin Planning Department. We got a call from the department head, I remember. He wanted me to look at the data that had been submitted in our name in their proposal. He had questions.'

'What I discovered was that someone at Ireland Visions had altered our data, literally changed numbers in a dataset we had provided. Not just a few numbers, but dozens. In such a way that they gave the exact opposite impression of our results. I called the fellow at the Planning Department about it. Within a day Ireland Visions withdrew that proposal. My impression was that they did so at the request of the Planning Department because of faulty data. That was the end of it.'

'The Planning Department doesn't seem to have any record of that. Do you know if there was anything in writing?' asked Cary.

'No, I'm afraid I don't. I'm looking at our file and I don't see anything about the withdrawal, the reasons, or any of that. But I'll keep looking.'

Cary thanked the man and accepted his offer of a copy of their report that they submitted to Ireland Visions. When he received the email with the pdf, Mr Swinton also included at copy of an email dated June 2015 that he had been able to locate. It was from the now-deceased head of the Dublin Planning Department. The email explained that his staff had found inconsistencies in the Hydrotech data that appeared to be intentionally altered. It went on to explain that Ireland Visions had been informed of this discovery and advised that the matter was being turned over to the City Attorney's office.

Cary could feel his pulse suddenly racing. Could it be that Ireland Visions, faced with a lawsuit, had been dissolved, perhaps to cover their tracks, to hide their past mistakes–or crimes?

Cary immediately sent an email to Professor Jurgenson, bringing him up to date on this development. A few hours later the professor called him.

'I just had a conversation with someone in the City Attorney's office who remembered the matter. In fact he has a letter, signed by the CEO and Board Chair of Ireland Visions. It seems the city was reluctant to proceed with an expensive lawsuit against the firm. Instead they reached an agreement. While not admitting to anything illegal, Ireland Visions agreed that mistakes had been made. Furthermore, they affirmed that their firm would no longer be allowed to submit proposals to the City Planning Department. And that, apparently, put an end to the whole matter.'

'Now what I suggest you do is research Ireland Visions and Emerald Isle further. I mean, that one case is serious enough. But if you have the time, you might want to look further, you know what I mean?'

'Yeah, sure, absolutely,' replied Cary.

'And Ciaran, a word of advice about presenting this kind of information. Be prepared for some grilling, both from Council members and those company reps. You know, there's a lot of money at stake, and they won't let it slip away without a fight. So do your homework. Have names, dates, documents, numbers.'

'Yep, a course.'

'Another suggestion: Don't try to present everything up front. But have it all ready, like backup, like reinforcements, when the big guns come out. Understand?'

'I think so.' He was remembering his professor's lectures on the dos and don'ts of environmental reporting.

'Oh, just so you'll know, I'm going on holiday with my family tomorrow, out to the west coast. We'll probably be out of cell range a lot of the time. But I'll be in touch as soon as we get back to Dublin.'

Cary thanked Professor Jurgenson several times before ringing off. His first instinct was to go to bed, to get some rest. But he knew he wasn't going to sleep until he had followed that lead further.

He was beginning to feel some queasiness in his gut.

You can do this, mate. Have courage!

'Cary, what on earth are you doing up this early?' asked his mother the next morning as she peeked into the study.

'Up early?' He laughed. 'I haven't been to sleep yet.'

He gave his mother a brief summary of what he had learned from Professor Jurgenson and the controversy regarding Ireland Visions, the predecessor of Emerald Isle Enterprises.

'Ma, I think I have to go to Cork to check out that shopping centre and talk to people in the City Planning Department. Do you suppose I could stay with Aunt Nell and Uncle Brian for a night or two?'

'Oh, Car, they'd love to see you, I'm sure.'

Finally, he found himself fading and after a cup of tea and a biscuit, he crawled into bed. As he was dropping off he was thinking, maybe, just maybe, the tide was turning on the Monster Mall.

Or, maybe it's up to you to turn the tide, mate.

When he woke up, Cary was tempted to call Gloria and give her a full report. And his mother was anxious for him to talk to her.

'She's very worried, Car. And Gloria doesn't worry easily, you know what I mean?'

Cary nodded. 'Yep. I do. But I'm not ready, Ma. I think I'm onto something, but I want to spend more time on it, really nail it down.'

'Well, you know what yeh're doing, I have no doubt. You are thorough, like your father was. Nothing wrong with that. And he would be so proud of you.'

She set her tea down and sat beside him. 'Yeh know, Car, things were very different in Ireland when your da and I were your age. People didn't challenge the authorities. Political leaders and church officials dictated everything. No one dared question them…' She paused, thinking. 'No one even *thought* to challenge them, Car.'

Cary looked at his mother and smiled. 'Well, times have changed, 'aven't they? It's a new world–a new Ireland.'

Later in the day Cary called Siobhan. He got her voice mail and left a cheery greeting, then asked her to call him back. That evening she called wanting to know how he was doing.

'Yeah, I'm fine, Shiv. Went up to Dublin yesterday to clean out my flat. Kinda sad, you know?'

'So, what's up with the special edition of the *Gazette*?'

'It's at the printer. They're supposed to deliver it this afternoon. What a relief. Yeah. I think it'll be good.' He paused. 'But, eh, Shiv, I got myself into another shite-load of work. The committee that's fighting that shopping centre proposal? They're really worried that the thing is gonna get approved and the chairwoman asked me to do some research on those companies that have submitted the proposal.'

'Oh?'

'So I talked to Professor Jurgenson–yeh've heard me talk about him, yeah? I went to see him in his office yesterday and he gave me a lot of help.'

'I remember how much you enjoyed his classes.'

'Yeah, he's great. Knows everybody. He gave me a lead on how to track down the people involved in the proposal. It turns out they've had some shady dealings in Dublin. They falsified some data in a report they filed with the city a few years ago. And they got caught. They barely avoided a lawsuit.'

'Wow, Car, that ought to make the Wicklow County Council think twice.'

'Yeah, exactly, so I have to follow up on that, get more information. I'm goin' to Cork next week to talk to some people there. Plus it sounds like Gloria, the committee chair, is expecting me to speak at the meeting. Which terrifies me.'

Siobhan tried to reassure him. 'You can do it, Car, I know you can.'

'Yeah, well, I hope you're right about that. I've not been sleepin' much the last few nights, worryin' about this. But I have to do it. They're depending on me. Gloria is really desperate. And my mom is talking like this could be the end of Glenkerry if that project goes through.'

Siobhan was trying to sound optimistic. 'It sounds like you should stick with it, then, eh?'

'Yeah–and it's interesting, Shiv–plus it's good experience for me, yeh know? Possibly a feather in my cap if I'm successful–and if I'm not, well, a blot on my soul, I suppose.'

Siobhan's voice sounded thin. 'So, what does all that mean about London?'

'I'm still comin', Shiv. It'll be just a few more weeks, for sure.'

10

MIDSUMMER'S EVE

It was Midsummer's Eve, the longest night of the year, a night traditionally devoted to celebrations. A bonfire was planned for midnight atop Signal Hill just outside the centre of Glenkerry. But earlier in the day a rally took place in Glenkerry's market square, a rally against the proposed Glenkerry Mall.

Save Glenkerry had decided not to dignify the plan with that name–instead they labelled it the 'Monster Mall.' Events began at ten in the morning with coffee, tea, sweets, and some lively fiddle music. Committee members were stationed at key locations around the square, passing out 'Stop the Monster' banners and buttons as well as copies of the special issue of the *Glenkerry Gazette*. The fiddler placed a tin on a stool asking for donations to the Committee and the coins and notes slowly began to accumulate.

By noon things were getting busy with many shoppers around ready to partake in the festivities. Cary was there, helping serve refreshments while receiving many compliments for his work on the *Gazette* special edition. He also enjoyed talking with many old Glenkerry friends and acquaintances whom he had not seen in some years. Soon Garda Samuels approached in uniform. 'Well, Glenkerry's finest, eh?' said Cary. 'Any good criminal activity to make your day today?'

'Nah, it's been pretty dull. But we've got a few irons in the fire on the O'Malley case.' He looked around. 'Call round at the station and I'll catch you up. Hey, great turnout today, lad. You and your people must be pleased.'

Cary nodded. 'Yeah, pretty fair.' They stood side-by-side, lattes in hand, watching the crowd mingle.

'So, whatta yeh hear from London?' inquired Del. 'That Siobhan mate been in touch lately?'

Cary nodded. 'Yeah, I talked with her just yesterday. Plus I check her Facebook page every few days, find out important stuff– like what's on her grocery list,' he added, rolling his eyes.

'Yeah, I know what you mean. I got friends who are forever updating their "Relationship Status." *Oversharing* is what I call it.' They both laughed.

Just then Rosie appeared smiling at the pair. 'Good *craic*, eh?'

'Yeah, I'll say,' replied Cary. 'And thanks again for all your 'elp.' He turned to Del. 'Rosie took those photos in the *Gazette*, have you seen it?'

'Yeah, sweet, Rosie, real sweet.'

'Plus she made that neat banner-masthead design.' He picked up a copy from the table and showed it to Del. 'See, it's got the town centre, the pastures, even some sheep. Notice the expressions on those sheep faces? Don't they look worried?'

Del chuckled, 'Nicely done, Rosie.'

'Shh,' she replied. 'My work has to be anonymous.'

Del understood. 'Oh, right.'

'Well, I'll be runnin' along,' said Rosie. 'See you lads later.'

They both watched her walk away, admiring the view. Then Del turned and looked at Cary, shaking his head. 'A real tragedy, it is. Will Shakespeare couldn't have written a sadder story.'

Cary clucked his tongue dismissively.

'But like the Bard once said, where there's smoke, there's fire.' Del sniffed the air, then smiled at Cary. 'And mate, there's definitely smoke between you two. But no flames yet?'

In spite of Del's constant teasing, it was kind of nice, thought Cary, having those two around. There were times when you wanted another guy to commiserate with, talk footie–or bump fists.

Also kinda nice to have a pretty filly's smile to greet you, mate.

As to the rest of Glenkerry's populace, Cary was noticing something curious. Nearly everyone who spoke to him about the special issue of the *Gazette* had the same question: When will the next issue be on the newsstand?

Kevin Leahy appeared at the rally later in the day, not wanting to miss an opportunity to schmooze with his constituency. As soon as he saw Cary he made his way through the crowd to greet him.

'Ciaran, me lad. Nice work on the *Gazette* special edition.'

Cary smiled.

'You have a knack, son, not only with the written word but with the design as well. Very effective. I'd say you've found your calling.'

Cary chuckled. 'Yeah, well, there's a good deal of writing and publishing in my blood. But I still feel like I'm makin' it up as I go along.'

Kevin leaned in and smiled that winning smile of his. 'That's what life's all about, Ciaran, makin' it up as you go along. Oh, I suppose some folks would tell you they had it all carefully planned from childhood.' Cary nodded, thinking of Siobhan. 'But for most of us it's a matter of trial and error.'

'Yeah, that sounds about right.'

Kevin sighed. 'So, you're off to London then, eh?'

'Nope, not till after the Council meeting.'

Kevin's eyes grew wide and he beamed. 'Really? That's news, lad. What brought on that change of heart?'

'You, Kevin–at Phinney's–you got me to thinkin'. I decided I ought to stay and see this business through. For my da.'

Cary then proceeded to fill Kevin in on the developments of the last forty-eight hours–his trip to Dublin, the meeting with Professor Jurgenson, Ireland Visions, their proposal, and the abrupt withdrawal of that proposal. And when Cary mentioned the threatened lawsuit, Kevin's eyes lit up.

'Do you think that will get the County Council's attention?' asked Cary.

'Oh, yes, I most certainly do. The idea that the folks we are being asked to trust have a skeleton in their closet, a serious one– oh, that will be very effective, lad. Even some of my colleagues that are hellbent in favour of the mall will think twice.'

'I'm worried though. Is that enough to turn the vote our way?'

Kevin drew in close. 'Here's what you need to do, Cary. Think about the kinds of responses you might get. Yeh know, ancient history, just a mistake, we admitted our errors and paid the price. That sort of thing. *Be prepared, son, be prepared with your response.'*

'Could you help me with that? I mean, think up some likely questions and how they could be answered?'

'Absolutely, absolutely. And Ciaran, how many others know

about this?'

'Only you, me, and my mother. And a course I should tell Gloria.'

'Okay, then. But other than the four of us, let's keep this under wraps. No need to tip off the enemy ahead a time.' Kevin smiled warmly, then took Cary's arm. 'Your da'd be right proud a you, son, right proud. See you later.'

Cary took another turn serving at the refreshments table. Then, in the evening, as the crowd began to thin, Gloria appeared at his side.

'Everyone loves your paper, Car.'

Cary shrugged his shoulders. 'It was a rush job, yeh know? Coulda been better.'

'Oh, I'd say it was just fine, lad, just fine.' She stood next to him, a paper cup of tea in hand, gazing out on the few folks still standing about.

'So, your ma tells me you've been busy–that you've turned up some interesting details on those Emerald Isle folks.'

Cary nodded, then repeated what he had just told Kevin Leahy. Gloria was ecstatic.

'Hallelujah, Cary, you are onto something there, son.'

Cary nodded but smiled weakly.

'You outta feel right at home up here tonight, Car,' noted Rosie. 'Isn't this s'posed to be the night that witches and dragons and sprites walk among us?'

Cary nodded. 'Yeah, well, I'm not into that stuff now like I was ten years ago, yeh know? I got more earthly matters to deal with.'

Rosie nodded. 'So, whatta yeh thinkin'? Can the Monster Mall be stopped?'

It was half eleven that evening and they were approaching the bald summit of Signal Hill where preparations were underway for the lighting of the Midsummer's Eve bonfire. There were other walkers ahead of them and behind, all with the same destination.

'Well, if yeh'd asked me two days ago, I'd a said not a chance. But my old environmental journalism professor gave me a big lead. I can't tell you any details yet, but we may be onto something.' He hesitated. 'It's just...'

'What, Car?'

'The research, the investigating–those things I can do. But they want me to speak to the Council at the meeting in Arklow, and public speaking–well, it's not my strongest point.'

'Well, like you said, win or lose, it could be good for you, I mean, a feather in yer cap, eh?'

'Maybe, but if I end up in London writin' advert copy, no one will care about the Monster Mall.'

'So London's still on, eh?'

Cary sighed. 'Yeah–I guess.'

It was now midnight, and the bonfire was lit. A plume of orange flame quickly consumed the stacked timbers and illuminated the sky above as well as the faces of a hundred or more townspeople gathered below. Rosie wrapped her hands around Cary's arm as they looked up at the undulating flames and incandescent sparks ascending into the night sky, now a deep purple.

'Hey-hey, wassup, mate?' asked Del Samuels the next day at the garda station as Cary entered.

'Not much.'

'Good day, yesterday, yeah?' said Del.

Cary nodded. 'Yeah, I'd say. Still lots to do before that Arklow meeting. Hey, so what's the news about Rosie's ma that you mentioned?'

'Well, coupla things. A garda search team covered the forest around Lough Beag the other day. They spent about six hours out there, didn't find a thing. And the CCTV from Bray and Dublin produced nothing either, I'm sorry to say mate. But we're not done.'

He turned and spoke to a young woman in uniform who was seated at a desk nearby. 'Officer Selkirk, got a sec? Sabrina Selkirk, this is Cary McGurk, an old schoolmate of mine and a friend of Rosie O'Malley.'

She stood smiling and offered her hand to Cary. 'Sabrina's been seconded to us for a time. She'll be our new FLO–Family Liaison Officer.'

'Well, good on you, Sabrina, and our good fortune,' said Cary with a warm smile. 'Welcome to Glenkerry. How are you likin' it so far?'

'Oh, it's lovely, just like Del told me it was. Very peaceful.'

Cary grinned sardonically. 'Yeah, sure, it looks like a peaceful place full of good, law-abidin' folk, but don't be fooled.' They all laughed. 'So, seconded to Glenkerry, eh, from where?' he asked.

'Wicklow.'

'Wicklow,' replied Cary with surprise, his gaze shifting from Sabrina to Del, then back to Sabrina.

Wait a sec, mate, a new garda, from Wicklow Town, a pretty young thing? Why is this ringin' a bell?

'Yes. And I've been assigned to track down any bank accounts in Mrs O'Malley's name. Del–eh, Garda Samuels–thought I might have some knowledge of the banks in Wicklow Town. I'm headed first to the Glenkerry banks, then off to Wicklow.'

'Oh, well, that's grand. I hope you'll be successful.'

Sabrina left, both Del and Cary watching after her with interest. As soon as the door shut behind her, Cary turned to his friend. 'Judging by that shite-eating grin on your face, I'm guessing there's a story here. Don't tell me she's that lady friend garda from Wicklow you were tellin' me about?'

'Okay, I won't tell yeh. But remember, Car, you made a solemn vow.'

'I did, Del. And I'll be callin' in that IOU one day soon, count on it.'

After a few minutes of additional give-and-take, Cary departed, Del promising to keep him informed of the progress of Sabrina's investigation.

Later in the day Sabrina returned from Wicklow and reported to Del. She'd visited and talked to the managers at five banks, two in Glenkerry, three in Wicklow. Each manager went into the bank's accounts database in search of the name Mary L. O'Malley. They found nothing. But when Sabrina provided Mary's National ID number, three accounts popped up in three different banks. They were in the name of Mary L. Malone, her maiden name. And all three accounts had been closed in early May, a few days before her departure.

When Del heard all this, he suggested Sabrina talk to Rosie. A few minutes later she drove up to the O'Malley home. She and Rosie stood by her garda car talking.

'I'm not surprised,' said Rosie after hearing Sabrina's account of her investigations. 'I shoulda suggested you look for her by her maiden name.'

This was a bit unusual, explained Sabrina. Most Irish women took the husband's name back when Harry and Mary O'Malley were wed some twenty-five years ago.

Rosie nodded. 'Well, that's just it. Yeh see, they were never married. I'm not sure why. I discovered this a few years ago when I needed a copy of my birth certificate and there was my ma's name, her birth name. I asked her about it and she was very embarrassed. She wouldn't explain. But now I wonder if it was about money. I know she had some money that she'd inherited from her parents that she didn't want Pa to know about. I think she had her suspicions about his drinkin' and gamblin' right from the start. So I'm not surprised that she opened those accounts in her birth name and probably kept them secret from my da all those years.'

'I'm afraid we're no closer to locating your ma, Rosie. You see, she closed those accounts back around the first a May.'

Rosie nodded. 'A few days before she left.'

'They were small accounts, a few hundred euro in each. And it looks as though she took it in cash.'

'Yeah, when she told me she was leavin' soon, she said she had plenty of cash on her. She didn't explain how she came by it, or how she could get it without my da's knowledge, but now we know, I guess.'

'Well, if that's all she had, we've kind a reached a dead end. But do you suppose there's more than those three accounts? That inheritance you mentioned. Did she say how much, I mean, did she give you any idea?'

Rosie shook her head. 'Nope. No idea at all.'

'The thing is, if there was a larger account in some bank, say ten or twenty thousand or more, we really should try to find out where it is, or was. Because she probably wouldn't be able to withdraw that much in cash, you see what I mean? So she might have taken a bank cheque or had it transferred electronically. Nowadays, banks can make electronic transfers of large sums so the customer never has to handle it. If your ma did either, got a cheque or authorised an electronic transfer, there would be a record of where the funds ended up. And that might just lead us to your ma.'

Rosie understood the possible importance of that information. 'But there's no way for you to search all the banks in the Republic?'

Sabrina shook her head. 'I don't think so, love. I'll ask Del and my Super, but I don't know as there is such a central database, even up in Dublin. Probably because of confidentiality concerns, yeh know? Some people just want to hide their money away. And for good reasons, often. Like your ma. Maybe for very large accounts, millions, where money laundering is a concern. But not for smaller accounts, I'm afraid.'

'Well, I wish I knew where else she might have been doing her banking. My da kept a close eye on her and so far as I know she rarely left Glenkerry except with 'im. But I'll give it some thought.'

With that Sabrina departed. Rosie went back to weeding in the kitchen garden, but she was thinking about her mother and her parents' relationship long ago, when she and her brothers were not yet in the picture.

Rosie spent some time the following day painting. She had done so little in recent months, and she needed to paint, perhaps to straighten out her head, to settle her rattled nerves. She arranged a still life on her kitchen table, with fruits from the family's little orchard–pears, plums, cherries, a few crab apples. The light was interesting, she thought, and cast shadows that would lend depth to the painting and expand the colour palette as well.

As she worked, her mind drifted, as it sometimes did while painting. This was often a good thing, she believed, because it meant her eye and her hand were working in such close synchrony that there was not a lot of thought required–pure aesthetics, she reasoned.

Then she began to think about her mother and the question that had dogged her for weeks now, where had she disappeared to? Was she safe, healthy, happy in her new situation, wherever she was? She hoped her mother was staying with a friend, perhaps an old classmate such as the ones her Aunt Marguerite had listed for her. But none of those had any information on her mother.

Then her thoughts went back to Roscommon and the times when she was a little girl and she and her mother visited with her aunts. There was a lovely pond in the town with ducks to feed and ice cream vendors to interest little ones like her. And suddenly it struck her. On more than one occasion, her mother had taken her along on errands in the centre of Roscommon. And one of those errands involved a bank. She remembered it clearly–it had polished granite floors and walls and a vaulted ceiling high above from which hung several huge crystal chandeliers. She recalled how quiet it was in the bank, how everyone spoke in low whispers, how her footsteps echoed in that vast space. She didn't know the name of the bank, but she remembered its location, not far from the duck pond. And she recalled very well its looming edifice with four shiny granite pillars. Within minutes Rosie was looking at that very bank online–it was still in business.

Early the next day, a Monday, Rosie telephoned the garda office and asked for Sabrina. Within an hour Sabrina had arranged for a garda in Roscommon to visit the bank and have a word with the manager. Several hours later, she received a return call.

'Good news, Rosie,' reported Sabrina on the telephone. 'Your mother had a large account at that Roscommon bank. About two weeks ago, she appeared in person and closed the account.'

Rosie's heart leapt. So her mother was alive. She breathed a sigh of relief.

Sabrina continued. 'The balance was nearly 20000 euro, Rosie. So perhaps that represents the inheritance your mother received long ago. The teller recognised her from that photograph you gave us. And the signature on the withdrawal slip looks genuine.'

'So that means you can find out her address, right?'

'Well, because of the amount of the withdrawal, your mom had to take a cheque for the balance. To date that cheque has not cleared. In other words, she must still have it. Perhaps she's nervous that your father might be able to somehow track her down if she deposited it near where she is now living. But the bank knows of our interest and that there is an active case involved, and the manager has promised to notify us as soon as they know the disposition of those funds.'

Sabrina took a breath. 'So we'll keep you posted, okay?'

Rosie thanked Sabrina again and again, then went back to her still life, somewhat encouraged. Her mother, Mary O'Malley, or Mary Malone, was alive. And the search for her seemed to be heating up once again.

11

ROAD TRIP TO CORK

When Cary was young the family travelled to Cork, Ireland's second largest city, once or twice a year to visit with their relatives, Catherine's sister Nell Harris, her brother William Flanagan, and their families. Cary and Aiden enjoyed spending time with their three Cork cousins who were roughly of their age. But it had been at least four years since Cary's last visit, before going off to uni.

Cary had called his Aunt Nell several days earlier. He planned to travel to Cork on Wednesday, he told her, then spend the day Thursday trying to find out what he could about the shopping centre project that Emerald Isle Enterprises was so proud of. Nell assured him that he was welcome to stay with them. In fact, before the telephone conversation had ended she had an entire menu worked out, making note of her nephew's gastronomic likes, dislikes, allergies, and preferences.

The drive from Glenkerry to Cork took nearly four hours, at first along lazy country roads, then on the faster moving motorway. The scenery was lovely but repetitive, green fields and pastures sloping away from the highway on both sides, sheep grazing, cows lowing, horses gambolling, and little else. Cary had his digital music player with him including hundreds of songs old and new that kept him company the entire way. He knew he was getting close to his destination when he heard 'Delilah,' 'Brown Eyed Girl,' and 'You Belong with Me' for the second time.

Nell and Brian Harris greeted him warmly and they sat in their yard in Cobh in the late afternoon sun, overlooking the harbour.

'Your mother, Ciaran, how is she doin'?'

'She's all right, Nell. She stays busy with her gardens, yeh know. Plus she's on a couple committees in Glenkerry–and she's still active in the church.'

'It must be hard for 'er, though, losin' your da so suddenly.'

Cary nodded. 'Yeah, it is.'

'And you? How 're you doin', lad?' asked Brian.

'Yeah, I'm all right. As soon as I got to Glenkerry the town started drawin' me back, yeh know? This old friend o' mine, Rosie O'Malley–maybe you met her at dad's funeral? Her mother's taken off, and I been tryin' to help locate her.' Then Cary gave them a brief account of Mary's departure, the promise to call Rosie, and the efforts of the gardaí to track her down.

'Well, she's lucky to have your help, I'd say,' offered Brian.

Cary shrugged. 'Well, I can't say I've helped all that much. And now there's this big shopping centre project. Ma is involved with a town committee that's fighting it. And I got myself mixed up in it, too. That's why I'm here, to see what I can learn about Emerald Isle Shops, that new shopping centre in Cork City.'

'We expected you'd be in London by now–wasn't that your plan?'

'Yeah, well, it's still the plan, but it's been delayed.'

'And that lovely American lass?'

'Siobhan? She's already in London. And I'm gonna be joinin' her right after this whole mall business is settled.'

'My goodness, you've got your hands full, I'd say,' said Nell.

'And what do you hope to learn in Cork, then?' asked Brian.

Cary explained the connection of the two projects. The same firm that built the Cork shopping centre was behind the Glenkerry project.

'I discovered that a company called Ireland Visions, Ltd, got into some legal difficulties a few years ago in Dublin. They had to abandon a multi-million-euro project there when they were caught fudging some of the figures in a development proposal back in 2015. That company went out of business, but Emerald Isle Enterprises it turns out is the same people, just with a new name.'

'Hmm, that sounds suspicious,' replied Brian.

'Yeah. So I want to find out anything I can about this Cork project. I have a nine o'clock appointment with the head of the Cork City Planning Department tomorrow morning, a Mr Smyth. And later I'm hoping to meet with a news reporter, Reynold Travers, who wrote several stories about that project while it was still under review. What I've read is all good, but I just want to hear it first-hand, have a chance to ask questions, yeh know?'

Cary was exhausted but wanted to check in with Rosie before going to bed.

'I'm so glad you called. I got some news, Car, about Ma.'

'What about her?'

'My dad's credit card statement came in the post today. I opened it and looked it over to see if there was anything important. Mostly it's just, yeh know, the usual monthly charges, like electric, phone, that sort. But there is one thing that's curious, Car.'

'What's that, Rose?'

'It's on the eighth of May–that's the day after Ma left. Somebody used that card to book a one-way ticket on the ferry from Rosslare to Fishguard in Wales–about 75 euro.'

'Whoa,' replied Cary, 'Wales? Can you tell where the purchase was made? Was it in Glenkerry? Or Dublin? Or Rosslare?'

'No. All it says is the name of the ship line, the date, and the amount. I looked it up. A one-way passenger ticket from Rosslare to Fishguard costs 75 euro.'

'Do you think your ma booked that ticket?'

'Well, I can't imagine my da buyin' it. So, yeah, I figure it must have been Ma.'

'But she musta known your dad would see it on the statement.'

'Yeah, she would have done. Although I found a whole stack of old statements on his dresser, like six months, never opened. So maybe she figured he wouldn't even look.'

'So, what are you thinkin', Rosie? Your ma went to Wales?'

'I guess.'

'Does she have any friends or family in Wales, or anywhere in the UK?'

'Not that I know of, Car. I'm worried, yeh know, that if she's left Ireland, I may never find her–I may never see her again.'

'Have you told Del or Sabrina about this yet, Rose?'

'No. I just discovered it a little while ago.'

'Well, you should call them tomorrow. They might be able to

find out more by contacting the credit card company or the ferry company, yeh know? I mean, if she got on that boat, the ferry line will have her name–they have to keep a list–whatta they call it–a passenger manifest, right?'

'Yep, right. A course.'

'And as soon as I get back home I'll see what I can do.'

Rosie sighed. 'So, how are your aunt and uncle?'

Cary gave Rosie a quick summary of the day's events, his visit with Nell and Brian, and his plans for the next day. 'I'm gonna be really busy tomorrow. I got two meetings in Cork and I want to spend some time at that new shopping centre, see what it's like. And I want to visit with Aunt Nell and Uncle Brian, and maybe my Uncle Bill, too. I'll either call you or text you, maybe in the evening, okay?'

'Yep, good luck, then, Car. And ta.'

'Yeah, you too, Rosie. See you Friday.'

The next morning Cary arrived at the Cork City Planning Department a few minutes before nine. The director, Harold Smyth, greeted him and led him to his office. Spread out on a table was a map of the proposed project, some photographs of the completed shopping centre, and a stack of reports and proposals. He proceeded to describe the project to Cary in a very orderly fashion, from its inception through the round of meetings and public hearings and finally to the City Council vote approving it.

'You should visit the shopping centre, Mr McGurk. I think you'll find it's very attractive and well managed.'

As to his dealings with Emerald Isle Enterprises, Mr Smyth had a favourable impression.

'They were well organised and very methodical in the planning process. They listened to our concerns and those of the public and by and large they were responsive. There was a bit of a kerfuffle over the carpark, its size and capacity, you know? But in the end they scaled it back and made some modifications to the runoff catchment system which is always a consideration with large tarmacked areas.'

Cary asked about the economic benefits of the centre.

'Well, yes, Emerald Isle's projections were perhaps overly optimistic. But the property is doing well–they've got nearly 100% occupancy and the tax revenues for the city have been encouraging. Of course, no one could predict the pandemic and the effects it would have on the economy, but the worst of that seems to have passed.'

After nearly ninety minutes, Cary took his leave of Mr Smyth, carrying a small stack of reports and thanking the man repeatedly for giving him so much of his time.

Then he drove about ten minutes to the Emerald Isle Shopping Centre. It was vast, even by Cork standards. It consisted of what looked to Cary like an endless carpark surrounding a series of unattractive, box-like buildings, all connected. As he walked through one of the main entrances he was immediately impressed by the cleanliness and attractiveness of the interior space. There was a central rotunda with a large shallow pool and a whimsical fountain of fish spewing jets of water twenty feet high. There was a food court with a dozen or more fast-food establishments. And there were two long, wide corridors, one to the east, the other to the west, onto which opened dozens of shops large and small.

Cary strolled up and down the full length of the centre, had a bite to eat in the food court, and sat for a few minutes by the fountain watching a steady parade of shoppers with bags of purchases, many pushing strollers. He had to admit it wasn't so bad as he had imagined it might be. But it was a far cry from a typical Irish town centre–it was sterile, predictable, utterly lacking in originality. Some of the storefronts were meant to look like small boutiques–with faux stone or stucco walls and names like 'Ye Auld Gifts' or 'Blarney Bling,' but inside they looked like every other chain store in Ireland, the UK, or America.

His next appointment was in Cork City Centre. But in the few minutes before his meeting, he strolled along cobblestone footpaths lined with boutiques, stalls, and street vendor carts. He browsed through quirky little health food shops, arts and crafts collectives, used bookshops, and second-hand furniture stores. The architecture was eclectic, the merchandise entirely unpredictable, and the people varied and colourful–a mime in an invisible box, a clog-dancing juggler, and a busker who played three banjos at once. What a different world this was, he thought, from the banal sameness of the Emerald Isle Shops. He purchased a pair of earrings made of sea glass for Rosie and a book on growing perennials for his mother whose birthday was just a few days away.

Okay, so you're skint. But it's all going on your credit card, mate, so don't worry about it.

Then he walked several blocks to the offices of one of the city's largest newspapers where he had an appointment with Reynold Travers, the reporter who had written several stories about the shopping centre project a few years earlier.

'As soon as the proposal was announced, the city government got excited. It was regarded as a great opportunity for Cork in a number of ways–shopping convenience, employment, tax revenues. So the proposal had a fairly easy time, I'd say. There were questions, of course, and a few councillors were worried about environmental impacts, effects on traffic, and so on. And there's always the concern that new businesses will merely take trade away from established businesses, especially those in the city centre. As you might imagine, the city centre retailers association raised alarms. But the Emerald Isle people were prepared for this. They argued that much of the new business would be from patrons living some distance away, people who didn't normally shop in the city. I'd say that was their strongest argument, that the centre would not simply divert business from established Cork retailers but bring in shoppers from far away.'

Had it achieved that goal? Cary asked himself.

'Well, it's probably too early to tell. The economy, locally and nationally, has been on a roller-coaster for the last few years. A few city centre businesses have closed, but it's hard to know whether that has anything at all to do with the new shopping centre.'

'What about the developer, Emerald Isle Enterprises? Any opinions about them?'

Reynold hesitated. 'Well, of course, their business is all about completing projects, about making money. But they certainly seemed to be trying to meet all the objections that were raised. They made some alterations to the plans in response to concerns, especially about parking. And they committed a large sum of money to a fund to be used in case of any economic disruptions caused by the shopping centre. That includes loans for downtown shops that might be struggling, funds for workers laid off by store closings, that sort of thing.'

'And have they made good on all of that?' asked Cary.

'Good question. I'm about to start work on an investigative

story about those funds. I'll be asking them to provide me with an accounting. So I guess we'll have to wait and see. You hear rumours that some of those funds have been used inappropriately, but those stories originated with individuals that I can't say I find trustworthy, you know? Some may have axes to grind, as they say.'

Cary thanked Reynold for his time and departed with copies of all the reporter's stories on the project.

Back in Cobh Nell had tea waiting for him.

'So, how did you do, Ciaran, in your investigations?'

'Well, both gentlemen were very generous with their time. And they seemed anxious to talk about the project. Overall they both gave high marks to Emerald Isle Enterprises.'

That evening the Harris's phone rang. It was Nell's brother Bill who lived in Cork City. His wife, Cary's Aunt Lily, passed away about five years ago. He had heard of Cary's visit and asked Nell if he could call around for a short visit. A few minutes later Bill Flanagan was in Nell and Brian's sitting room getting caught up with his nephew.

'So, Nellie tells me you're here on a mission, eh?'

'Yes, you could say that.'

'Something to do with Emerald Isle Shops?'

Cary described the project in Glenkerry and the concerns that the townspeople had. Bill was impressed to learn that Cary had met with Mr Smyth at City Hall and Reynold Travers, the reporter.

'You know, Ciaran, your Aunt Lily had a friend, Eleanor Wright. She lives on Prince Street, right across the way from the new shopping centre.'

'Oh, really?'

'Yeah. They wanted her to sell them her land—and several of her neighbours—for the carpark. But she and the neighbours refused. It got rather nasty.'

'Nasty?'

'Yes. She was very upset at the time.'

'Is she still around? Do you suppose I could talk with her?'

Bill made a call on his mobile and minutes later he and Cary were seated in Eleanor's parlour, looking out on the shopping centre. Bill inquired after Eleanor's health, her children and her grandchildren.

'Well, Ciaran, Bill tells me you're lookin' into the shopping centre,' said Eleanor, her gaze drifting toward the view out of her front window.

'Yes, ma'am. He told me you had some difficulties with the developers over your property?' inquired Cary.

The lady was tiny, grey-haired, and a bit frail, but her eyes shone intensely as she recalled the occasion.

'Oh, my, they were persistent.'

'Now who was this?' Cary asked.

'Oh, some attorney for the company. I don't recall his name. But he came to the door one day and offered to buy my house. Just like that. And for an outrageous amount.'

'That must have been tempting, yeah?' asked Cary.

She shook her head. 'No, not at all. I've lived here since a girl. Where am I gonna go? And my daughter may want it when I'm gone. So I said no.'

'How did he react?'

'Oh, he was a cool number, he was. He had this slippery smile. He said he hoped I'd reconsider–that all my neighbours were sellin'. Of course the next day I talked to Miriam next door and Ellery on the other side. They heard the same story. But they were not inclined to sell, neither.'

'Was that the end of it, then?'

'Oh, he came back a couple more times. Offered even more for the house. And the third time he said something like that they could make life pretty unpleasant for me if I refused to sell. Of course I had no idea what he was talkin' about. But my late husband's friend is an attorney and he helped me. And he assured me that no one could force me to sell. And those threats were probably just talk–bullyin' tactics, he called 'em.'

'So the project went through anyway.'

'Yes, and they decided they didn't need our property, that they could make do with fewer parking spaces. Which the city approved. I think the City Council was hearin' complaints from neighbours like us and decided it was better to let them scale back the project a bit. I suppose it saved them a few quid, too.'

'Mrs Wright, are you sure you can't remember the man's name? Is it possible that you wrote it down somewhere?'

She thought for a moment, then shook her head. 'I'm sorry, son, but I don't think so.' She paused, still thinking. Then she drew out her mobile.

'Miriam, it's Eleanor, dear. Do you have a minute?' She explained about Cary's interest in the shopping centre. Moments later Miriam Porter, Eleanor's next-door neighbour, appeared at Eleanor's door with some papers in her hand. Eleanor introduced her neighbour to Cary and Bill.

'Cary's interested in the name of that attorney that tried to get us to sell our houses. Remember him?'

A look of disgust spread across Miriam's face. 'Aye, I do remember him.' And she handed Cary a business card.

'Michael Monahan, Attorney,' read Cary. He recognised the name at once. It was one of those names on the proposal submitted to the Wicklow County Planning Board. 'And did he make any threats to you?'

'Oh yes, he got very angry and started fumin' and fussin' right on my front step. I wouldn't let 'im in the house, you see.'

'Exactly what did he say, do you recall?'

'Well, just that I would regret it if I didn't sell. And they wrote me this letter.' She handed him the letter. Cary read it. It asked her to sell her property to Emerald Isle Enterprises, stated a large sum, and reminded her that it was a very generous offer, one that she would regret passing up.

'May I take a picture of this?' asked Cary, pulling out his mobile. Miriam agreed.

Later that evening, just before he went to bed, Cary received a text message from Rosie. She hoped Cary had a productive day in Cork. And she had talked to Sabrina about the credit card charge. Her message ended with, 'see you tomorrow, mate.'

The next day Cary made the return trip to Glenkerry, listening to his music but all the while ruminating on what he had learned in Cork. True he had not uncovered any misrepresentations by Emerald Isle Enterprises people of the kind that had gotten them into so much trouble in Dublin. Maybe the Cork project had passed on its own merits, and maybe the environmental data submitted were accurate and unaltered. But he suspected that the tactic of bullying abutters, making threats to elderly ladies, would alarm the Wicklow County Council, even if it hadn't happened in Glenkerry. And it might add weight to the concerns over Ireland Vision's dirty dealings in Dublin.

By the time he got back to Glenkerry, Cary was exhausted. But at the same time he was exhilarated by what he had learned and anxious to move ahead with his research. He shared his excitement with his mother over tea.

'Those two ladies, Mrs Wright and Mrs Porter, had stories to tell about that attorney for Emerald Isle, a Mr Monahan. He badgered them about sellin', then got angry when they refused. And he threatened them, Ma. Mrs Porter said he told her they could make life miserable for her if she didn't sell. That's what she said. And she showed me this letter she received.' He had printed out a copy of the letter which he handed to his mother.

'Oh, that is wonderful, Car,' she said, glancing at the letter. 'And wasn't it nice of Bill to come round and visit with yeh? It sounds like a stroke of luck that he did. So what's next?'

'Well, I'm not sure. I gotta talk to Professor Jurgenson, see what he thinks.'

Late in the afternoon he called Rosie. 'Anything more on that credit card charge?' he asked.

'I talked to Sabrina and she's lookin' into it. But I haven't heard back from her yet. So what about Cork? Anything interesting?'

Cary gave her a quick summary of what he had learned.

'Hey, I have to run. I got some old rugby mates from uni coming by tonight. We're goin' to Phinney's. Then some footie in the morning.'

'Phinney's, eh? Maybe I'll see yeh there.'

Cork

12

GLENKERRY AFTER DARK

That evening two of Cary's rugby teammates from uni, Brendan Canty and Cian Mahoney, arrived in Glenkerry for a short visit, perhaps a few pints. Cary suggested they meet at Phinney's. He was waiting in front of the pub on High Street that evening as a sporty Mazda pulled up to the kerb.

'Hey, lads,' he said as he leaned down and peered in the car window. 'Welcome to Glenkerry.' They parked and tumbled out of the car onto the footpath, shaking hands and bear-hugging with their old teammate. The pair looked like rugby players, big, broad-shouldered, square-jawed, with close-cropped hair, Brendan's dark brown and curly, Cian's a tangled thatch the colour of carrots. Both wore impish smiles as they greeted Cary, suggesting that they were ready for a good time.

'Sweet little town you got 'ere, mate,' said Brendan. 'Wild nights 'round these parts, I bet.'

Cary nodded. 'Like you wouldn't believe, Bren. Party-party-party–dawn to dusk–and sometimes even after dark, too.'

They all laughed. Then Cary opened the door and ushered them into Phinney's, the closest thing to night life that Glenkerry had to offer. He'd reserved a booth in the corner and the trio slid into the curved pew and stretched their legs.

'So, boys, what'll you have?' asked the young waitress with a smile.

'Just you will do me, lass,' replied Cian.

Cary spoke up. 'This is Gráinne Phinney, lads. Her dad and grandad own this place.' Then he turned to her. 'You gotta excuse these fools, Gráinne. They're from Dublin and they have no detectable manners.'

'Yeah,' she replied with a wink, 'but they make up for it with charm.'

Soon their pints arrived along with platters of fried calamari, barbecued wings, and 'feckin' hot fries,' and the evening was on. As they tucked in, the trio were reliving some of the highlights of the past rugby season at DCU when Del Samuels walked in the door. Cary beckoned him to join them.

'Gents, like you to meet an old buddy of mine, Del Samuels, Garda Del Samuels that is. Del, meet Brendan Canty and Cian Mahoney.'

They shook hands. 'Garda, eh?' noted Cian.

'Yep,' replied Del with a proud grin. 'So you betta behave or I'll be wantin' to see your IDs, maybe take away your keys.'

All laughed. Cary had told his friends of Del's achievements in rugby at *Coláiste* and they quizzed him further, then regaled him with stories of their own scrumming exploits over the last three seasons at DCU.

'Sounds like your team was brilliant, lads.'

Cary suddenly got serious. 'The truth, Del? We sucked. We totally sucked. But we had a good time doin' it, din't we, boys?'

Again there was laughter.

'And lads, that's about the strongest language you'll ever hear outta this guy. Ever notice, he like *never* swears–*ever*.'

'Well, Del,' replied Cary, 'I suppose yeh're right. Maybe I got put off a bit when we were on the football team at *Coláiste*. Remember? About 90% of those blokes' vocabulary was sex organs and sex acts. And the other 10% was about excretion, yeah?'

Del smiled. 'Yeah, probably. But don't you feel, just once in a while, like a good cuss?'

Again everyone laughed.

'Who knows, maybe the ladies would really go for the Gurkman if he had, yeh know, more street cred? Machismo.'

Cary tried to ignore his friend's taunts and he proceeded to tell them tales of Del Samuel's other athletic achievements. 'He's a whiz at cricket, lads, pretty fair at Gaelic football, too. And he's the perfect gentleman when he's in uniform. He treats everyone with respect. I know. I seen 'im in action–he's a true professional.'

Del laughed. 'I'm afraid I'm gonna have to have your keys, Ciaran, 'cause from the way yeh're talkin', I'd say yeh're already scuttered.'

While all this was going on the crowd was growing. Lights had been set up on the small stage at one end of the room and several local musicians were tuning up, a fiddle, a penny whistle, and an electric guitar. There was a microphone and the usual 'tap-tap-tap-testin'-testin'-testin'.' Finally, Liam Phinney, the proprietor, stepped up to the mic.

'Welcome, ladies, gents, to our weekly talent night. We got our usual house band here, Seamus, Bart, and Mike, you all know them. And we got some good listenin' for yeh this eve, I promise yeh that, includin' a few surprises.'

For the next hour or so the audience was entertained with all manner of amateur talent, with the emphasis clearly on 'amateur.' There was a grammar school fiddler-in-training, a couple of cringeworthy vocalists, and a fifteen-year-old accordionist who played 'Lady of Spain' like it had never been played before and probably never will again.

But then there were three young lasses from Aughrim who did themselves proud, channelling the Dixie Chicks, first with 'Cowboy Take Me Away,' then with 'Long Time Gone.' And they nearly brought the roof down with their final number, a soulful rendition of 'Landslide.' They were good, really good, setting a high bar for anyone who had the misfortune to follow them.

'Okay, folks,' said Liam once the cheering had abated, 'we're gonna take a short break now, give the performers a chance to arrange rides home. But when we come back we got a special treat fer yeh.'

The crowd cheered their appreciation and many, many more pints were pulled, poured, and downed.

'Car, me bye, this is brilliant,' said Brendan. 'Who'd a guessed this little town would be like some Irish Nashville or Branson, eh? And there are some nice little ladies hereabouts, too, by the looks of it. I'll bet they're all hankerin' to take a ride with the Gurkman.'

Cary laughed and even blushed a little, although it was hard to tell the blush of embarrassment from that of strong ale coursing through his bloodstream.

Then Del spoke up. 'You lot apparently don't know young Ciaran, here, or maybe he's been tellin' yeh tales. But this guy's got the sorriest record with the fairer sex this side o' Dublin. Not that he 'asn't had his admirers. Even goin' back to primary school, the girls were always up in his grille. And at *Coláiste* he was mighty popular with the ladies, too. But I don't know, his heart was never really in it, ain't that so, Car?'

Cary was starting to get annoyed at his friend's mockery.

Sensitive nerve there, mate?

'Well, Del,' replied Cary, 'there's a lot you don't know about me, I'll tell yeh. A lot.'

'Yeah, heard it before, mate–heard it *all* before.'

Del knew how to work a crowd, and even though his audience consisted of only three somewhat blitzed Irish lads, he had them in the palm of his hand. Just then Liam Phinney stepped up to the mic once again.

'All right, then. We're back, folks. Now, I told you we had a special treat for yeh. She's a local lass with a voice as clear and sweet as a bubbling Wicklow stream. So please put your hands together for Glenkerry's own, *Miss–Rosie–O–Malley.*'

Cary was stunned as he watched Rosie step out of the shadows and up to the microphone wearing a plaid kilt and a lacy cream white blouse. She looked out briefly on her audience with that shy smile of hers and for one brief moment her gaze met Cary's. Then she turned to her host and spoke softly: 'Thanks, Phinney.' The fiddle began to play softly and sweetly, and Rosie began to sing:

I once loved a boy, just a bold Irish boy
who would come and would go at my request;
and this bold Irish boy was my pride and my joy
and I built him a bow'r in my breast.
But this girl who has taken my bonny, bonny boy,

let her make of him all that she can;
and whether he loves me or loves me not,
I will walk with my love now and then.

Her voice was delicate and pure, and it travelled up and down the scale like a nightingale's, tender and sad. There were several more verses, each ending with the line, *'and whether he loves me or loves me not, I will walk with my love now and then.'*

When Rosie finished, the crowd jumped to their feet, shouting and cheering their appreciation.

Del looked at Cary. 'Oh my God, Car. Were you listenin'? Did that not pierce your very soul, lad?'

Then he turned to Cian and Brendan. 'Rosie and Cary go back forever, boys, and I mean *forever*. So believe me when I tell yeh, that sweet serenade you just heard? It was sung for the benefit of young Ciaran here–it so was.'

Cary shook his head. 'Yeh've put away too many pints, Del. That's just an old Irish poem set to music, is all. Folk been recitin' those words for centuries.'

But Del was shaking his head. 'No one ever sang 'I Will Walk with My Love' like that before, mate. Never. Like I said, boys, he's got sweetie-pies everywhere, but he's like a bad estate agent: *he can never close a deal.'*

Brendan and Cian roared at that, but Cary was not amused.

Del went on. 'What this boy needs is a matchmaker, someone to, yeh know, speak for 'im, match 'im up.'

Cary turned to Brendan and Cian, smiling from ear to ear as he anticipated his comeback line: 'Yeah, Del? Well here's a match for you, dude: *your lips and my ass.'*

Once again Brendan and Cian erupted. 'Ooooo–the Garda gets

burned by the Gurkman.'

Now the crowd began to thin out. It was pretty clear that no one was going to top Rosie's performance. And when 'Lady of Spain' boy decided to take an encore, that pretty much shut down the evening's festivities.

The four young men stepped out onto the street where Cary assured Del that his two inebriated friends would not be driving. He led them the short distance to 1 Upton Road, let them in and up the narrow flight of stairs.

'You lads can doss 'ere. There's a double bed in the bedroom and a couch in the sitting room. Suit yourselves. Footie starts at eight, so rest yer bones.'

'Oh, man, that Rosie,' said Cian, 'she's one sweet little lady. And she's got it for you, but bad. Can't close the deal, eh?'

'You know, mate,' chimed in Brendan, not willing to let the opportunity pass. 'These days there's pills for guys with those kinda problems.'

Cary shot him a look of disdain. 'See you lads in the morning– or not, depending on how I feel.'

Cary had a hard time sleeping that night. Maybe it was worry over the Glenkerry Mall proposal, or too many pints of Guinness, or the torment he suffered at the hands of his so-called friends–or maybe it was the strains of that tune, that lovely Irish ballad, and its singer, that kept him awake.

Somehow he found himself flashing back to that Skype call with Siobhan nearly two weeks ago. What was it about that call that he found so unsettling? In part it was the realisation of what it would be like, sharing that tiny flat with Siobhan Sullivan. If they were a couple, well, of course, that would be fine–that would be perfect. But as mates? As roommates? Torture, he admitted to himself, it would be torture–because of the attraction, the gravity, that inexorable force drawing him toward her.

Now, if she felt the same, that would be one thing. But she didn't, that was clear. Her walking around in her skivvies? 'No problem,' she had said, 'we'll be roomies.' Him walking through her bedroom to the loo at night? Again, 'No problem.'

There it is, the cold, hard truth: Siobhan doesn't think of you in that way. To her you're a eunuch, or worse, just one of the girls. Face it, mate, maybe Del was right after all.

The next morning Cary was still miffed, mostly at Del, for skewering him at Phinney's, but also at his rugby mates for encouraging Del. Despite his lingering resentments, Cary appeared bright and early at 1 Upton Road, intentionally making loud noises on the ground floor to raise his mates as rudely as possible. Eventually he clomped up the stairs and spoke loudly: 'Up 'n at 'em, lads. The match starts in twenty minutes.'

The Gaelic Athletic Association is a national organisation dedicated to preserving and promoting traditional Irish games such as hurling, camogie, and Gaelic football with clubs in nearly every city and town in Ireland. Glenkerry's GAA grounds stretched out along the River Kerry a short distance from the town centre. The football pitch was still wet with dew when Cary, Brendan, and Cian arrived at eight o'clock sharp.

'Now, listen to me, mates. This match is just for fun, yeah?

Everyone in Glenkerry loves footie, watching it or playing it. And nearly everyone joins in, young and old, lads and lasses–so go easy on the body tackles and headbutts. And no rows or shemozzles, yeh hear me?'

Brendan and Cian nodded that they understood. They were subdued after all those pints of ale of the previous evening and that abrupt awakening this morning. Plus Cary had provided them only the barest of breakfasts, lattes and plastic-wrapped biscuits from the Glenkerry Minimarket consumed while leaning against Cian's car in the warm sun.

Just then two small vans pulled in and unloaded more competitors including the entire Phinney family–Liam, Niamh, Timothy, Gráinne and her schoolmate, Eileen–plus Father O'Ryan, the young vicar of the Glenkerry Church of Ireland, and his wife, Laura. Soon Del Samuels appeared on foot with four of his garda colleagues, three burly young men and Sabrina Selkirk.

'I think we got a quorum, lads,' said Cary to his two bleary-eyed friends. Sides were formed and the match was on.

Gaelic football is a cross between soccer and rugby. The ball, slightly smaller than a soccer ball, can be carried, bounced, kicked, or passed. There are goals at either end of the pitch, with a goalkeeper in each. In a pickup match like this, there are few rules and no one takes it too seriously. Normally there are fifteen players to a side, but this match proceeded with only seven, everyone expecting that a few latecomers would arrive after play had begun.

The match got off to a slow start with some of the players still processing their morning's caffeine. But the pace soon quickened and the shouts of players and onlookers became more strident. At one point Cian displayed some fancy footwork evading defenders along the side line, then passed the ball to the centre where his teammate, Sabrina, kicked it over the crossbar for a point. Everyone cheered. Del embraced Sabrina and spun her around, even though she was on the opposing side.

Soon Catherine arrived and stood on the side line watching with concern. Then Rosie appeared next to her.

'Any broken bones yet?' asked Rosie.

'Oh, good morning, lass. No, not yet. But I'm holding on to my rosary beads here for dear life, praying that this will be over and done with before anyone gets hurt. Those little lasses, I worry so...'

A few minutes later the ball was passed to Cary around mid-pitch and he tried to kick it toward his side's goal, only to have Laura intercept his kick and carry the ball away in the opposite direction. She lost it at one moment to Timothy, but Father Ryan was there, snatched the ball away, and kicked it directly at the net, only to see his shot blocked by goalkeeper Brendan.

Then to everyone's amazement, Gráinne and Eileen, who played soccer and camogie together at Coláiste, moved the ball quickly downfield, each soloing, then passing it to the other with exceptional finesse, adroitly evading several of the hulking gardaí. Gráinne centred it out just short of the goal. This time the female garda popped up right at the opportune moment, grabbed the ball, and kicked it in the opposite direction. But Laura was there to trap the ball and kick it straight into the goal for three points, with cheers and adulation from both sides.

Cary approached Rosie on the side lines. 'Care to join us, Rosie?'

'Yeah, thanks, mate, but I value my life too much. Besides, those lasses seem to be carryin' the day out there. If I joined 'em it might make you blokes look even sorrier, so.'

'Yeah, well, yeh're probably right. Hey, loved your song last night,' he said with a wink as he returned to the pitch.

'You be careful now, Car,' added Catherine.

Cary rejoined the match. Moments later he collided with one of the gardaí. He lay motionless on the grass for several seconds, his mother and Rosie calling to him from the side line. But soon he was back on his feet, although moving a little more slowly now.

A couple more kicks between the posts by Cary's teammates evened the score and the match ended in a tie about half nine. Two of the gardaí had to be on duty at ten. And Phinney's pub would be opening soon.

'Thanks for comin', lads,' said Cary to Brendan and Cian after the match. 'It's been great seein' yeh.'

'Yeah, and say hi to Siobhan for us once you get to London.' added Cian.

'Will do,' replied Cary. 'For sure.'

'You headed to work now?'

Cary groaned, rubbing his bruised side. 'Maybe not straightaway. Think I'll go home first an' have some breaky.'

Maybe a wee soak for these aching muscles, too. Then it's back to work.

After a soak in the hot tub, Cary went back to work on mall business, emailing Professor Jurgenson an update on his trip to Cork and attaching the photo of the letter Mrs Porter had sent. At midday he took a break and went down the hill for chips and chowder. There he ran into Del.

'Mate,' said Cary curtly.

'Good match, eh?'

Cary nodded.

'What, you still miffed with your old schoolmate about last night? Can't take a little ribbin'?'

'A little ribbin'?' replied Cary. 'I felt like a bloody stirk in a pasture, about to be gelded while passers-by looked on in amusement. You might as well have surgically removed my bollocks right there, Del.' He stared into his huge pile of chips, then at last looked up at his friend. Finally, he smiled.

'Okay, I apologise,' said Del. 'So I was a little harsh. But it's only 'cause we're mates, yeh know?'

'Well, okay, but mark my words, I will get even with you, one day, Garda Samuels. Just you wait.'

'But you must admit, yeh've left a long trail of broken hearts in this town, and at *Coláiste*. And I'm bettin' there's more than a few coeds up to Dublin City that are lickin' their wounds. Like that Siobhan you claim is just a friend.'

'That's crap.'

'Right, and I suppose Glenkerry Rose and you, that's crap as well?'

Cary stood up. 'I'm gonna finish my chippies elsewhere.' And he walked out.

That afternoon Sabrina–Garda Selkirk–called Rosie.

'Good news, Rosie. That cheque from the Roscommon bank? It's been deposited. In a bank in Galway.'

'In Galway?'

'Yes. And the new account is in the name Mary Malone with her proper ID number and all.'

'Galway. So my ma's in Galway?'

'Well, maybe, maybe not. You see, she set up the account online, then mailed the cheque to the bank. You can do that nowadays pretty easily.'

'But the bank must have an address for her, if she has an account?'

'Yeah, well. The address she gave them was her Glenkerry address.'

Rosie sighed with disappointment. 'I'm kind of surprised she would give that address. I'd think she'd be worried that the bank would write her there and my father would find out.'

'Yeah, right,' replied Sabrina. 'But she set up a paperless account, so all communications will be online. So you see, she could still be anywhere.'

'Have you been able to find out anything more about that Rosslare ferry ticket?'

'No, not yet. The company's computer system has been giving them some problems. But they say they'll try to have an answer for us within a few days, whether she was on that boat and if so was she travelling alone or with another person.'

'But if she did take that ferry, why did she travel up to Dublin?' asked Rosie. 'Rosslare is in the opposite direction.'

'Yeah, good question. Of course, we don't know for a fact that she took that bus to Dublin. Del concluded that from the CCTV footage in Ballinoch. But yeh know he never found her on the video from Bray or Dublin. It's possible she took the southbound bus from Ballinoch, not the northbound. That connects with Rosslare. Or maybe she got off the bus at Bray, then travelled south by rail to Rosslare.'

Rosie was trying to make sense of this. 'But why would she

open a bank account in Galway, then take a ferry to the UK?'

'Another good question. But Rosie, do you know if your mother had any contacts in Wales–or anywhere in the UK? An old friend, a schoolmate?'

Rosie shook her head. 'No, not that I ever heard about. But I'll ask my aunts. Me 'n Cary are driving to Roscommon to visit with them tomorrow. Maybe they'll know of someone.'

Rosie thanked Sabrina for all her efforts and rang off. She stood in the kitchen gazing out the window, trying to imagine what was going through her mother's mind. Did she have some particular destination in Wales or England, an old friend perhaps? Or was she simply trying to get as far away from Glenkerry, as far away from Harry O'Malley, as fast as possible?

13

ROSCOMMON MEMORIES

The drive to Roscommon took Cary and Rosie through the high country from Glendalough to Wicklow Gap where mist still hung over the steep mountainsides on either side of the road. They startled some deer at Tonelagee before descending to Hollywood. Now in the central lowlands they travelled through Counties Kildare, Westmeath, and Offaly, passing herds of cattle and fields of wheat and barley before entering the motorway that would take them to Roscommon.

They spent much of the drive reminiscing about school days, Rosie about her old girlfriends, Cary mostly about sport. They avoided any discussion of their time together, as a couple, perhaps acknowledging by the omission that the memory was painful even now for both.

'You always loved writing, didn't you, Car? I remember even when we were chisslers, those fantastic stories you wrote, with witches and ogres and demons and all. Do you remember?'

Cary admitted that he did. 'I was really into the supernatural back then–and horror stories.'

'And at *Coláiste* you reported on sport for the school paper.'

'Yeah, I did that a bit. But I also wrote about music. Remember, I did a piece on David Bowie, like he was a personal friend–like I knew the inner workings of his mind? Now there's a horror story for yeh.' They both chuckled.

'I remember you spending most of your spare time in the art studio, painting. Remember that little watercolour of Glenkerry you gave me when I left for uni? I kept it right on my bedstand in Dublin for three years. And now it's on my desk at home. I love lookin' at it. Do you still paint, Rosie?'

'Yeah. I took a class in Wicklow last spring on drawing human figures.'

'Ah, with naked models?'

'No, nothing like that. We drew one another–clothes on.'

'No fun, that,' replied Cary.

'I also took a course in Taekwondo.'

'Really?'

'Yeah, surprised?'

'Very. Somehow, I can't picture Rosie O'Malley as a female Bruce Lee in the films.'

She chuckled. 'Yeah, well, I never got all that good. But be warned, I can throw a mean kick when necessary. So my advice, whenever I'm around, protect your crotch, mate.'

'Good to know,' replied Cary with a laugh.

'Did you do a lot of writing at uni?' she asked.

'Yeah, I did. Mostly for the student literary magazine–short stories–essays–poems. Just personal stuff, mostly.'

'I'd like to read some sometime, if yeh let me.'

Rosie brought Cary up to date on her conversation with Sabrina the previous day including the information on the credit card transaction in Rosslare for the ferry to Fishguard.

'Rosslare? Well, that changes things, doesn't it?'

'Sabrina thinks maybe she actually boarded a southbound bus in Ballinoch that morning. She could have been in Rosslare in a couple hours. And in Wales by the end of the day.'

'So she used your father's credit card. Does that surprise you?'

'Well, my guess is that she didn't want to spend that much in cash, so she took the chance. He wasn't likely to follow her to Wales, yeh know? Plus my da was in such a bad way for a time there, I doubt he even looked at the monthly statements. They come in the post–there's a stack of those envelopes unopened, just sitting on his desk. Maybe she took the chance, hoping he would never even notice the charge.'

'Wales, eh?' said Cary.

Rosie shrugged. 'I don't know–I got my doubts.'

Finally, they entered Roscommon. It was a bit larger than Glenkerry with a busier centre. Rosie remembered the location of her Aunt Marguerite's home and directed Cary right to it.

'Oh, love, it's so good to see you, dear,' said Marguerite Hurley as she greeted her niece. She was tall, rosy-cheeked, with long brown hair that was greying but still glistened in the sunlight.

'And this must be Ciaran, eh? Now there's a handsome young Irish lad, if I ever saw one.'

Cary blushed. 'How d'yeh do, ma'am?'

'Och, call me Maggie. That's how I'm known hereabouts. Well, come through won't yeh, and let me lay in some tea for yeh. I hope you brought yer appetites, I do.'

Within minutes she presented Rosie and Cary with a pot of tea on a silver tray accompanied by all manner of sweets and the obligatory bowl of clotted cream. It was more a feast than a cup of tea.

Once those niceties were attended to, Marguerite looked glumly at Rosie. 'I'm guessin' yeh've still not 'eard from your ma, eh?'

Rosie shook her head. Then she recounted the story of her mother's disappearance, her plan to be in touch, and the efforts of Rosie, Cary, and the Glenkerry gardaí, to locate her.

'Is Aunt Elizabeth about?' asked Rosie. 'She'll want to be hearing this, too, I imagine.'

Marguerite smiled weakly, then looked sadly at Rosie and Cary. 'Oh, Rosie, love, I shoulda tol' yeh on the phone, but I couldn't.' She started to cry and took a tissue from her apron pocket to wipe her eyes. 'Lizzie's not well, dear. Mentally, I mean. She's in a care home now, almost a year. Can't remember much of anything, I'm afraid, not even her old sister.'

'Oh, Auntie, I'm so sorry. That must be terribly hard for you,' replied Rosie.

Rosie and Maggie exchanged stories of the past, of visits in Roscommon and in Glenkerry. They spoke of Rosie, Buddy, and their mother, but Cary noticed that neither Harry O'Malley nor Rosie's brother Jimmy figured in any of their reminiscences.

'And Buddy, how's he doin', love?'

'Buddy's okay, Auntie. He's working in a car repair shop in Dalkey. I don't hear much from him, actually. But the last time I saw him, at Christmas I think, he was pretty chipper. He's got a girlfriend, so they say.'

'Oh, good. He's a darling boy, that one. Do give him my love, now, won't yeh?'

Rosie promised she would do so.

'Well, dear, you said on the phone that you thought I could help you search for yer ma, that you wanted to try and track down some of her old friends from school days?'

Rosie nodded, then explained. It seemed unlikely that her ma would go off unless she had some place, or someone familiar, to go to, at least for a time. Perhaps she had some old schoolmates that she might have visited or at least been in touch with.

Maggie pulled out a stack of high school yearbooks from her years in secondary school. 'I been paging through these and I made a list for yeh, mostly girls that your ma was friendly with.' She showed Rosie the list. Next to each name she had made notes of married names, where they were living now, even phone numbers for the few who were still right around Roscommon. There were several who had passed, and Maggie made notes of that fact next to the names Maura Killam, Eleanor Reynolds, and Gerry Flaherty, all of whom had died within the last five years or so as best she could recall.

'Your ma and Gerry were quite an item for a time, Rosie. Did she ever tell you about 'im?'

Rosie couldn't remember anything of her mother's boyfriends of long ago. She never spoke of them, so far as Rosie could recall, probably for fear her husband would be jealous.

'Very sad, it was. Pa scared 'im off, I fear. Didn't approve. He was a Protestant, you see. Anyway, they parted ways and pretty soon Gerry is engaged to some gal, Marion something, from out of town. I think he met her at uni. He became a teacher, 's I recall.'

'Auntie, do you know if Ma had any friends in Wales or England?'

Maggie thought for a moment. Then she shook her head. 'I'm sorry, dear, but I don't recall anyone. But I'll keep thinking.'

Then Maggie took Rosie and Cary to the care home for a short visit with her sister Elizabeth. Cary had never met her before but Rosie was stunned to see how her dear auntie had declined. She looked frail and unsteady on her feet. She brightened at Rosie's face.

Who wouldn't, thought Cary.

Back at Maggie's house, they thanked her and said their goodbyes.

Marguerite hugged her niece tearfully. 'You call me now, dear, soon as you hear anything from your ma, okay? And I'll see if I can find out anything more about her old friends.'

Rosie was silent for a time on the return trip, thinking about her once lovely Aunt Lizzie and her grieving Aunt Maggie. Cary tried to console her, but, as he told her, he had no experience with Alzheimer's or other forms of dementia.

'No, a course, but you lost your da.'

'Yeah, but it was sudden, yeh know? At least we didn't have to watch him age decades in a year, or have to be helped to the toilet and the tub. And I can't imagine what it must be like to have someone you love who doesn't even recognise you anymore.'

The next day Rosie spent several hours in the garden weeding, trimming, fertilising, and harvesting some lettuce, beans, and cabbage. She was just about finished and heading back to the house when her mobile rang.

'Rosie, it's Sabrina. Say, I'm working on the Rosslare ferry business. It looks like they're still having some difficulties with their computer system. So they can't put their hands on the passenger manifests for the eighth of May just yet, yeah? But they're working on it. I wondered, did you and Cary get to Roscommon yesterday to visit with your aunts?'

'Yes, we did. Unfortunately, my Aunt Elizabeth has dementia. This was the first I knew of this. It's very sad. Just a few years ago she was so pretty and full of life. We went to visit her in the care home. I barely recognised her.'

'Oh, dear, I am so sorry.'

'But her sister, my Aunt Marguerite, was able to help us quite a good deal. She made up a list of my ma's old friends from school days. She even had addresses and telephone numbers for some of them. She's talked to several, but none of them knew anything about my ma. And several have passed away.'

Sabrina asked about any friends in Wales or elsewhere in the UK. 'No, I'm afraid my auntie couldn't think of anyone. But I been doin' a little web surfin' early this mornin' to see if I could find any more of the names on my aunt's list and try to contact them. I'll let you know if I learn of anything. Oh, and Del asked about Ma's cousin Eileen in Virginia. But I can't find an address for her anywhere, and Aunt Marguerite couldn't either.'

That evening, after Rosie had done the supper dishes, she was tidying the kitchen counter when she came across her father's wallet. Protruding from it was a slip of paper with some writing on it that caught her eye–it looked like her mother's hand. There was a name that was unfamiliar to her, Margaret Ahearn, with a telephone number that looked unusual. It started with 44, the prefix for the United Kingdom. She took a photo of the paper with her mobile, then carefully replaced it in her father's wallet.

Minutes later Rosie was sitting at her laptop. The area code was for Cardiff in Wales. She did a reverse number search to see if she could find the name and address associated with the number. But the search was unsuccessful. She stepped out into the front yard and tried to call the number, but quickly realised that her mobile service did not include calls to the UK.

She walked down the lane and found Catherine in her garden.

'Is Cary around, Mrs M.?'

'Yes and no, love,' she answered with a wry smile. Then she gestured toward the back yard.

Rosie walked around the corner of the house only to find Cary in a pose that made him look like a figure from a Grecian urn–or possibly an Egyptian sarcophagus. She stood watching for a minute. Finally, he looked her way, broke his pose, and stood hands on hips.

'So, martial arts?' she asked.

Cary shook his head. 'Tai chi–for stress relief.' He shrugged his shoulders, then chuckled. 'It helps.'

Rosie told him about her conversation with Sabrina, then showed him the photo on her mobile of the name Margaret Ahearn and the telephone number.

'It's in Cardiff, Car, in Wales. But I can't dial it on my phone. I don't have UK service. I thought maybe you did.'

He already had his phone in hand and started to dial. Then a series of tones sounded.

'Number does not exist.' He could see Rosie's disappointment. 'Maybe it's an old number, a landline maybe that she gave up for a mobile. Come inside.'

For the next few minutes Cary sat at his laptop searching for a Margaret Ahearn in Cardiff. But he could find no listing for the name. There were a number of O'Hearns including several Margarets, but no Ahearn. 'Maybe that's her maiden name and she's listed under a married name. Or vice versa. Or maybe it's just an unlisted number.'

Rosie was disappointed. 'Well, I'll call Aunt Maggie tomorrow and ask her if the name Margaret Ahearn means anything to her.' She sighed. 'I'm worried, Car. If my ma really is in the UK, I wonder if I'll ever be able to find her.'

The following morning Rosie and Cary walked to the garda station. Sabrina wasn't in but Del was. Rosie showed him the photo of the name on her phone.

'Well, that together with the Rosslare-Fishguard ferry starts to make sense. She took the bus to Rosslare, booked a ferry ticket to Fishguard, then travelled to Cardiff to the home of this Margaret Ahearn.'

'But we've had no joy reaching that number or finding anyone of that name in Cardiff.'

As she spoke Del was clicking away at his keyboard. 'Let me see what I can find. We have access to some city directories in the UK that you might not be able to get to.'

After several minutes of clicking, he looked up.

'I see a Margaret Ahearn, not in Cardiff but in a place called Twyn-yr-odyn.' He chuckled. 'Irish language is hard enough. I pity schoolkids in Wales having to learn Welsh.'

He turned the monitor so that Cary and Rosie could see the name. 'The telephone exchange looks right, too. But the number shown here is different than the one your ma wrote. There are a few other Ahearns in that area code, too, one Megan and one Marilyn, but that's the only Margaret.' He thought for a moment. 'Listen, let me contact the police department in Twyn-yr-odyn. I'll see if they can send an officer to the house. I'll call you if I learn anything. It might not be today, though.'

Only a few hours later Del called Rosie. 'An officer went to the home of that Margaret Ahearn. Sounds like she might be about your ma's age. But she told the officer she knew no one by the name of Mary Malone or Mary O'Malley. She also said she's never been to Ireland. The officer felt pretty confident that the woman was not hiding anything–or anybody.'

'Wow, Del, they really acted fast, didn't they? I expected to have to wait days.'

'Yeah, well, I told them the circumstances, yeh know, domestic abuse and so on, and they wanted to get right on it. But Rosie, I also heard back from the Rosslare ferry company. They have no record of your mother travelling to Wales. They say that ticket was never used.'

'Oh, Del, now I feel bad that you had to go to all that bother about Margaret Ahearn for nothing.'

'No worries, Rose, it's all part of the job.'

Rosie was feeding the chickens the next day but thinking all the while about her mother and where to search next. Back in the house, she sat at the kitchen table reading over her Aunt Maggie's list of some of Mary's old friends. After each name Maggie had made note of where that person had lived in recent years. Several were still in Roscommon, one in Tralee, one in Limerick.

Next to Gerry Flaherty's name Marguerite had written 'Galway – deceased.' Suddenly she had an inspiration. She immediately opened her laptop and began searching the web for an obituary for Gerald Flaherty of Galway.

Minutes later Cary received a call from Rosie. 'Remember how Aunt Maggie mentioned a beau of my ma's–Gerry, Gerry Flaherty? The one she wanted to marry but her father objected to?'

'Yeah, the one that died.'

'But *he* didn't die, Car. It was his *father*, Gerald Flaherty, Senior, who died. Maggie must've seen a death notice in the Roscommon paper and assumed it was Ma's old boyfriend. I found the full obituary on the web, Car. He was eighty-five. Listen to this.'

She read the obituary on the laptop screen. 'It says, "survived by a son Gerald Flaherty, Junior." And "predeceased by a daughter-in-law, Marion Flaherty." '

'Oh, that's excellent, Rosie. Do you suppose you can get in touch with him?'

'Car, it says Gerald Flaherty, Junior, is a teacher, that he teaches in a secondary school, in Galway.'

'Whoa, Rosie. Galway. I think yeh've clocked it.'

'Car, I'm lookin' right at his picture on the Galway National School Facebook page. There's an email address and a mobile number for him. He looks like a nice fellow, yeh know?'

'Geez, Rosie, yeh're way ahead of me. Have you called him yet?'

'No. I thought I'd wait till evening when he's likely to be at home. But I'm a little nervous. Could you call round, please? For moral support?'

Rosie was a bundle of nerves as she fixed her tea. Then she saw Cary walking up the drive. She greeted him at the door.

'Thanks for comin' round, Car.'

'No problem, Rosie. I'm curious, though, how'd you happen to look up Gerald Flaherty? Your aunt was sure he'd passed away.'

Rosie nodded. 'It was Galway, Car, *Galway*. On her list Aunt Maggie wrote 'Gerry Flaherty–Galway–deceased.' I'd looked at that again and again and I suppose my eye just skipped to the word 'deceased.' But the other day Del mentioned Galway as a possible rail destination, yeh know, from Heuston Station. And then Sabrina called to tell me Ma had opened a bank account in Galway. All of a sudden, it hit me. So I right away went searching for that obituary, thinking maybe Maggie had been mistaken. Which, as it turns out, she was.'

'Wow, that's really something, Rosie. Good work.'

But despite his words of praise, Cary could see she was distressed. 'Gee, Rosie, I thought you'd be chuffed.'

'I don't know how to feel. What if Gerald Flaherty knows nothing about Ma? I'll start worrying again that I'm never gonna find her. Or what if she's there but doesn't want to talk to me? Or maybe she'll be unhappy there, or depressed, or frightened.'

She was shaking as she spoke. 'I'm a bit of a mess, Car.'

'Come 'ere,' he said, and he drew her into his arms and gave her a hug. 'Somethin' good'll come of the call, I'm sure of it.' He hated those kinds of false promises, but he couldn't think of what else to say to reassure his anxious friend.

Finally, they went out to the yard where the mobile reception was a little better. Rosie sat on the garden fence while Cary stood watching, starting to feel nerves himself over the call.

'Uh, Mr Flaherty? Gerald Flaherty? Hi, my name is Rosie O'Malley.' She spoke louder and slower. *'Yeah, Rosie–O'Malley–I'm tryin' to locate my...'* She could hear him talking to someone.

'It's Rosie, love,' she heard him say.

The phone was jostled and then Rosie heard a thin voice that brought a big smile to her face.

'Ma? It's Rosie,' her voice cracking.

Cary was hearing only half the conversation but he got the gist.

'I'm fine Mama. But how are you?'

She flashed a smile at Cary and gave him a thumb up.

'Oh, well, it took quite some doin', Ma. Marguerite remembered Gerald Flaherty. I thought I'd try to contact him.'

Now she was listening again, nodding, and smiling.

'Well, on the internet, a course. I found his picture and his mobile number.'

A confused expression spread across her face as she listened.

'Really? Well, I never got 'em, Ma. I kept that prepay with me day and night, hopin', and worryin' something awful. But I never got your texts.'

She listened again.

'Well, at least we finally got connected, Ma. Yes.'

She listened again, then looked at Cary.

'I'm fine, Ma. Ciaran McGurk, you remember, Cary? Yeah, he's been an angel. He's been helpin' me. And Del Samuels, too. Yeah, right. Well, he's a garda and he's been a big help, too.'

She paused, listening to her mother's reply.

'Yes, Ma. We reported you missing weeks ago. Your face is probably on the wall in every garda station in the Republic by now, we been so frantic to find yeh.'

Tears started to run down Rosie's cheeks.

'Well, you're safe, right?'

She smiled at the response.

'Good, Ma, I'm so glad of it. And you and Gerry are old friends.'

Rosie was nodding in relief.

'You sound happy, Ma.'

Now Rosie was beaming.

'Oh, that's wonderful, Ma.' She paused. 'Ma, Pa's in hospital. Yeah, not too good. I guess it's the emphysema. Yeah. I'm goin' to see 'im tomorrow.'

'I talked to Buddy, yesterday, Ma. Yeah, he's okay. I'll call him straightaway and tell him where you are.'

Cary noticed that Rosie made no mention of her other brother.

'Yeah. And Cary's pa died just a couple weeks after you left.'

She listened and looked at Cary.

'Yeah, he was, yeah, a proper dad.' She listened again.

'Mrs M.? Well, she's okay, I guess. She's got Car with her, yeh know. And I been doin' what I can to help her. But it's been mostly them helpin' me, it seems.'

She nodded.

'I'd like to visit you, Ma, sometime, maybe soon?'

She listened, again looking at Cary.

'Well, Cary said he'd drive me one day. Yeah.'

She rolled her eyes at Cary.

'No, Ma, it's not like that, Ma–we're just–Ma–Cary's right here, Ma. Yup, he says hi.' Rosie's face was bright red.

'Hello, Mrs O'Malley,' called Cary.

'Ma says hi.'

'Okay, well I'm so glad to know yeh're okay, Ma. And I'll call you again as soon as we can make the trip to Galway. Okay.'

'Love you, Ma. Bye.'

Rosie collapsed against Cary, first crying, then laughing, then crying some more. Finally, she dried her eyes and looked up into his.

'Ma's okay.'

'Yeah, well, I kinda figured that out. Sounds like she's tryin' to hitch us up, just like mine, eh?'

Rosie shrugged. 'Yeah, well, that's just what mothers do, eh?'

They both chuckled.

'I better give Del a call right away,' said Rosie. 'Tell him the news.' She left a message on Del's voice mail: her mother was safe and sound.

'Let's go for a stroll,' said Cary.

They walked out across the pasture to where they could look down on the village, with the river beyond, the sea in the distance.

'Yeh know, I been hyperventilating so much these last few weeks,' said Rosie. 'Sometimes it was like I forgot how to breathe.' She looked at her hands. 'Look, I'm still shakin'.'

'Well, you can relax now–take in some summer air. You know what we should have up here?' asked Cary. 'One of those Chinese sky lantern thingies to light and send up. Then you could put all your worries in it and watch them sail off into the universe.'

'Yeah, that would be nice, Car. But I feel like they are floating away, at least some of them, already.'

'That's good, Rosie, that's real good.'

'Thanks mate,' she said with a shy smile. Then she looked him squarely in the eyes. 'Yeh're brilliant.'

Wicklow

Fitzwilliam Square

14

A WARNING IN WICKLOW

The next morning Rosie took the bus to Wicklow Town, then walked the short distance to the hospital where her father had been for more than two weeks. As she entered, she came face to face with her brother, Buddy.

'Hey, bro,' said Rosie. They hugged.

'How's Da?'

Buddy was grim-faced. 'Not good, Rosie. He's–well, he's sleepin'. They got him dosed up, so he's out of it, pretty much. I only stayed a few minutes. What's the point?'

Rosie nodded.

'But listen, you may not wanna go in right now. Jimmy's in there.'

'Jimmy? How the hell…'

'They let him out, on parole. Can you believe that? I guess they took pity on 'im that his da was sick.' The young man scoffed. 'Like he cared a plug nickel, eh?'

'Parole? Really?'

'I guess he was up for it–he's served nearly two-thirds of his sentence. But like I said, they took pity, gave him special consideration. That son of a bitch don't deserve nothin' special, is what I say. And he's ripped, Rosie, I gotta warn you. Maybe we oughta go in together.'

They walked side-by-side down a long corridor, through some double doors, then down another long corridor till they came to their father's room. Just as they approached, the all too familiar figure of James O'Malley emerged from the room. He was tall, several inches taller than his brother, with a shaven head, heavily tattooed arms, and a permanent sneer on his face.

'Hello, Jimmy,' said Rosie.

'Well, look who it is. My little sis. Ain't this just the perfect family reunion. You gonna throw a party?'

'Nice to see you, too, Jimmy,' replied Rosie. 'I hear someone sprung you from Arbour Hill. Not that you ever deserved a favour from anyone.'

'Look at this. Once a bitch, always a bitch. And not a friendly word to spare on her bro.'

Buddy held back but Rosie stood her ground. 'Friendly? When did you ever deserve friendliness? The way you treated your olds and your brother and sister. All you ever did was look out for your own arse, and not very well, as your enrolment at Arbour Hill shows. So no, you won't get a bit of friendliness out of me. And if that makes me a bitch, then I'm a bitch–and yeh're a bloody bastard.'

'I'm outta here,' replied Jimmy. 'Don't expect to get anything outta the old man. He's toast. Oh, yeah, and by the way, I know what's up with Ma. And just so you know, I'm gonna find her, and I'm gonna bring her back, you hear? Pa will want to see her before he croaks. And I'd like to see her, too.'

'Forget it, Jimmy, she's long gone, and yeh're a good part of the reason.'

'Yeah? Well, my sources tell me you and that uni nob McGurk know where she is. So I'll find out, if I have to break every bone in that eejit's body. And my guess is he'll spill the information as soon as he sees my fist comin' at his ugly face. So be advised, it's on.'

'Stay away from him, from me, and from the house. I got a safety order against you, and the first time I see your ass within sight of the place, I'll have the garda there in minutes. And you'll be back where you belong, where your true friends are, at Arbour Hill. And I'll bet you got some pretty good friends in there, eh? They probably miss you on those long, lonely nights.'

He sneered at Rosie. 'You are a bitch, and a feckin' freak of nature.'

Just then a burly attendant came walking toward them. 'Everything all right here?' he inquired, looking anxiously at the red-faced, heavily tattooed young man, then at Rosie and Buddy.

'Yeah, we're finished,' replied Jimmy. With that he stalked off.

Rosie was shaking.

'Sure yeh're okay, miss?' asked the attendant.

'Yeah, ta.'

She looked into her father's room, then turned to her brother. 'Maybe best to let him rest, eh?' The pair stepped out into the corridor.

'Excuse me,' said a man in green scrubs walking toward her. 'Are you family members of Mr O'Malley?'

'I'm his daughter, Rose O'Malley, this is my brother, Brendan.'

'How do you do. I'm Doctor O'Connor. May I have a word?'
He gestured toward a small waiting room where they sat.

'We've been trying to reach you two, or Mrs O'Malley.'

'Yes, well, Ma is–away.'

'I see. Well, then, can we talk about your father?'

Rosie and Buddy nodded anxiously.

'Your father is very ill. Perhaps you are aware.'

Rosie nodded. 'Ma and I have been trying for months to get him to see the doctor. The only way he came here is that the gardaí in Glenkerry insisted.'

'Yes, so I understand.'

'Is it emphysema? We've known for some time...'

'Well, yes, there's that. But we did x-rays and scans of his lungs. We found tumours.'

'You mean lung cancer?'

The doctor shook his head. 'Not exactly, miss. They are secondary tumours, you see.'

'What does that mean, secondary?'

'It means that there is a primary tumour elsewhere. His cancer didn't originate in the lungs. It spread to the lungs.'

'Well, where is this primary tumour, then?'

'His liver, miss. Your father has metastatic cancer of the liver. I'm sorry. It's quite advanced.'

Rosie was shaking, trying to take in this information, trying to understand what it all meant.

'Can you operate? Or give him, yeh know, chemo or radiation or whatever?'

The doctor looked gravely into her eyes, then Buddy's. 'There's too much tumour, too many tumours, in his liver and lungs, to make surgery feasible.'

Rosie started to sob and Buddy put his arm around her. 'So, can you do anything?'

'We can keep him here–provide palliative treatment–make sure he is comfortable.'

'I'm pretty sure he won't want to stay here a day longer than necessary, doctor.'

'Yes, well, he's made that pretty clear.'

'So, doctor, how long does he have?'

'A month, maybe two. I am sorry, miss. What about your mother, perhaps I should speak with her?'

She shook her head. 'No, doctor. Thank you. We'll talk to her. Can we go in and see him?'

'Of course.'

Rosie returned to her father's bedside. He was still sleeping. She held his hand for a moment and looked down at his wan and wrinkled face. He looked years older than he had just a few days before. She leaned down and kissed him on the forehead as Buddy stood silently. Then they left.

'I'll call Ma and let her know where things stand.' She sighed. 'I'm not sure how she'll feel about comin' to see 'im.' Then she looked at her brother. 'You all right, Bud?'

He shrugged. 'I guess. I don't know, I suppose I feel bad for 'im, but I can't just forget everything…'

'I know. Me either.'

They hugged, then parted.

As she waited for her bus, Rosie drew her mobile from her pocket and left a message for Cary, warning him that Jimmy was out and might well be coming for him. She made no mention of her father's condition.

On the bus ride back to Glenkerry, she was thinking about her father. He was a mean and spiteful man, but for a time in her childhood he had done a good deal on her behalf, and maybe she could in the present circumstances cut him a little slack. He wasn't all bad. Jimmy, on the other hand...

Back in Glenkerry, Rosie went to the McGurk house looking for Cary. She found him working on his laptop at the kitchen table with stacks of papers all around.

He smiled uneasily. 'So, yeh see your da?'

Rosie nodded but looked glum. 'He's in a bad way, Car, I'm afraid. Did you get my text?'

Cary had been so immersed in his work that he hadn't thought to check his phone in several hours.

She told him about her encounters with her brothers. 'I'm worried, Car. Jimmy's daft, he's outta control, and there's no tellin' what he might do next. I'm worried for me, for Buddy, and most of all for you. He already suspects you of helping me. He said you know where Ma is and he promised to get that information out of you, by force if necessary.'

Cary looked worried.

'I told him I already had a safety order against him. I better see Del about gettin' one, maybe you, too. But in the meantime maybe you should go into hiding for a while.'

Cary shook his head. 'I can't do that, and I don't want to do that. I'll be okay. But Rosie, I think we better go see your ma soon, before he has a chance to tail us.'

'How soon?'

'How about early early tomorrow morning, before sunrise.

And let's take my mother's car. He'd recognise your dad's car easily, but maybe not Catherine's.'

Rosie nodded. 'Uh, Car–I talked to the doctor today.' He could see from her face that this was serious.

She gestured toward the pasture. 'Walk with me?'

Claddagh, Galway

15

ON GALWAY BAY

Early the next morning, while most of Glenkerry's citizens were still buried under their quilts and blankets, Catherine McGurk was awake and fixing a small breakfast for three. Cary showered, shaved, dressed quickly, then tapped lightly on the guest room door.

'Rosie, you awake, mate?'

Minutes later the three were seated around the dining room table making quick work of poached eggs, sausage, and toast. Catherine had also prepared road snacks for the two in an insulated container. Then, at half four, with only the faintest glow in the eastern sky, Cary and Rosie set out in Catherine's Hyundai, bound for Galway.

They took the back roads out of Glenkerry, watching anxiously for the headlamps of other cars, fearing that Jimmy O'Malley might be on their tail. But they encountered not a single other vehicle for the first twenty minutes or so, by which time they were on a little used country road headed north. Still they were uneasy until they entered the motorway toward Dublin. Finally, they were able to relax, convinced that they had evaded the one potential spanner in their plan.

Even then, Rosie remained anxious, but now it was the prospect of seeing her mother after more than two months that had her stomach churning. Their telephone conversations had convinced her that she was in good health, but Rosie needed more than anything to see her ma, to touch her, and to know she was safe, happy, content in her new life.

After nearly three hours they began to see signs for Galway. Shortly after eight they rolled into the town, found their way to the public facilities in the city centre, then had coffee and a Danish in the sun looking out on that eponymous bay. At half nine they climbed back into the Hyundai and followed the directions provided by the vehicle's GPS system to the home of Gerald Flaherty.

It was a quiet neighbourhood of brick homes, each with a postage stamp sized garden in the front yard. As soon as they stepped onto the footpath the door opened and Mary O'Malley appeared, smiling sweetly, arms held out prepared to embrace her daughter. Tears flowed between the two for several minutes as Cary stepped up to the front stoop and introduced himself to Gerald Flaherty, Jr. The man was in his mid-fifties, balding, with a round, jovial face.

'Mr Flaherty, sir, I'm Cary McGurk, a friend of Rosie's.'

'Well, come through, please,' said Gerry after all the greetings had been had and the tears had abated. It was a neat house, with comfortable but not lavish furnishings. Tea was served and they sat in upholstered chairs. Chintz drapes hung around the windows, several glass-fronted cabinets displayed a collection of lovely china. A large black and white cat sniffed curiously at Cary's trousers, then rubbed up against his legs as if in approval.

Mary wanted to know everything about her daughter, her health, her painting, her herb garden. 'I been thinkin' about you so much these last weeks, pet, and hopin' you were aright. Are yeh eating well?'

Rosie assured her that she was fine.

Then Mary O'Malley turned to Cary, offered her condolences on the death of his father, and asked after his mother and brother. She had many generous comments and fond recollections of the McGurks.

'Ciaran, I remember when you used to come up the lane with a football under your arm. You and Buddy would kick it about in the yard by the hour.'

'Yeah, well, we did love our footie back then, so. Rosie had some good moves, too, as I recall.'

'I hear you did yourself proud at university, eh?'

'Well, I passed, anyway.'

'And what next for yeh, then? More school?'

'Not for now, no.'

'Car's a writer, Ma,' chimed in Rosie. 'Remember how he used to write for the *Coláiste Machnaimh*? Plus he worked on the DCU literary magazine.'

'Really? Oh, well, we always knew you'd do your folks proud, Ciaran.' Her eyes watered at that, perhaps thinking about her own sons. Then she smiled at Cary. 'I understand you been takin' care of my Rosie lately, Ciaran. I want to thank you. I was so worried for 'er, with her father the way he is.'

'Well, we go way back, Rosie and me, eh? And I was only too chuffed to help out.'

'And Rosie, dear, I feel terrible about leavin' you in the dark for all that time. I really thought I was sendin' you those text things. But only after you called and told me you hadn't gotten any did Gerry look at my phone and explain. I never really sent 'em, you see. I wrote 'em, and saved 'em, but I didn't know about that little button for 'send'. We oldsters got a lot to learn about such things, don't we, Ger?'

'Well, with Cary's help, and Del and another garda named Sabrina, we finally found you, ma.'

She told her mother about Heman Murphy, the CCTV at Ballinoch, and the search for her bank accounts.

'In the end it was Aunt Marguerite who led us to you. She remembered Gerry.' Rosie turned to Gerry. 'I located your father's obituary in the Roscommon newspaper. It said that you were a teacher in Galway. That's when I found you on the National School web page.'

'But Ma, I got one question for yeh. Did you book a ticket for the Rosslare-Fishguard ferry and charge it on your credit card?'

Her mother flashed a guilty grin. 'I did, lass.' She looked at Gerry and smiled. 'That was Gerry's idea. I was so worried about your father findin' me. So Gerry suggested I buy that ticket online. He helped me do it on his computer. But of course I never used it. It was just a diversion. And I left a slip of paper in your da's things with a made-up name and telephone number in Wales.'

'Margaret Ahearn,' cried Rosie.

'Oh, he told you?'

'No, but I found that paper sticking out of his wallet. We figured out that the number was no good. But I was gonna ask you about Margaret Ahearn.'

'I'm sorry, dear. I hope you didn't go to too much trouble trying to locate her.'

Rosie's and Cary's eyes met. She had decided she would spare her mother the details of how much gardaí and Cardiff police time had been wasted looking for Margaret Ahearn, Megan Ahearn, and Meg O'Hearn. 'Oh, no, not at all, Ma.'

'So Gerry, yeh're a teacher, right?' asked Cary, sensing the need to change the subject. 'I'll bet technology is important in secondary schools nowadays?'

'Oh, absolutely. And I do my best to keep up. We spend lots of time these days being trained in the latest technology, only to have it all change six months later. I'm interested to hear that you want to go into newspaper work, like your father. It sounds like yeh're swimming against the tide there, so?'

'Yeah, I guess so. And you, yeh've been teaching English at the National School a long time?'

'Oh, my, yes, going on thirty years now. As I say, it's challenging. But I do love it. My wife Marion passed about five years ago. We have two children–well, they're all grown up now, a course. Julia works in Dublin, Gerry is in New York. It was pretty lonely hereabouts for a time, but then Mary wrote me and…'

He turned and smiled at Rosie's mother.

Just then a knock sounded on the front door and Gerry went through the passageway to answer it. There were loud voices and footsteps in the passage, and then Jimmy O'Malley emerged into the parlour, all six foot two of him, with that malevolent scowl on his face, a look that had been his trademark as long as Cary could remember. He was accompanied by a fellow traveller with even more tattoos than Jimmy.

'James,' called out Mary. 'What in heavens…'

Rosie blanched. 'How the hell? What are you doin' here, Jimmy?'

'I heard all about your little family gathering and thought, gee, I wish I'd been invited. So I decided to crash the party, yeah.'

Cary and Gerry instinctively stepped in front of Mary and Rosie.

'Well, if it ain't McGurk the Jerk?'

Cary's knees were shaking but he stood his ground.

'I don't know how you found us, O'Malley, but yeh're not welcome 'ere. So get out, now.'

'Oh, pretty boy talks tough. And just whatta yeh gonna do if I don't, arsehole?'

'James, don't be like that,' said Mary.

Momentarily distracted by his mother's voice, Jimmy turned toward her. In that split second Cary lunged at him, shoving him as hard as he could toward the front hallway. Jimmy's companion went for Cary then and the two got into a wrestling match.

'Enough,' hollered Jimmy. And he drew a knife with a wide blade. Everyone stood stunned, wondering what he would do next.

'Now here's what's gonna happen. Ma, yeh're comin' with us. Pa will want to be seein' yeh, and you should be back in your own 'ouse.' He took a step toward Mary.

At that moment Rosie pivoted on one leg and in a flash her other leg flew up like a bolt, her trainer slamming hard into her brother's hand, sending the knife flying.

'Why you little bitch.' Jimmy reached for her. But another kick was already on its way, this one delivered directly to the groin. He doubled over, groaning.

By now Jimmy's companion had subdued Cary from behind,

securing both his arms behind his back in a full Nelson. But Cary had not forgotten his rugby and another weapon at his disposal that his assailant had overlooked. He jerked his head back, ramming it into the guy's face. Bones and cartilage crunched, the arm hold was released, and his attacker teetered unevenly, blood squirting from his nose and mouth.

Just then a siren could be heard. Gerry had dialled 9-9-9 seconds after the intruders had entered the house and pushed past him. Jimmy and his friend turned and rushed out the front door, right into the hands of three gardaí who were approaching on the footpath. They handcuffed the pair, helped them into patrol cars, and sped off while the other garda talked to Gerry, then Mary, Rosie, and Cary.

When the garda finally departed, the four went inside. That ugly encounter had lasted less than five minutes–there were blood stains on the carpet as a reminder should anyone wonder if they had imagined it. Gerry hugged Mary who was in tears.

'I'm sorry, Gerry, for bringin' my family troubles right into your parlour this way,' she said.

But Gerry stroked her hair gently. 'Well, dear, every family has its troubles.'

'Not like this family, I'm afraid, love.'

Then it was Rosie's turn to apologise. 'I'm the one who should be sorry, here. I was so sure we had slipped outta Glenkerry unseen. He must a been waitin' for us and tailed us, but I can't figure out how he did it, there were no headlamps in sight.'

Then Gerry spoke up. He was holding a small transmitter. 'This was hangin' from the undercarriage of your car. I saw it when you pulled up but thought it must be just a loose muffler clamp or something.'

Cary looked at it. 'Well, I gotta hand it to your brother, Rosie. The gardaí sometimes clamp those things under the cars of known drugs dealers, then map their routes and identify their contacts. He must've planted it under my ma's car sometime overnight.'

Rosie nodded with a look of disgust on her face. 'Yeah, well, if there's one area that my brother knows all about, it's drugs.'

After all that drama it took some time and lots more tea, but eventually the four were able to relax. Gerry wanted to know more about Cary's university experience and his career plans. As they spoke Mary and Rosie shared a few minutes in the kitchen.

'Love, I feel terrible leavin' you all alone with your pa.'

Rosie shook her head. 'Don't, Ma. I'm glad you left. You deserve so much more in life than bein' with 'im. Anyway, I'm a big girl now and I can take care of myself.'

'Well, lass, that fancy footwork proves that all right.'

They both laughed. Then Mary's expression changed. She reached out and took her daughter's hand.

'Don't let your pa ruin your life, love, the way he tried to ruin mine. Yeh hear? Yeh know, I had a sweet spot for Gerry way back in secondary school, and I let my pa come between us. I just hope that doesn't happen to you...' She nodded toward the parlour. 'To you two, understand?'

Rosie nodded. 'But Ma, I talked to dad's doctor yesterday, at the hospital.' She told him of the cancer and the grim prognosis.

'Well, I am sorry to hear it, love. And I wish I could be there for 'im...'

Rosie shook her head. 'No, you got your new life here, Ma. And he's got me 'n Buddy to take care of him in his last days, if he'll let us.'

They talked for several minutes more. Then Mary looked into

her daughter's eyes. 'Young Ciaran there, he's a fine young man.'

'Yes, Ma, he is.'

'And yeh have feelin's for him, don't yeh? Always have.'

Just then Cary and Gerry entered, and the conversation shifted. Soon Cary and Rosie prepared to leave. Tearful goodbyes were exchanged on the footpath between mother and daughter. Cary shook Gerry's hand and leaned in and kissed Mary on the cheek.

The trip back to Glenkerry held a mixture of relief and worry for Rosie and Cary.

'Listen, Rose, what Jimmy did back there, forcing his way into Gerry's house, threatening us with a knife. His parole–for sure it'll be revoked now. So with luck he won't see the light of day for at least a few years, yeah?'

The thought relieved Rosie somewhat. 'I just want my ma to be happy. But look what I did to her? And Gerry. I can see what yeh're saying–maybe yeh're right. But I feel awful for what I did to my ma.'

Along the way, Cary called his mother and told her of their misadventure in Galway. It was late afternoon when they finally rolled up to the O'Malley house. Cary shut off the engine and he and Rosie sat in silence for a moment.

'Now I don't want you stayin' alone in that house, Rosie, especially after all you been through today. Ma is expecting you for supper and to spend the night, yeah?'

Rosie accepted the invitation gratefully. 'But sooner or later I gotta come back here, Car, yeh know? I'll have a talk with Buddy. Maybe he's ready to move back to Glenkerry–maybe he and I could live here together, for a time, anyway. I don't know, Car, it's too much to think about right now.'

Rosie retrieved a few things from her house, then walked down the lane to the McGurks. Catherine was very happy to have Cary and Rosie back home, safe and sound. She put on a lavish meal, fish chowder followed by mushrooms and pasta. After supper Del Samuels showed up and talked to Cary and Rosie in the drive.

'We got the full report from the Galway gardaí. Sounds like a nasty bit of doin' you got yourselves into, eh?' Then he reassured them. 'Jimmy's already on his way back to Arbour Hill. And that'll be his home for the duration of his drugs sentence, at least three years with no chance of another parole, that's for sure. And as to today's hijinks, well, I'm guessing he'll get another five, at least, for that. And his mate, he has a list of outstanding warrants against him as long as your arm, so he'll be in court tomorrow.'

As Del prepared to leave, he had some advice for Rosie and Cary. 'You two are quite a team. Look at how you worked to track down Rosie's ma. Cary, you figured out Mary's route over to Ballinoch. And Rosie you got that list of names from your aunt, and clocked that Gerald Flaherty was an old flame o' your ma's and livin' in Galway. You two are like a couple a Sherlock Holmeses, I'd say. Did you ever consider startin' a private detective agency? I'll bet you'd be an overnight success.'

Rosie laughed. 'Yeah, I like that. And you could be a partner, too, Del. All we need is a catchy name.' She glanced toward the house to be sure Catherine was not listening. 'How about the Wicklow Dicks, eh?'

The three friends laughed together.

'She's a one in a million, this lass,' he said to Cary with a wink.

'Don't yeh think?'

Cary put his arm around Rosie's waist and they waved as Del backed out of the drive and drove off down the lane.

'She is that,' he said softly into Rosie's ear.

And don't you forget it, mate.

Just then Rosie's mobile rang. She walked away from Cary for a moment, then returned.

'That was my da. He's home from hospital. I better get goin'.'

He watched her walk slowly up the lane. Back inside, Cary told his mother about Patrick O'Malley's cancer diagnosis. Catherine shook her head.

'I'm sorry for the old guy. But I'm even sorrier for that lass.'

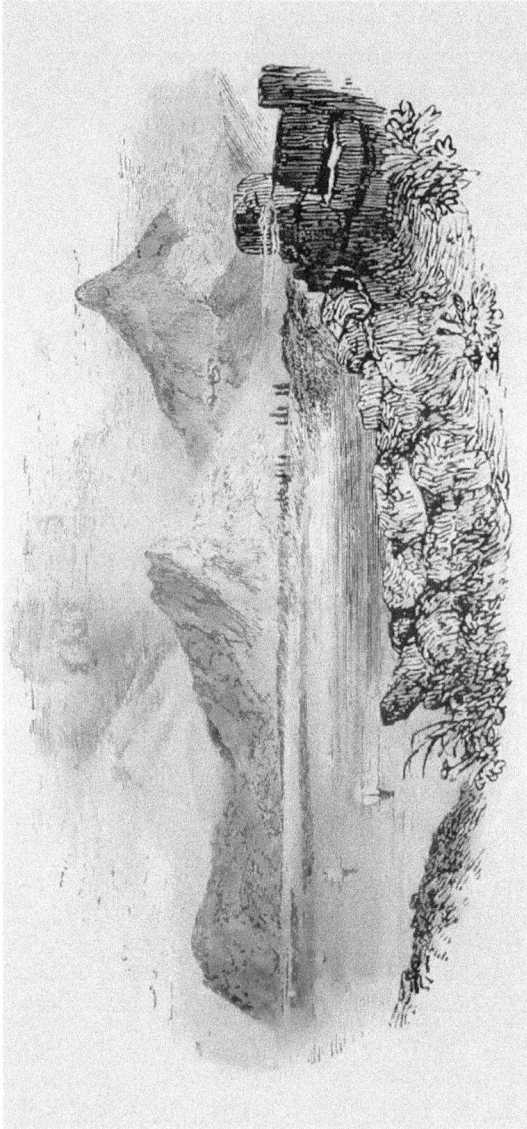

Wicklow Mountains

16

RETURN TO GLENKERRY

'So, yeh're back 'ome,' said Rosie to her father. He was leaning against the kitchen sink, a bottle in one hand, looking out the window.

'Don't care for hospitals–never 'ave.'

'How're you feelin'?'

He shrugged. 'Been betta.'

'You hungry?'

'Nah, I waited for tea at the hospital before I left. Wanted to get my money's worth, yeh know?'

He chuckled, looked briefly at Rosie, then turned back to the window.

'Buddy and me talked to that Doctor O'Connor. He told us.'

'Eh, don't believe what those eejits say. They get paid by the disease, yeh know? So they're always finding new things to charge the HSE for.'

'Well, I'll be here for you, yeh know, as long as I can help.'

It was a perfect opening for the old man to say thank you to his daughter, but all he could manage was a perfunctory, 'I'll be fine.' She thought she saw the slightest glistening in his eyes, but then he turned and looked out the window again.

'I saw Ma today,' said Rosie softly.

No response.

'She's doin' real good, Pa. She's happy and healthy. In Galway.'

'She say when she's comin' home?' he asked without turning.

Rosie hesitated. 'She's livin' in a nice house with a nice man, an old friend. He cares a lot about her. He treats her well. I think she feels like she *is* home, Da.'

'And how'd you get all the way to Galway?'

'Cary, Ciaran McGurk. You remember him. He's been so good to me since Ma left. Without his help we never woulda found her.'

'Never cared for that kid. Know-it-all. Eejit.'

'Well, Pa, I happen to be in love with that eejit.' She laughed at her own admission.

'Well, good on you,' he replied dismissively. 'Jimmy came to see me in hospital. He's gonna go get your ma, bring her back home where she belongs.'

'Don't count on it, Pa. Jimmy's back in Arbour Hill.'

She gave her father a quick summary of events in Galway earlier in the day.

With that Harry turned to his daughter. 'Well, I hope yeh're happy, gettin' your brother locked up again. Thanks to you and that McGurk kid.'

Rosie might have broken into tears at that point, but her anger at her father overrode any sadness.

'I'm goin' to bed, Pa. Let me know if yeh need anything in the night, yeah? And I'll fix you breakfast in the mornin'.'

She spoke calmly, without ire.

How is it possible for me to be so civil, so polite, to that man?

Once around midnight Rosie was awakened by the sound of coughing. She found her father in the loo, standing over the sink. She patted him on the back.

'Pa? You all right?'

'Yeah, I'm fine. Just a little tickle is all.'

She looked down. There were spots of blood on the white porcelain.

'Go back ta sleep,' he said gruffly.

In the morning Rosie fixed her father his usual breakfast, fried eggs, baked beans, and sausage. He ate very little, just sat sipping his tea.

Rosie did some laundry, then took her easel into the garden to paint. As she worked she could hear her father's voice in the house. He was talking on the telephone. By the sound of it he made several calls. She wondered if he was having second thoughts about leaving the hospital. Perhaps he was considering going back.

At midday she was making herself some tea when her father appeared.

'I'm goin' to a meetin' Monday night, in Arklow. The County Council is voting on a project. They want to buy some of my pastureland down along the river road.'

'Yes, I've been hearing about that. Stirred up quite a kerfuffle, it has.'

Harry groaned. 'Do-gooders and tree-huggers. They don't know what's good for 'em.'

Rosie offered no response.

'I need yeh to come with me. You don't need ta stay for the meetin', just help me in and at the end help me out.'

'Can't you get one of your friends to drive you and help you?'

'Friends,' Harry groaned. 'Judases more like it. Nope, I need you.'

'I don't think you should be drivin', Pa. Not in your condition. Takin' those pills and all?'

'You could drive me.'

'Don't you remember, Pa? I don't have a licence. You never let me get my driver's licence.'

'Bah, that's no matter. Yeh've driven that car up the lane and back, with your brother, quite a few times 's I recall.'

That evening Cary received a call on his mobile from Professor Jurgenson. He apologised for being out of touch; he and his family had been on holiday on the Dingle Peninsula and were out of cell range for several days.

'Thank you for sending me that information from Cork. It sounds like you learned a lot about that new shopping centre, and Emerald Isle Enterprises. Anything new on that?'

'No, not really, professor. The firm seemed to work hard to meet all the criticisms about that project. And they made a commitment to local businesses as well. The city planning director had only good things to say about them. And that reporter, the same.'

'But it sounds as though they were a little heavy-handed with neighbours of the project, am I right?'

'Yes, that's what I learned. I talked to two ladies who own homes next to the shopping centre. They felt a lot of pressure to sell. But they refused. And apparently that attorney, Monahan, badgered them, with phone calls, visits, and a letter.'

'And you said in your message that he threatened one of them?'

'Yes, that's right. Did you see that letter?'

'Yes, I did. And he was definitely trying to convince that Mrs Porter to sell, saying it was a very generous offer and there would never be a better offer.' The professor paused. 'But Ciaran, I'm not sure your Council members will see that as threatening. He was trying to persuade them, true, and he may have been a little strong in his language about never getting a better deal on their property. But it wasn't exactly a threat, do you see what I mean?'

Cary hesitated. 'Yes, sir, uh-huh. She said she felt threatened. But now that you mention it, the letter doesn't really read that way.'

Professor Jurgenson went on. 'So I think unless there's some more specific evidence of a threat, a real clear effort at intimidation, I wouldn't present it to the council.'

'Uh-huh, yeah, I guess you're right, sir. I…'

'Remember, you still have the Ireland Visions business, falsifying data, facing a lawsuit, and so on. That's pretty significant. So maybe on balance Emerald Isle Enterprises behaved themselves in Cork–and put the Dublin matter behind them, or hoped they had. Your best bet with the Wicklow Council is to convince them that Emerald Isle's reputation was tarnished and they should not be trusted just because they changed their corporate name.'

'Yes, right, of course.'

'Your meeting is Monday, am I right? Just two days from now.'

'Yes.'

'And you are making the presentation? Is that right?'

'Yes, sir.'

'My advice would be to write out a script for yourself, exactly what you plan to say. Think carefully about your language, about not overstating your case, as we talked about. Send me a draft if you like, I'll be glad to look it over. And do a rehearsal with some of your committee members, I think that would be important.'

'Okay, yes, I will do that.'

'And most importantly, Ciaran, try to anticipate the questions you may face from supporters of the project on the Council. So when they ask, you'll be prepared.'

'Yes, I will for sure. Thank you, professor.'

'And good luck, Ciaran. I'm sure you will do a fine job, whatever the outcome.'

After ringing off, Cary sat at his desk thinking, and worrying. He reread the letter to Mrs Porter. The professor was correct, he realised–that letter contained no threat. Yes, it was intended to convince her to sell, but it was carefully worded. Maybe he had been too quick to condemn that attorney without looking carefully at the evidence. If that was the case, then there wasn't really anything about the Cork project that he could use in his argument to the Wicklow County Council.

Cary had a hard time getting to sleep that night, worrying that he would not be able to make a convincing case against the Monster Mall before the County Wicklow Council. And time was running out.

The first thing next morning Cary was reading over his notes from his Cork trip, still brooding on the matter of threats. Didn't both ladies say they felt uneasy with that attorney? And didn't Mrs Porter say he told her if she refused they could make life miserable for her? Over his usual bowl of porridge the next morning, Cary reported to his mother on his conversation with Professor Jurgenson.

'I've been thinkin' that letter was the key, Ma, that it contained a threat. But now as I read it, it really doesn't say anything threatening. So I feel like I have nothing from Cork now to strengthen our case.'

Catherine took a sip of tea. 'Why don't you call your Uncle Bill today, Car? He was there, right? And he knows those ladies. Maybe he can help.'

A few hours later Cary called his uncle in Cork. There was no answer, so Cary left him a long voicemail message. Did Bill recall anything more specific about threats received by his friends? Perhaps Mrs Wright received a letter as well, but one that was more intimidating, more threatening, than the one to Mrs Porter he had copied.

The Vale of Avoca

17

SHOWDOWN IN ARKLOW

I t was the evening before the council's decision on the Monster Mall and a vigil was held in Glenkerry's market square. It began with several brief but emotional speeches, encouraging all to be in attendance in Arklow the next evening when the decision would be made.

Then came refreshments. Half a dozen of the town's restaurants offered finger food including stuffed dosas from Punjab Palace, spring rolls from Paddy's Chinese Takeaway, corn fritters from Siam Bistro, and cod crunchies from the Glenkerry Fishmonger.

Next came musical entertainment, the trio from Phinney's– Seamus, Bart, and Mike–Emma Stewart with her electric cello, and Buster Hanley of Ballinoch on the uilleann pipes, Ireland's own bagpipes.

At the end Father O'Ryan outdid himself with his benediction, a heartfelt prayer for God's guidance in difficult times, for peace in war-torn Ukraine, for wisdom on the part of leaders near and far, from Wicklow to Washington to Warsaw. At Cary's urging, the evening was capped by the honeyed tones of Glenkerry's own, Rosie O'Malley. Not a dry eye was there to be found as she intoned those words that are seared on the very soul of every man, woman, and child in Ireland, and so many others across God's green earth:

Oh, Danny boy, the pipes, the pipes are calling
From glen to glen, and down the mountain side.
The summer's gone, and all the roses falling,
It's you, it's you must go and I must bide.

But come yeh back when summer's in the meadow,
Or when the valley's hushed and white with snow,
It's I'll be here in sunshine or in shadow,
Oh, Danny boy, oh Danny boy, I love you so!

When Rosie was finished, a roar of admiration and appreciation rose from the crowd. Cary had been standing in the front row gazing upon that sweet colleen with a voice to match. He stepped up to her, kissed her on the cheek, then held her in a tight embrace.

'Rosie, that was beautiful. And so are you.' At that she leaned back and looked into his eyes. Unnerved by the intensity of her stare, Cary added, 'Ta, mate, for everything.'

The spell was broken when Rosie was suddenly surrounded by other townspeople, embracing her, praising her, and thanking her. Cary stood back and watched with pleasure as attention was lavished on her. Just then Del appeared at his side.

'She's something, ain't she?'

Cary nodded and smiled. Then Del took Cary's arm and pulled him away from the hubbub.

'Listen, lad, I been jawin' with folks all day. And everybody's talkin' about you and that paper. Everyone.'

'Get out, mate.'

'Nope, no lies. You, my friend, have a following–an audience–a posse. It's up to you to step up, bring it back, resurrect the *Glenkerry Gazette*. You have to. And you want to, lad, admit it.'

Cary shook his head. 'Yeah, well, that's great, mate, if it's true. But–a newspaper, a print newspaper, in these times? It would be dead in the water the first issue. I swear.'

'Well, what about a hybrid?'

Cary looked at his friend, confused.

'Yeh know, print and digital. A few hundred print copies a week, mostly for the older folks, with some in the shops for tourists and visitors. And a digital edition that people would receive on their mobiles or tablets or laptops or whatever.'

Cary paused, trying to imagine what Del was describing. Then he shook his head.

'It would never fly, Del, not today. No one has time for newspapers anymore, print or digital. Forget it, mate. Anyway, I'm leavin' for London right after the Council meeting.'

Del looked sad eyed at his friend, then turned to watch townspeople gathered around Rosie. He shook his head.

'It's a shame, mate, a real shame.'

Back home, Cary sat in his mother's rose garden, feeling as low as he'd been since his father's death. Okay, Rosie had been reunited with her mother–a good thing, a very good thing. And her older brother was behind bars for the foreseeable future. But the Monster Mall, well, it was inevitable, that much was clear.

Maybe, he thought, maybe that mall is the future of Glenkerry, of Ireland. An artificial world, a pseudo-community of anonymous, unconnected shoppers wandering around a place that could just as easily be in England, or America, buying cookie-cutter merchandise from cookie-cutter people in cookie-cutter shops.

He kept rethinking his visit to Cork, about those sweet old ladies who seemed so put out by change in their neighbourhood and threats to get on board or regret it forever. He was disappointed for them, but most of all, he was disappointed in himself. He had worked so hard on the Ireland Visions/Emerald Isle Enterprises business and thought he had really found something of importance there. But he doubted now that that alone would be sufficient to sway many votes in the County Council. And more to the point, he wondered whether he had the courage, the confidence, to state the case and make it stick. Surely he would stumble and fall. Maybe Del was right after all–Ciaran McGurk was like the bad estate agent who just couldn't close a deal.

After tomorrow night, your work here is done, mate. London, that's where it's at.

Just then he heard a skylark calling from the meadow. It felt like it was beckoning him, and he rose and walked across the lawn, over the wall, and into the pasture to his favourite spot. His harbinger was perched on a fencepost not far beyond, singing that song as if his life depended on it. Cary listened to that heartfelt song as he gazed on the village below, those slate-roofed houses clustered along High Street, chimney stacks protruding like saw teeth from the rooflines. Out of the corner of his eye he saw the stump of the hawthorn and once again the memory of that old tree triggered an aching in his chest.

But then he noticed something unexpected and new, several small green stems protruding from the cut stump, each bearing a single leaf. The tree he had known since a boy, the tree that once framed his view of Glenkerry, that tree wasn't dead after all.

He stood looking at that hawthorn reborn, that fresh-cut stump glistening with sap, and those new shoots ascending toward the light, full of vigour, full of hope, full of life. Faith, that was what he needed, faith in life, in rebirth, in the future.

It's there, mate, in that tree stump, all you need to know is right there in that gnarly stump.

Finally, he rose and walked back to the house. He felt exhausted and fell onto his bed. Several hours later he woke, took off his shirt and trousers and pulled on his running shorts, then fell back to sleep.

When he awoke the next morning, Cary felt as well rested as he had in weeks. True, the meeting in Arklow was only about twelve hours away. But he had achieved a new comfort, a certain inner peace. He believed in his cause and would give it all he had, let the chips fall where they may.

After breakfast he went to work preparing his notes for the meeting. He would present his case regarding Ireland Visions as forcefully as he could, emphasising the false data in the Dublin project, intentional misrepresentation of the facts, the threatened lawsuit by the city, the admission of errors, and the agreement to withdraw the proposal and accept the city's sanction. Furthermore, he would argue, the abandonment of the name Ireland Visions should count as an additional mark against the firm, an additional deception, amounting to little more than an effort to hide their past.

The critical point, he would conclude, is trust. Can we trust this firm, these individuals, knowing what we now know about their recent past? Should we, the citizens of County Wicklow, enter into a partnership with such untrustworthy, discredited individuals?

Around noon Gloria arrived. She and Catherine listened as Cary delivered his speech, notes in hand. Gloria had some valuable suggestions for rewording as well as some additional ideas he might want to include. About his delivery, she urged him to make more eye contact with his audience.

'Look up as often as possible, Cary, look at the Council members. Smile. You have a wonderful smile and an honest face. Let them see it. Show them that you are smart, you are well prepared, and you are sincere.'

As to content, she had only compliments.

'I like how you have presented this as a series of deceptions. If the Council sees it as one small mistake seven years ago, they probably will be inclined to overlook it and approve the project. You remind them that this is much more than one mistake, it is a series of intentional distortions all designed for the purpose of covering the truth, of persuading the Dublin Planning Board that their project was something other than what they knew it to be, deeply flawed.'

'And the way you treat the corporate name change as a separate offense, a separate effort to hide the truth, that is perfect as well. It's part of a pattern of deliberate deception.'

At Cary's request Gloria also came armed with a series of questions or responses he might expect from the Council members or from the Emerald Isle personnel. They included several provided by Kevin Leahy who knew as well as anyone what might be going on in the minds of his fellow councillors:

> *This all happened seven years ago. We fail to see how this has any relevance to us here today.*

> *These were errors, nothing more. Ireland Visions was fully prepared to correct those mistakes and resubmit the proposal. They never got a chance.*

> *But no charges were ever brought against Ireland Visions, isn't that so?*

Finally, they talked about the Cork project. Reluctantly, they agreed that it in the absence of more evidence of threats against the property owners, it might be better not to bring up the subject at all.

After Gloria left, Cary went to the yard to do his tai chi. Just as he was finishing, his mobile sounded.

'Hey, Rosie. What's up?'

'Are you ready for tonight's meeting, Car?'

He took a deep breath. 'Yeah, I think so. Gloria Hennessey came round earlier and she and my ma listened to my presentation and gave me lots of good feedback, yeh know?'

'So you're not too nervous?'

'I'm beyond nervous, Rosie. I've decided I need to float above it all, let it play out as it will. I've done my part, best I can.' He exhaled loudly. 'I been doin' my tai chi, yeh know? Destressing.'

'Well, good for you, mate. I know you'll do well.'

'You comin'?'

'Eh, well, I'm not sure. My da wants me to, in fact he wants me to drive him. I don't want to, honestly. But he might even need my help gettin' in and out of the building–he's not too steady on his feet. We'll see.'

The Wicklow County Council convened a special meeting that evening in Arklow. With all the attention focused on the 'Monster Mall' proposal, they met in a school auditorium. The scheduled starting time was seven in the evening, but the crush of attendees resulted in a delay while additional seating was brought in. A video link was also provided in the school cafeteria where more seating was available.

At last the Chair, Councillor Kelly, spoke: 'Ladies, gentlemen, we apologise for the delay. The Wicklow County Council has scheduled this special session to consider the proposal of Emerald Isle Enterprises, Limited, for a project known as the Glenkerry Mall.'

A low groan could be heard.

'We thank the gentlemen and ladies from that firm who are in attendance this evening to present their proposal, to entertain questions, and to hear comments.'

More groans.

'We understand that emotions are running high on this matter, but we beg your cooperation in maintaining a polite, civil atmosphere in these proceedings. The Chair will not tolerate outbursts of any kind. Without further ado, let us proceed.'

For the next forty minutes a woman representing Emerald Isle

Enterprises made an illustrated presentation on the proposed project. She began by describing the scope of the project, its location and siting. She then addressed some of the concerns that had been raised on the subject including environmental considerations such as soil, water, and air quality, traffic and road impacts. Finally, she expounded on the project's economic impacts, arguing that it would attract business to the village and surrounding towns, provide over one hundred new jobs for the county, and generate significant tax revenues.

When she concluded, she invited questions. The floodgates, it seems, swung wide open. For the next two hours the questions and comments came, and the tone was decidedly negative. In the spirit of civic order, the exchange was mostly polite, with only a few 'arses' and 'feckers' interjected. Save Glenkerry had pleaded with its members and supporters to maintain civility, and that request was honoured–in the main.

Midway through the public comment period, Cary's mobile buzzed. He stepped out into the foyer to take the call. It was from his uncle, Bill Flanagan, in Cork. Cary was back in his seat in the auditorium just as Gloria Hennessy was about to speak. He whispered in her ear. She nodded, then she stood to address the Council.

She began with a spirited and forceful commentary on the proposed project, paying particular attention to the projected economic benefits. The developers had argued, as they did in Cork, that the mall would not harm local businesses because most of its customers would be coming some distance to shop. Gloria took aim at that argument, citing examples in Limerick, Waterford, and Sligo where such 'out-of-town' developments had gutted established shopping districts in city centres.

She then introduced Mr Harlan Pierce from Keep Ireland Green, a Dublin-based organisation, who attempted to raise concerns about the environmental impacts of the project. But his delivery was halting and disorganized; some council members seemed unimpressed.

Gloria then introduced Cary McGurk, a native of Glenkerry just graduated at Dublin City University in journalism. She reminded the Council of his father and mother who were known to many of them.

Cary stepped up to the microphone. He was grateful that the mic was mounted on a podium so the council members couldn't see his legs shaking as he prepared to speak. He looked down at his notes, then up at the Council seated across the stage. Kevin Leary was smiling at him as if to say, 'Have courage, lad–you can do it.'

'I'm Ciaran McGurk. I'm–eh–from Glenkerry. I–eh–would like to share with the Council some–eh–some information I have recently come across in–eh–in my study of the proposed project.' He had been urged to make plenty of eye contact with the council members, but each time he looked up from his script, he lost his place and had to pause while relocating it.

This is not working–just talk to them, mate, tell them what you know.

He placed the script on the podium, looked up at the Council, then spoke ex tempore.

'I would like to give the Council a little background on a firm called Ireland Visions Limited.' Several of the councillors shook their heads dismissively. But as he said the words 'Ireland Visions Limited' he felt certain he saw some squirming and the exchange of glances between members of the Emerald Isle team. Now his eyes were fixed on the Council. He knew what he wanted to say, what should be said, and he didn't need those carefully prepared notes.

'Ladies and gentlemen, several years ago Ireland Visions Limited submitted a proposal for a commercial development in Dublin, to be sited close to the banks of the River Liffey. Concerns were expressed regarding the possible impacts of that project on the river, in particular to possible runoff of hydrocarbon contaminants such as petrol and oil from vehicles to be parked on the property.'

He held up a copy of their submission.

'Ireland Visions submitted a lengthy report on the question including data collected by a subcontractor, Hydrotech, a hydrological engineering firm in Kingswood.'

The Chair interrupted. 'Mr McGurk, can you get to the point here?'

'Yes, sir. Here it is, sir.' That prod was just what he needed. His voice became firmer, more confident. 'The Dublin Planning Board found errors in the data, forty-five to be exact, and they were not really errors but alterations they believed were intended to cover up the actual findings and suggest that the project would have no impact on water quality. I have here a copy of a letter the Planning Board sent to Ireland Visions detailing their concerns. A day later the firm withdrew their proposal.'

A buzz could be heard among the councillors and in the audience. Again the Chair interrupted. 'What relevance does this matter have to us this evening, sir?'

'Mr Chairman' replied Cary, 'shortly after Ireland Visions withdrew their proposal, the company was dissolved. But a new firm was formed by the principals of that firm. That new company is known as Emerald Isle Enterprises.'

There were gasps and a few shouts from the audience at this

revelation. One council member, a known supporter of the Glenkerry Mall, spoke up.

'Mr McGurk, companies often reorganise, change their names, for a variety of reasons. I see no evidence that this firm has done anything wrong.'

Cary was prepared for that question. 'Well, sir, Ireland Visions, its top staff and board members, were cited by the Dublin City Planning Board as potential targets of legal action. The words 'fraud' and 'misrepresentation' were mentioned.'

One of the Emerald Isle representatives stood up.

'Mr Chairman, I am Michael Monahan, legal counsel for Emerald Isle Ltd. I know a few things about this matter. What the young man has failed to point out is that no action was ever taken against that firm or those individuals. Am I right, sir?'

'That is correct,' replied Cary, now speaking forcefully. 'And the reason for that was their willingness to admit to having falsified data. They did that in a letter to the city dated 15 June 2015, a copy of which I have right here.'

He held up the copy.

'Not only did they admit to those actions. They accepted the decision that no charges would be filed against the firm on condition that it would be barred from filing any future development proposals within the city of Dublin.'

The attorney sat down.

'If that firm was banned from submitting any further projects in Dublin, I believe this Council should have serious reservations about approving a proposal from Emerald Isle Associates, now or in the future, in Glenkerry or anywhere in County Wicklow.'

The chair spoke again. 'Thank you, Mr McGurk.'

'If I may, sir, I'd like to make just one additional point. It pertains to the Cork project that has been mentioned.'

The chair nodded.

'I spent some time in Cork City last week. I met with Harold Smyth, head of the city's planning department, and I had a conversation with Reynold Travers, a reporter for one of the city's largest newspapers. I was introduced to three Cork residents whose properties abut the Emerald Isle Shops. These are elderly folks, pensioners, and all three reported that back when the project was in the design phase, a representative of Emerald Isle Associates badgered them on several occasions about selling their property. All three found his tone and manner upsetting. They also reported that that representative threatened them. That person was Mr Monahan.'

Again the Attorney stood. 'Mr Chairman, if I may. It is true that I spoke to some of the neighbours of that project. And we made them very generous offers for their properties, far above the market value of those homes at the time. But Mr Chairman, I categorically deny that there were any threats made. I simply informed them that the offer being made was a generous one and that they might regret it if they passed it up. That was not a threat but a simple statement of fact.'

Cary spoke up. 'Mr Chairman, I would like to show you a short video clip, approximately forty-five seconds, recorded by one of those neighbours at her front door. Gloria?'

At that Gloria held Cary's mobile in front of the video camera set up at the back of the room. The image was projected on a large screen where all could see and hear.

She played the clip. There was Mr Monahan, just visible through Mrs Porter's partially opened door. His voice could be heard:

You may never get another offer like this, ma'am. You could be very sorry if you passed it up. Life could get very miserable for you, believe me.

'Life could get very miserable for you, believe me,' repeated Cary. 'Those were Mr Monahan's exact words to one of those neighbours I met. I think it is clear, members of the Council–what you just heard was a threat.'

The audience rose to their feet, clapping and shouting, while the Chair tried valiantly to gavel the meeting to order. When the room was again quiet Kevin Leahy spoke up, calling for an end to discussion. The Chair hesitated.

'I will allow one more speaker, then consider a motion for a vote.'

Just then a throaty voice came from the rear and a figure rose to speak. It was Harry O'Malley.

'Sir?' said the Chair.

Harry spoke slowly. He was a bit unsteady on his feet, grasping the back of the chair in front of him for support. And his words were slurred.

'I been livin' in Glenkerry for nearly thirty years and seen that town struggle to survive. Most o' the stores and shops we used to have are gone. About all you can buy in the village now are toys for your poodle, unicorn hats, candy floss, and all that malarky. And the restaurants, all they serve are fortune cookies and crap from China. Now here's a chance to turn this town around, and I say let's do it. Don't let a small bunch of know-it-alls tell you how to vote. Vote for jobs and money for our town and for all a County Wicklow. That's all I gotta say.'

Not a sound was heard in the auditorium as Harry O'Malley took his seat.

Finally, the Chair called for the end of discussion. The motion seconded, the council proceeded to a vote. There was a proposal tabled to delay the decision until the questions Cary had raised could be investigated. But there seemed to be little interest in more delay and the motion was defeated.

'We shall now turn to the question at hand, the proposal submitted known as the Glenkerry Mall.'

It was a verbal vote, with each councillor asked to step up to the microphone and vote yea or nay on the project. The first two voted yea, leaving the committee members with a sinking feeling. But soon the nay votes were in the preponderance. When the last of the votes had been announced, a cheer went up from the crowd. But the Chair called for quiet while the count was checked. Finally, he made the announcement.

'On the matter of the proposed Glenkerry Mall, the vote is 12 in favour, 22 against. The proposal is rejected.'

A wild scene ensued. The Committee members and their supporters hugged one another, cheered, and shouted. Gloria Hennessy hugged everyone in sight including Catherine and Cary. She planted a loud kiss on Cary's cheek. Meanwhile, amidst all that mayhem, Harry O'Malley rose without a word and staggered out of the auditorium. A few minutes later, Gloria, Catherine, and Cary walked out into the night together, their spirits soaring.

Catherine drove herself and Cary back to Glenkerry, following the winding road along the river. The surface of the road was still wet from a rain shower earlier in the evening. As they approached the bridge over the River Kerry, the flashing lights of garda cars warned them of trouble ahead. Finally, traffic came to a halt, but they were now near enough to see that the trouble was at the bridge. Cary opened his door and stepped out onto the Tarmac, trying to see what was going on up ahead.

'Hey, lad,' came a voice from behind him. It was Del in his yellow garda jacket.

'What's goin' on, Del?'

Del shook his head. 'Some poor sod didn't make the turn onto the bridge. Car jumped the guardrail and went down into the river. Musta been goin' awfully fast, mate. Car's in the water.'

Catherine overheard Del. 'Oh, dear. How awful.'

'Heard the good news from Arklow, eh?' said Del.

'Yeah,' replied Car. 'Pretty one-sided vote, almost two to one against.'

Just then traffic started to move. 'See yeh, Del,' said Cary as he climbed back into his mother's car. As they crossed the bridge, they could see the beams of spotlights and torches arcing down the steep riverbank, then across the dark waters far below.

Back home Cary was busy reading a series of text messages from Siobhan about her work. At that moment he heard a car pull into the drive and a door slam. It was Del. Cary opened the front door and stepped out onto the porch, still in his bare feet.

'What's up, garda?'

Del's expression was glum. 'Bad news, Car, real bad news. That car, the one that went over the rail and into the river? It was Harry O'Malley's. They found him in the water. He didn't make it.'

Cary stood motionless, unconscious of the light mist that was swirling about him. His legs suddenly felt weak under him.

'Was–was anyone in the car with 'im?' asked Cary fearfully.

'They don't know. They're still searchin' the water.'

'Oh, jeez, Del–oh, God,' said Cary. Then he took a deep breath, thinking. 'He was sitting alone at the meeting, I know that, but Rosie told me he wanted her to come with 'im.'

'Hop in,' said Del.

Cary ran back into the house, pulled on his trainers, and gave his mother a very brief account of what happened.

'But, what about Rosie?'

'I don't know, Ma. We're headed up there now.'

Cary thought he would be sick to his stomach on the less than one minute drive up the lane to the O'Malley's house. The garda car had barely come to a halt when he was out the door and across the lawn to the front door. He knocked. There was no reply.

'Rosie,' he called, his head feeling like it was about to explode. 'Rosie.'

Finally, he heard a sound, a light came on, and then, as if by a miracle, the door swung open and Rosie was standing there in her nightshirt.

Cary lunged at her and hugged her. 'Oh, my God, Rosie. Yeh're okay.'

Then Del appeared at the door.

'What's wrong?'

'Rosie,' said Del, 'you wanna sit down, love?'

Bridge at Shillelagh

18

HARRY, WE HARDLY KNEW YE

'How am I feelin?' asked Rosie. 'I don't know, Car, I don't honestly know.' They were sitting together on a couch in the O'Malley parlour. Del had departed, reassured that Rosie was in good hands.

'He was a bastard is all I can say. It's hard to grieve for someone as mean as he could be. And I can never ever forgive him for how he treated Ma.' Rosie started to cry. She teetered and leaned against Cary. He held her and stroked her hair. Then she regained her composure.

'But Car, I gotta say, he was there for me, for a time, when I needed my da. He really was.'

'When was that?'

'Oh, a few years back, when I was so sick.' Cary remembered the several years when Rosie missed nearly as much school as she attended. He had no idea back then what it was all about, and he knew no more to this day.

'Well, maybe you can try to put his memory in a good place, then, block out some of the bad?'

Rosie nodded.

'What about Buddy? How's he gonna take it?'

'Well, he's a bloke, yeh know? Stiff upper lip–all that.' She looked up at Cary and smiled. 'He grew up in the old man's image–gotta be tough, always. But inside, it'll be a struggle for him at first. For me, too.'

'And Jimmy, I imagine.'

She nodded and they sat together lost in their thoughts.

Finally, Rosie spoke. 'But Car, I gotta wonder...'

'What, Rosie?'

'If–if maybe it wasn't an accident.'

Cary was stunned. 'Rosie, you don't think...'

She nodded. 'Well, it was just two days ago he heard from the doc that he had inoperable cancer, yeh know? And he didn't have long. And losin' Ma, and then losin' the vote tonight.'

Cary sighed. 'Yeah, I can see that, I suppose.'

Rosie's jaw was now set in anger. 'Yeh know, in a way, it mighta been just like 'im. He was so damned proud and unwilling to give in to anyone, to anything. He probably hated the prospect of us takin' care of him in his last days. It would have been humiliating, with his twisted concept of family, to admit that he needed us. Do you see what I mean? He wanted to be in control, to the very end.'

'And Car? He really wanted me to go with him to that meeting tonight. Even if I didn't drive, I think he thought I would take his side, or maybe make him look better, yeh know? That his daughter was with 'im? I didn't want that, and anyway, I knew he'd be drinkin' right up till he left the house. So I said no.'

'Oh, God, Rosie, I hate to think, if you'd been with 'im…'

By now Rosie was fading. She pulled her feet up onto the couch, leaned against Cary, and fell asleep. Cary sent his mother a text to tell her that Rosie was okay, but he was staying with her for the night.

The next morning, after she had brewed tea for herself and Cary, Rosie made a call.

'Hey, Buddy, it's Rosie. Yeah. Sorry to call so early, but I needed to talk to you before you went to work.'

She could hear little more than muffled groans from her brother.

'Buddy, Pa died last night. Yeah. Car accident. Down on the river road.'

She went on to tell him what she knew, about the meeting, the slippery roads, the sharp turn at the bridge. But she spared her brother her personal thoughts on the possible cause of the 'accident.'

Buddy took a deep breath. 'Well, that's that, eh?'

'Yeah, I guess so.'

'So, whatta we do?'

'Well, how about I talk to the undertaker, Mr Wilson, here in Glenkerry? He'll know what to do, I suppose.'

'And Ma?'

'Yeah,' said Rosie. 'I'll call 'er.'

'So, I guess there should be a funeral Mass?' asked Buddy hesitantly.

'Yep, I suppose there should.'

'We need to talk to Father Desmond, then?' asked Buddy.

'You wanna talk to him, Bud? You know 'im better 'an me.'

'Yeah, I'll give 'im a call on my break this morning, then I'll let yeh know.'

There was a long pause.

'Rose, you still there?'

'Yup, uh-huh.'

'You okay?'

'Yeah, Bud, I'm okay. Say, why don't yeh call round tonight, or tomorrow? I'll make us a meal of some sort. Get caught up, you know? Ask Danielle to come, too, if you like.'

'Sound. See you later, Sis.'

'Yup, catch you round.'

'How'd he take it?' asked Cary as he sat sipping his tea.

She nodded a few times. 'He's okay, yeah, I think so.'

'Good,' replied Cary. 'It's tough, yeh know, for a bloke–losin' his da. Even a nasty old one.'

'He's gonna talk to Father Desmond, see if he can set up a funeral Mass.'

'Well, good, Rose, that's good. You two are workin' together.'

'Yeah, we've always been on good terms. It was just that, when Jimmy was around, Buddy stayed away as much as possible, and then when Jimmy was gone, Buddy still kept away to avoid Da.'

'What about your ma?'

Rosie grimaced. 'Yeah, I know. I gotta call her. Straightaway. Maybe before Gerry leaves for school, yeh know? So he can be there for her.'

Cary felt like he needed to give Rosie some space now, some time to sort things, in her head. Maybe in her heart, too. Alone.

No one else can do that for her, mate.

'Maybe I'll go along then?' he asked. 'See you later?'

She gave him a hug. He hugged her back and she discovered to her surprise that he wasn't too anxious to release her from his grip. He sniffed and she turned his head so their eyes met.

'What?' she asked.

He shook his head.

'For a few minutes last night, after Del told me about your da and the car in the river…'

His breathing was heavy and his voice cracked as he spoke.

'For just a few minutes, I thought I'd lost you, Rosie. And I thought–*I can't handle this–there's no way that I can fucking handle losin' her, not now, not ever.*'

She brushed back his hair.

'Well, yeh're not losin' me, Car. Yeh're not, okay?' She looked into his eyes, then kissed him on the forehead.

He wiped his eyes, embarrassed at his sudden outburst.

'Go,' said Rosie. 'I'll be okay, yeah? And I'll see yeh later.'

Cary stood up and walked to the door.

She added, 'and ta, mate.'

Cary was planning to walk down the hill to the hardware shop later that morning. His mother offered to drive him, explaining that she was meeting a friend at Phinney's, next door to the hardware shop. As he stepped out of the car on High Street, Gloria Hennessy appeared.

'Ciaran, just the man we been looking for. Got a minute?' Without waiting for a reply, she grabbed his arm and pulled him through the entrance to Phinney's. Inside he was greeted with cheers. Several dozen members of Save Glenkerry were gathered and stood as one to welcome him. As they cheered still more well-wishers came through the doorway.

Gloria spoke. 'Ciaran McGurk, you are the man of the hour in Glenkerry.'

Cary smiled, then blushed. 'Huh?' Someone handed him a pint of Guinness.

'We're celebrating, Cary, celebrating the death of the Monster Mall.' A cheer went up.

'Of course, we were all shocked and saddened to learn of the accident on the bridge last night. And we will honour our fellow townsman as we should.'

Gloria then turned to Cary.

'But right now, we are celebrating a great victory for Glenkerry. And we are honouring you, Ciaran McGurk, the man who made that victory possible.' Just then Kevin Leahy came through the door.

'Uh, well, I don't know,' replied Cary. He gazed around the room at all those familiar smiling faces. 'I was just one of the folks who spoke, who worked on this. I couldn't have done it without you, Gloria, and Kevin, and my mother, and Rosie O'Malley, and all you Save Glenkerry people. Heck, I didn't even know about the project until I came to that meeting right here just a few weeks ago.'

'Cary, you are much too modest, young man. You saved Glenkerry, almost single-handedly. You are a model for us all, of what the future of this town can be.'

Maybe it was the Guinness that was responsible, but Gloria started to tear up. 'You and your generation, young man,' she gushed. 'It gives us old folks hope. Because most of us have been around long enough to remember darker times in Ireland when we allowed ourselves to be bullied and cowed by those in authority. We learned a sad lesson, a lesson I hope and pray Ireland never forgets. And you and your generation, you give us hope.'

'Well, thank you, but…'

'And I know I speak for everyone here today, and for everyone in Glenkerry, when I say thank you, Cary McGurk.' Again there were cheers from the still growing crowd.

Kevin Leahy stood, cleared his throat, then spoke.

'One more thing, young man. It's about the *Gazette*. Your special edition was what started the ball rollin' and rallied the opposition to the mall, Cary. It was factual and persuasive–and it showed heart and courage. So I think I too can speak for everyone here today and in this town in asking you–in begging you…'

Kevin paused, looking around the room, then at Cary:

'Bring back the *Gazette*, permanently.'

Cheers rang for nearly a minute and Cary stood speechless. Then he turned and looked at his mother who was beaming and nodding. He raised his hands to quiet the uproar and all eyes were on him. He shook his head.

'Uh, I don't know what to say. I'm flattered, but…'

A hush fell over the crowd as everyone stared at him, anticipating his next words.

'But who would buy the paper, and read it?'

'Everyone!' came a united shout.

He smiled, his eyes directed first at Kevin, then Gloria, and finally to his mother.

'You know what this means, don't you? It means I'll be depending on every one of you to sell ten subscriptions to your friends and neighbours.'

Everyone cheered.

'And when I say subscriptions, I mean *paid* subscriptions.'

Everyone laughed. Then more cheers.

Just then Liam Phinney spoke up. 'A course, you will accept major credit cards, right?'

Everyone roared.

'And one more thing,' added Cary with a twinkle in his eye. 'If I say yes and this thing flops, it's on you, everyone one of you, right?'

Again there were cheers.

'I guess I have no alternative.'

He took a deep breath and smiled.

'Ladies and gentlemen, you win. The *Gazette* is back.'

Mayhem ensued. More pints were poured, and the merriment continued for some time still.

When at last the crowd had dispersed, Cary, Catherine, and Gloria sat in a booth enjoying cups of hot coffee to help offset the earlier libations. Gloria and Catherine were now in a reflective mood.

'Katie, you remember my sister, Diana? She's a couple years my senior.'

Catherine nodded. 'Of course, where is she nowadays?'

'She's in Canada. I went to visit her and her husband in Ottawa a few summers back, the first time I'd seen her in, oh my, twenty years or so.'

Gloria looked at Cary. 'Diana got pregnant, Car, when she was just fifteen. In those days that was an unspeakable sin in Ireland, a blot on the mother, on the child, on the entire family. Diana had to leave Ireland. Can you imagine, fifteen years old and banished from her homeland, from her family? They sent her to Canada to live with an aunt. She had the baby and eventually married a Canadian man.' Gloria's lips trembled as she spoke. 'She's never returned to Ireland.'

'That's so sad,' replied Cary.

'But that kind of thing happened all the time. In those days in Ireland, the only solution to the problem was to pretend it hadn't happened, that there was no mother, no pregnancy, no baby. And no one, not even my parents, thought to resist. It was simply the way things were.' She shook her head. 'So, you see, that's what I meant when I said I hope Ireland never goes back to those days.'

Catherine nodded in agreement. 'And the censorship. My goodness, they wouldn't let us see movies like "Last Tango in Paris," or read books like *Ulysses*–by our country's greatest writer. It would pollute Ireland, they said. Can you imagine?'

'That's why we're so grateful for your generation,' added Gloria. 'And we hope you never have to experience what we did. It's all up to you and your friends now. We're counting on you.'

Cary smiled. 'Well, I hope we don't let you down, Glo. And yes, things are better. But you know, it's not just up to us. We need your generation more than ever these days, to remind us of what it was like. It's true, me and my friends, the only Ireland we've ever known is the new, modern Ireland–at peace with itself, prosperous, independent. We have no memory of the Troubles, of the Magdalenes, of censorship and corruption. But there are still problems, even right here in Glenkerry. There are abusive fathers and husbands. And as much as we hate to admit it, there are still abused children. That's why we need you folks to remind us of what it was like, to keep us from going back.'

At home, Catherine was over the moon–no, even farther–more like out among the stars.

'Oh, Car, this is wonderful, dear, for you, for me, and for this town, I'd say. I'm certain the new *Gazette* will be an instant success.'

They spent some time discussing his plans for 1 Upton Road, all the improvements and repairs that would be needed. And how he could live upstairs once it was ready. Catherine assured him that she would be good for the cost of all that. And Cary promised his mother that he would do as much of the work as possible himself and pay her back in time.

As promised Rosie appeared at the McGurk house late that afternoon. Catherine met her at the front door.

'Rosie, sweetie,' she said, and reached out with both arms and hugged her. 'I'm so sorry, love.'

Rosie nodded. 'Thanks, Mrs M.'

Cary appeared then and the three sat together in the parlour.

'Buddy talked to Father Desmond. The funeral Mass will be tomorrow at ten. Not a big deal, yeh know, no afters or anything. Will you come?'

'Of course, love,' replied Catherine.

Cary nodded. 'Did you reach your ma?'

Rosie bit her lip. 'Yeah, I talked to 'er. She's havin' a hard time with it. Doesn't feel inclined to make the trip.'

'Yeah, I can understand that.'

'And Jimmy?'

'The chaplain went to see him, told him about Da. But I don't think he'll be at the funeral Mass unless some family member makes a plea to the Arbour Hill warden. And honestly, I don't know that any of us even want 'im there. He made his bed, yeh know?'

It was after nine o'clock when Rosie finally took her leave. Both Cary and Catherine had pleaded with her to stay but she declined. 'I gotta get used to bein' in that house alone. I'll be okay.'

Cary and Rosie walked up the hill hand-in-hand.

'Gloria Hennessy spoke to me this afternoon, Car, in the fish shop. She tol' me you were the hero, last night–she said you single-handedly saved Glenkerry.'

Cary shook his head. 'Are you kidding? I was shakin' like a leaf up there. Besides, I had lots of help, including you. I'm no hero, Rose, believe me.'

Rosie hesitated for a moment, distractedly twirling a plait of hair in her fingers.

'She also told me you've decide to stay in Glenkerry, to revive the *Gazette*.' Now she was looking squarely into his eyes. But Cary looked away, avoiding her gaze.

'So, when were you gonna tell *me*?'

Slowly he looked up. He paused awkwardly for a moment, as if unsure of his words.

'I'm sorry, Rosie, I meant to, I really did.' He gulped. 'I–I wasn't sure how you'd react.'

'What do you mean, did you think I wouldn't approve?'

'Well, honestly, I wasn't sure. I thought maybe you'd think I was giving up on my dream, or something.'

'Well, that's just nonsense, Cary. I want what you want. If you're happy, then I'm happy.'

'Really?'

'Of course. But what made you change your mind?'

'Yeh mean about London? Well, for one thing I started to feel guilty about leavin' Ireland. I mean, the Irish have been emigrating for centuries, and many with good reason–famine, poverty, lack of work. But that's all in the past now. Ireland is my home, and it's different now, right? It's prosperous, full of hope, why should I leave? Maybe I feel I have a duty to stay and contribute.'

'Well, Ciaran, that's grand, then, for you and for Ireland. And Siobhan?'

'What about her?'

Rosie shook her head. 'For a smart young lad, Cary, you amaze me, you really do.'

'I'm sure I don't know what you mean, Rosie. Siobhan is just a friend, a mate, and she's got her own dreams. She'll do just fine.'

'You're sure of that?'

'Yes–absolutely–one hundred percent.'

'Well, then I congratulate you on your decision. I'm sure you will succeed. In fact I'm thinkin' a nominatin' you for County Council next term: *Comhairleoir* McGurk.'

Cary laughed. 'Yeah, that'll happen, Rosie–in donkey's years.'

They stood face to face in the O'Malley front yard. 'You are somethin' else, Ciaran McGurk.' And she leaned forward and kissed him. 'Somethin' else.'

Back home Cary took his mobile out to the garden, then sat for several minutes. He dreaded this. He felt like a traitor. He felt so much remorse that he even for a few minutes tried to imagine living in London but still publishing the *Gazette*. Not possible, he concluded. Not unless he was prepared to hire an editor.

Forget it. Man up, mate. Call the girl.

Siobhan's voice was bright and cheery this time. And he quickly twigged that her good humour had to do with his imminent arrival which made him feel even worse than before.

'Oh, Car, I can't wait to see you. And to show you this place.'

No response.

'Car? You there?'

'Yeah, Shiv. I'm here. I...'

'What's wrong, mate? Your mom okay?'

'Yeah, she's fine, Everything's fine. Hey, Shiv? Listen, eh, I've decided to stay in Glenkerry.'

There was a pause. Then, 'What?'

'Yeah, things just started happenin', see. Everyone in town was tellin' me they want me to revive my dad's paper. And my ma is willing to let me fix up the old office and live upstairs. So I said yes, I'll do it.'

'Oh, yeah–sure,' replied Siobhan in a voice filled with bravado that didn't quite ring true.

'It'll be different, yeh know. And it might come to nothin'. But I have a feelin' about it–I just have a feelin' that it might be good.'

'Well, I'm glad for you, Car. I really am.'

'Well, good, I feel better hearin' you say that.'

'Gotta go, mate, yeh know? Things to do.'

'Yeah, sure, okay. Well...'

'Talk soon.' And she rang off.

'Yeah, talk soon,' said Cary to the evening air. He was shaken. He felt like the lowest of the low. But at least Siobhan seemed to understand.

Several hours later Cary was lying in bed, just dropping off to sleep when his mobile ringtone sounded. It was Siobhan.

'Hello,' he said groggily. 'Shiv?'

'Hey. Cary. I, uh…' Her voice was cracking. 'I, uh, I'm…'

'What's the matter, Shiv? Is something wrong?'

There was a long silence. Then he heard her voice, weakly. 'Car, I'm not doin' so well, mate.' And she began to cry.

It was a long call, and for a while Siobhan was barely able to make herself understood, she was so distraught. Cary's alarm grew by the minute as did his guilt in setting off this emotional meltdown in his friend. But eventually she began to settle down. Cary didn't try to defend his decision, just to reassure her that everything would be okay. At length Siobhan was sounding like her old self.

'You have to do it, mate–I understand–it could be great–sure–go for it–yep–you should do it–I'm happy for you–you'll do great things for Glenkerry–yep–for sure–how awful would I feel if you gave up your dream for my sake?'

It was after midnight when the call ended, Cary now somewhat mollified about Siobhan's emotional state. But sleep was not an option. And he went to the kitchen for more 'seafood.' His mother appeared in a robe and slippers.

'Car, everything okay?'

He nodded. 'Oh, yeah,' as he opened a small package of bacon fries.

'I heard you on the phone. Was it Siobhan? Is she okay?'

Cary nodded. 'Yeah, she's fine. Took her by surprise at first, but she's fine. Sorry if I woke you.'

Then he was back in bed, staring at the ceiling, trying to think himself asleep–which never worked, he reminded himself. And then the question forced itself: *Is it possible that Siobhan, through all that 'mate' business, had come to think of you as more than just a mate?*

You better hope not, because, if it's true, then you are well and truly an eejit, a right eejit.

The following morning, Cary placed a call to Siobhan's friend, Ellen, in London. She and Siobhan were mates at DCU until Ellen graduated, a year ago. He asked her if she might give Siobhan a call, maybe invite her for a meal or to go out for an evening.

'I think she's havin' a bit of a rough patch, yeh know?'

Then he called his old uni friend, Brendan Canty, in Dublin. Good to talk to old mates, especially lads, at a time like this. Get some perspective. They made plans for a mini-uni-rugby-reunion.

Later in the day Cary received an email from Siobhan. That was unusual, he thought. He couldn't recall the last time she sent him an email message.

> *Hi Cary, Sorry about the other night. I had a bad week at work and was discouraged. But today my boss called me in, complimented me on my work, and gave me a new assignment all my own. I'm designing a whole new system from scratch for an on-line retailer that's expanding and wants to add a number of features to their user interface. I can't wait to get started. Best wishes to you on your new endeavour. You are awesome. All my love to you and your mom, Always, Siobhan*

Gusty winds drove a heavy rain against the stained-glass windows of St. Brigid's Church as a few family members and friends gathered for Harry O'Malley's funeral Mass. Rosie and Buddy sat up front as several dozen townsfolk, mostly old timers, filed in, knelt, then were seated in the pews. Buddy's girlfriend, Danielle, was seated next to him. When Cary and his mother came down the aisle and took seats right behind the two O'Malleys, Rosie turned and smiled at them. Her gaze drifted to the rear of the sanctuary where she saw two women, one older and grey-haired, the other thirty or so, sitting apart from the other guests. They were not familiar Glenkerry folks, not to Rosie nor to Buddy.

Father Desmond was about to begin the Mass when he looked up to the back of the church. His gaze shifted to Rosie and Buddy, then back to the rear. Rosie turned to see what had caught his eye.

'Ma,' she said. And she stood, walked back up the aisle, hugged her mother and Gerry, then escorted them to the front. Mary then kissed Buddy and introduced him to Gerry.

Before Rosie sat down, her eyes met Cary's. She smiled, and he nodded back.

When the Mass was over, the family members stood in the entryway at the rear of the church speaking with friends. Mary approached the two unfamiliar women as if she knew them. They talked for several minutes, then went along without speaking with Rosie or her brother.

Cary shook Gerry's hand. 'Wonderful you could come.' Then he spoke to Rosie's mother. 'Mrs O'Malley, nice ta see yeh again.'

She acknowledged his words with a nod. 'I was reluctant at first, Ciaran. But in the end I realised I should be here. Not for me, yeh know, but for them.' She gestured toward her daughter and son.

After the guests had departed, Rosie thanked Father Desmond.

Then she spoke to her mother.

'Ma, will you folks come up the house for tea?'

Mary sighed. 'Ta, lass, but I think we'll go along. Too many memories in that place that I'm tryin' to put behind me, yeah?'

'I understand, Ma, yep.'

'But love, your pa was not entirely a bad man, was he? He was there for us when we needed 'im.'

'Yes, Ma, he was.'

Then she turned to her son. 'Buddy, I want to hear more about your work. You got my mobile number now, right?'

He nodded.

'And Danielle, I am very glad to meet you.'

'The two of you are welcome to come to Galway for a visit sometime,' added Gerry.

At last the rain had let up and they walked down the weathered granite steps to the street. Buddy and Rosie said their goodbyes to Mary and Gerry, then stood side-by-side watching their car pull slowly away.

Catherine and Cary then stepped up beside Rosie. 'We want you, Buddy, and Danielle to come up to our place and have tea, yeh hear? Maybe a few biskies?'

They nodded. Rosie hugged Catherine. Then she turned and hugged Cary. 'Thanks again, mate.'

That evening Rosie received a call from her mother. 'I'm sorry we didn't have a chance to talk today, just the two of us.'

Rosie agreed.

'So, how ya doin', love?' asked Mary.

'I'm okay, Ma. It's still, yeh know, an adjustment. Maybe it hasn't hit me yet. He was my da, a course, but I can't say I'll miss 'im a whole lot. I suppose I'm a terrible daughter for thinkin' that.'

'Now, don't punish yerself, Rose. I feel the same, believe me. He was mean and spiteful. But he was the father of my children and in that way he was important to me. But, well, life goes on, eh?'

'Yeah, Ma, that's right.' Rosie sensed something in her mother's tone that surprised her. 'And yer happy now, with Gerry, right so?'

'Oh, yes, dear, very happy. He's a wonderful man–always was. But Rosie, I'm concerned fer you. You all alone there in that house, in Glenkerry. Have yeh thought about what yeh might do now, dear?'

Rosie sighed. 'I'll stay put fer now. I like it here, this house, this town. I suppose it's all I've ever known, but still, I like it.'

'And that lad? How about 'im?'

'Cary?'

'Yes, dear, Cary. He's been awful good to yeh. He cares fer yeh, don't he?'

Rosie didn't answer for a long time. 'We've been friends– forever. I'm not sure he wants to change that, yeh know?'

'Love, listen to me, okay? If you care for 'im, I mean, more than as a friend, you have to tell 'im.'

Rosie sighed.

'Listen to yer ma, dear. Tell 'im how yeh feel. Let him decide how he feels about it. You don't want to live the rest o' your life in regrets, eh?'

'Yeah, Ma, I hear yeh.'

'And sweetie, there's a few other things–things about yer da– things yeh should know.'

The next day Rosie called Cary on his mobile, asking if she could stop by 1 Upton Road to see him for a few minutes. He agreed and soon she appeared. He was indisposed, his legs and butt all that were visible as he suspended himself down into the crawl space under the ground floor where the mains were housed.

She tapped his buttock with her foot.

'Havin' fun down there, mate?'

With some effort he extracted his upper body from the pit, brushed cobwebs from his hair and face, and looked up at Rosie. 'Sorry—got myself in an indelicate position, eh?'

'Just showin' off your hind quarters, I reckon.' She laughed, then reached up and pulled some dust balls from his hair.

'So what's up?'

'Ma called last evening. We talked for a long time. I guess she felt bad about not stayin' longer after the Mass for my da.'

'Well, I'm guessin' she was torn, right?'

'Yeah. And she apologised, though I told her that wasn't necessary. Then she got very chatty and she told me some things I never knew.' Rosie hesitated for a moment, then continued. 'I was gobsmacked. They blew my mind, Car, the things she told me.'

Now his curiosity was piqued. Rosie didn't seem upset. She seemed more amazed than bothered and anxious to share her amazement with him.

'For one thing, she admitted that she had her doubts about Pa from the beginning. She was worried about his bad habits even then. Which is why she had those bank accounts that she never told him about all those years. Almost like she was expecting to leave him eventually. And she kept her maiden name. I knew they never married, Car, but I never heard the whole story.'

'That's a shocker, Rosie. And it's amazing she could keep that secret all those years, especially in the Glenkerry fishbowl.'

'I know, I was shocked. But Cary, you better sit down for this one. My da, it turns out, could not have married my ma even if she had agreed. Because he was already married. And was till the day he died, apparently.'

'Get out. That is outrageous, Rosie.'

She nodded and smiled. 'Her name is Sarah, she's from Wexford, and they were married in 1990. She 'n Pa lived down in Wexford for a couple a years, then they split up. And that's when he moved to Glenkerry. And no one knew but Ma. And of course, gettin' a divorce was no simple matter in Ireland in those days. So he and Ma couldn't a been married, even if they'd both wanted to.'

Cary shook his head. 'And is Sarah still alive?'

'She was at the funeral, Car. That woman in black near the back?'

Cary sighed. 'Ahhh. So that's who she was.'

'And Car? There's more.'

His eyes nearly popped out of his head as he anticipated where this was leading. 'Yeh're kidding me, Rosie, yeh've gotta be fecking kidding me. That young woman with her?'

She nodded. 'So you see why my mind is blowing? Yeah, I have a sister. And get this, Car. Her name is Rose–Rosemary, actually–how weird is that?'

That evening Rosie, Buddy, and Danielle sat at the kitchen table eating a stew Rosie had prepared. They talked about the startling new revelations about their father's past, then about the future.

'What now for you, Bud? Any thoughts of goin' back to school?'

He shook his head. 'Nah, I like mechanicking, I really do. I'm only like a lowly apprentice now, but my boss thinks I'm ready to advance. So we'll see.'

'You could move back 'ere, if you wanted, both of you. I know you hated bein' 'ere with Da, but now, well, we get along, right?'

Buddy nodded. 'Thanks, Rose. We'll think on it. Danielle has a decent place in Greystones, so I stay over hers a few nights a week.'

Rosie turned to Danielle. 'Don't take any crap from this one, understand?'

Danielle smiled, shaking her head.

'Are you kiddin' me?' said Buddy. 'She's a real scrapper, this one. If we fought, she'd win, every time. Hey, Rose, how 'bout we take a road trip up to Galway sometime? Spend a little time with Ma and that guy, Gerry? He seems pretty chill.'

'I'd like that, Buddy, and I know Ma would, too.'

There was a long pause. Rosie could tell there was something else on her brother's mind.

Finally, Buddy spoke. 'But Jimmy? I'm done with 'im. Once and for all. Done. For what he did in Galway, for how he treated you, and everything.'

Rosie nodded. 'He's pretty hard to like, I admit. But Buddy?'

He looked up from his stew, his eyes fluid and soft.

'Let's not say never, okay? He might need us one day, and he might change. You never know. Miracles do happen, yeah?'

They finished their meal in silence, thinking about the ties that bind and sometimes divide.

The Black Castle, Wicklow

19

ONE UPTON ROAD

Cary rose early the next morning. He was determined to fix his mother a special breakfast for her birthday. She loved a traditional Irish breakfast, this he knew—rashers, sausage, eggs, tomatoes, baked beans, the whole deal.

And yet I, her own flesh and blood, get bilious at the very thought of fatty meats for breakfast. What's up with that?

Catherine was delighted when she stepped into the kitchen and saw that luscious platter waiting for her along with a birthday card and gift from Cary plus several more cards that had arrived by post, including one from Aiden.

'Oh, love, you didn't have to do all this. My goodness, look at all that food. Now my doctor tells me I should cut back on saturated fats. Oh, well, that can wait till tomorrow, so?'

They both laughed and Cary gave his mother a hug.

'Happy birthday, Ma.'

He could see tears welling up in her eyes, no doubt wishing her Paddy could be there. But she smiled bravely, sat down, and began to tuck in. Then she looked across the table. Her son had just one small bowl in front of him.

'Where's your platter, Car?'

'Oh, I'm just havin' porridge, Ma.'

'What, are you not feeling well, dear?'

'I'm fine, Ma. Go ahead, eat.'

A few minutes later the conversation had drifted to the *Gazette*.

'I meant to tell yeh, Ma, I'm goin' to Wicklow tomorrow to talk with Mr Hadley, the printer. I need to be sure I know what my printing costs are gonna be. And talk about stock–paper, I mean. And be sure about his formatting requirements.'

'It sounds so complicated, Car. I'm glad you understand it all. You know, when I was a girl, my cousin Thomas worked for the newspaper in Cork. He took me into the pressroom one day and, my land, I will never forget it. That machine filled the whole room– it must have been thirty or forty feet long. For every issue they made up these heavy metal plates and attached them to drums on the press. And when that machine started to run, goodness what a racket it made, like a freight train.'

'Do you suppose that press is still running?'

'Oh, no. Thomas told me they sold it for scrap decades ago.'

'Someday you should come with me to Wicklow and see Mr Hadley's shop. It's very quiet. The *Gazette* will run on a digital printer not much bigger than this table. Can you believe it?'

'That is amazing, Car, isn't it? Now, in the old days there'd be a queue a boys outside that pressroom waiting to take away their papers for delivery. How will your paper be distributed, have you thought about that?'

'Yeah, well, I'm already taking subscriptions by mail and online. And I've personally talked to quite a few businesses on the High Street that will take a stack of papers each week to sell. I'm hopin' to find a couple of local kids to do most of the delivery, maybe on bicycles.'

'Oh, just like the old days, Car,' she replied.

'But I'm expecting we'll have lots more digital subscribers than print. You know? So the *Gazette* will pop up on your tablet or mobile automatically every week.'

'Now that is just too much for me to comprehend, Car.'

Cary smiled. 'It is pretty amazing. In a way I'm walking in dad's shoes, carrying on his work. But in other ways it seems like a totally different world. It's kind of scary, actually.'

Catherine looked at her son. 'What, Cary, are you having doubts?'

'Of course I have doubts, Ma. I'm all about doubts. But I'm plunging ahead–I have to–I promised Rosie–and Del…'

'And half of Glenkerry,' added Catherine. They laughed together. Then Cary was reminded of one of his concerns since deciding to revive the *Gazette*.

'Ma, did dad enjoy writing editorials?'

'What do you mean, Car?'

'I mean, he was kind of soft-spoken, yeah? So was it hard for him to, yeh know, take a stand on difficult issues?'

'Well, your da saw himself mostly as a reporter. He tried to keep his personal feelings at bay most a the time. Maybe to a fault, but that was the way he was. Once in a while he'd speak out in his editorials. He chose his topics very carefully, though.'

'Like what?'

'Well, after 9-11. You were too young to remember, thank God.

But all of Ireland was shocked by the events of that terrible day. To the core. And your da wrote a fine piece on it. About how every Irishman should show solidarity with America at such a time. Especially considering all America has done for this country, you know, going way back to the Revolution a century ago. And the Good Friday Agreement in 1998 that put an end to the Troubles. So how could we fail to stand by our American cousins now when they were under attack? He wrote with a lot of feeling, he did, and folks were ringin' his phone off the wall thanking him and congratulating him. I've got a copy somewhere. Oh, but you can find it on the internet, I'm sure.'

'Yeah, I wanna read it.'

'And then, just a few months later, he wrote another editorial, this one against sending Irish soldiers to Afghanistan to fight with the Americans. Now there were opinions on both sides on that hereabouts as I recall. But your da was opposed to the idea. And to the American invasion of Afghanistan in the first place. He said it would end badly, that there was no winning in a place like that.'

'Yeah, well, he was right there, Ma, wasn't he?'

'You might do well to take a lesson from your old man, Car. When the time comes, don't hesitate to speak your piece, but choose your battles carefully.'

Cary nodded.

'I miss him, Ma. I wish I could just walk into the study, sit down in that chair next to his desk, and talk to him about these things. And I can't believe now that I never did it while I could.'

Tears were sliding down his cheeks.

'Car, love. It's the oldest story in the world, regrets. That's why we have to do what we can when we can. That's why I bother you so...'

They both chuckled. 'Keep botherin' me, Ma. I'll complain, but I'll still listen, I promise.'

'Okay, Car. And I'll try to listen to yeh, too.'

After breakfast Cary prepared to leave. 'I'll be paintin' today, Ma, pretty much all day.'

'Better wear a mask, Car. And take your inhaler, just in case.'

'Yeah, Ma.'

And now we see the editor of the new Glenkerry Gazette reduced to a ten-year-old!

At midday Del appeared. He had apologised, in a way, for his perhaps over-the-top skewering of Cary the week before at Phinney's, although Cary was still harbouring a bit of resentment for that. But he needed Del's expertise and had asked him to call round for a 'lunchtime consult,' as Cary termed it. As he stepped through the doorway to 1 Upton Road, Del found Cary sitting at his desk staring intently into his laptop.

'Wow, this place is really comin' round, lad. Look at all yeh've done, eh?' said Del.

Cary smiled. 'Yeah, well, the *Glenkerry Gazette* is now officially open for business. Can't you tell by all the hustle and bustle in here? Just like a newsroom of the old days. Would you believe, I actually got a phone call a few minutes ago—my first at the new *Gazette* number?'

'You are gettin' stuck into it now, Car, for sure. And upstairs?'

'Yeah, well, I spend my first night there tonight. And don't start goin' on about my love life, Del. It's just me, solo—for the foreseeable future.'

Del huffed, shaking his head. 'What are we gonna do with you, boy?'

They sat at a picnic table behind the shop in the warm sun, spreading their lunches on paper towels before them. Del had a pile of chips from the Fishmonger that he offered to share with Cary.

'So, talk to me, Del. About those ideas of yours for the digital edition of the *Gazette*. How'll that work?'

'Yeah, well, I did a bit of surfing and there are some pretty good apps available for setting up a page, like a Facebook page, for your paper. I'll send you links.'

'And letting readers give feedback?'

'Oh, yeah, that's all built in. You can have a little dialogue box after each article where readers can respond. Or one place in each edition where you invite feedback.' Cary winced.

'You mean, anyone will be able to say anything in my paper?'

'Not exactly, lad. Relax. You'll be the moderator, see? Everything will come to you. You decide what goes out to your readers, right? You–or your people.'

'What people?' said Cary, laughing and shaking his head.

Del laughed. 'Well, that could be a problem at the start.' Then Del's expression turned serious. 'Fair warning, my friend. When you invite comments, public input, you have to be very careful.'

Their eyes met and locked. 'Even in a little town like this, there's stuff out there, nasty stuff, hateful, downright offensive stuff. Especially against people of colour, people of the Islamic faith, Hindus, you name it. It's all out there. You have to be the voice of reason, lad, and of compassion. It's all on you, bro.'

'We deal with this stuff a lot, the gardaí. There's a Syrian family livin' out at Dunbraugh. Nice folk, quiet, law-abidin'. You wouldn't believe the crap they've been gettin' from a few neighbours. Even their kids in school have been targeted. And these two Welshmen who own a farm on the Rathdrum road? They're married. And you wouldn't believe the things they've heard said—to them or behind their backs. It's only a few, but still it makes me ashamed, sometimes, yeh know, of some of our countrymen and women.'

They sat in silence for a moment. Then Del broke the contemplative spell.

'Hey, I gotta get goin'. But I'll send you those links. See what you think. Pick a couple and I'll be glad to sit down with you and look 'em over.'

A few minutes later Cary received a text message from Rosie. She was sending him a folder that she said contained a web page design she'd been working on, but she wanted him to see it on his desktop computer. He sat down at the terminal, clicked a few keys, and looked in amazement at a mock-up of the *Glenkerry Gazette*, online edition. It was beautiful, with Rosie's exquisite masthead of pastures and sheep above, the title of the paper in elegant calligraphy in front of the design. She had taken several of the stories from his special edition and reformatted them with a classic serif font. She had inserted some images as well, wrapping the text artfully around the photos. And there were unobtrusive dropdown menus to allow a reader to move from one section to another.

What impressed Cary most was the simplicity of the design—not too dense, not a lot of distractions or crazy animations that he found so off-putting in much web design. It would appeal to his digital subscribers, no question about that, but it might even find devotees amongst the older citizens who were not so web-comfortable.

Within minutes he texted Rosie.

'You are hired, Miss O'Malley. Can you start today?'

'Uh, how 'bout tomorrow?' she replied.

'Whatta yeh say we talk about it over dinner?'

Bray

20

GLENKERRY CONFIDENTIAL

A light drizzle was falling the next evening as Rosie walked down the lane to the centre of Glenkerry. She stepped up to the front door of 1 Upton Road and knocked. The tread of heavy feet could be heard on the stairs, then Cary opened the door and smiled.

'All right, then, Miss O'Malley. Come on through. You look nice,' he said, admiring her green knit skirt and matching sleeveless top.

'I was gonna wear dungarees but decided against it. Here.' She handed him a small rosemary plant in a ceramic pot. It was covered with blossoms. 'Thought this might cover up the mildew odour a bit.'

Cary nodded. 'Oh, that's pretty. Yeah, this place needs some decoration–and deodorizin'.' They laughed together. 'So, let me show you around the newly refurbished offices of *The Glenkerry*

Gazette.'

Beaming with pride, he walked her through the four small rooms on the ground floor. First he showed off a ragtag collection of office furniture, desks, tables, chairs, in assorted colours, styles, and conditions.

'I got 'em for a song at a used furniture store in Dublin,' he explained.

He showed her an old Underwood manual typewriter and they both laughed.

'It was my da's. I decided to keep it mostly for its sentimental value. The National Museum will be wantin' it one day, no doubt.' Again they laughed together. 'We'll be working on laptops, a course. And then, when we get our full-featured desktop publishing system in place, that will do it all for us. But that's a bit more than we can spring for right now.'

He showed her a rank of grey metal cabinets where stories could be filed. Except, of course, most of the 'files' would be digital and reside in that high-end computer system he was anticipating. Rosie slid open one drawer. It contained a 1980s vintage coffee maker, a crumpled-up rugby shirt, and an empty whiskey bottle. They both chuckled.

'Wow, Car, this place is really something. It's all so clean. Fresh paint everywhere. You been busy, mate, eh?'

'Yeah, I have been. And for now it'll be just me, bangin' away at the keyboard. But in time I'll hope to have a few employees, mostly stringers–reporting local news from the surrounding villages. And of course my crack photographer, artist, and now web designer. This can be your desk.' Rosie smiled.

Then he led her up the narrow stairway to the first floor, that tiny flat that was now his home. Rosie pivoted in the diminutive kitchen.

'Dishes, a tea pot, a fry pan, a microwave–and a can opener. Wow, I guess you'll be dinin' in style, eh? Battered hot dogs and the like? And look at that, a French cafetière. What, no instant coffee here?'

Then he showed her his bedroom.

'Pretty plain, Car. Needs a little something, like curtains, don't yeh think?'

'What, you think I should be worried that the neighbours'll be peering in on me?'

'Yeah, for sure they'll be lookin' to see who that lad is entertaining of an evening.'

Cary laughed.

'And look at your en suite. Isn't that a cute little loo?' Then she added, 'So long as you don't need to turn around, eh?'

'Yeah, I may have to back into it.'

Rosie looked squarely into his eyes. 'Congrats, Car, you done it.'

Cary shook his head and chuckled. 'What I've done is spend a shite-load of lolly on this place–mostly my ma's, by the way. And what I haven't done yet is sell a single paper.'

'Well, baby steps, eh?'

They climbed back down the stairs. 'Well, shall we?' asked Cary. He opened the front door and they stepped out onto the street. The rain was falling a little harder now and Cary took along an umbrella.

A few minutes later they were seated at a table Cary had reserved in a cosy corner of The Grenadine, the newest and by all reports the poshest restaurant in Glenkerry, though, as he conceded, that wasn't saying much. Almost immediately the waiter brought them a bottle of champagne on ice and two flutes.

'Oooh, champers, eh?' said Rosie. 'Classy. Do you do this for all the girls you take out?'

He shook his head. 'Only the very special ones, to be sure.'

When their glasses were full, Rosie raised hers. 'To Cary and his dream,' she said. And they clinked their glasses and sipped. 'Your da would be so proud a yeh, Car.'

Then Cary raised his glass. 'To Rose of Glenkerry,' he said. She blushed, then took another sip.

'Yeh know, you don't give yourself enough credit, Car.'

He nodded and sighed. 'Sometimes I feel like I can't do anything right. But then sometimes I surprise myself.'

Soon they were tucking into a several courses meal including leek and potato soup, mussels and linguini, champ, and a side dish of fresh greens. Cary was surprised at how much Rosie ate and with what gusto.

'I love mussels, Car,' she noted with a giggle. 'The marine kind, that is.'

Cary laughed. 'Oh, that kind. For a minute there I thought you were hintin' that I better start workin' out some more.'

He laughed, then looked into her eyes warmly, admiringly. He seemed to be about to say something, but the words just wouldn't come.

'What?' asked Rosie.

'You are amazing, yeh know? How yeh've coped with all the trauma in your family and kept a level head through it all.'

'A level head? Yeh've gotta be kiddin' me. How many times did I lose it? But fortunately there was always one strong shoulder to cry on.' Her face flushed. 'Ta, mate, for everything.'

The meal was capped with a mocha soufflé. It was, both

agreed, 'to die for.'

'When did you learn about web design, Rosie? I mean, not that I'm any expert, but what you sent me today was impressive.'

'Thanks, Car. That's been one of my hobbies since I left school. I took an on-line course. And I do a lot of surfin' about, lookin' at websites good and bad, tryin' to figure out what I like and what I don't like, how it looks and how it feels, yeh know? And truth be told, I been workin' on that *Gazette* idea for a few weeks now, even before you told me you were stayin'.'

Cary shook his head. 'Rosie O'Malley, you never stop surprisin' me, yeh know?' Those words of his seemed to transfix her, to draw her eyes to his and hold them.

Neither wanted the evening to end. But end it must and they stepped out onto the High Street and walked along hand-in-hand in the darkness as a light rain fell. At 1 Upton Road Cary started to open the door. But Rosie hesitated.

'Well, Car, this has been lovely.'

'What, you think I'm gonna let you walk home alone in the dark? And the rain?'

'Don't worry about me, Car. I'll be fine. I'll take your brolly.' And she wrested it from his hand.

Then he took her free hand and held it in both of his. He leaned in to her and kissed her, a soft, gentle, lingering kiss. When their lips finally parted, they stood inches apart, each breathing lightly.

Steady on mate, stay cool.

'Yeh know, Rose, you could stay 'ere–if you wanted–for the night.'

She smiled, then blushed a little bit. 'You mean, with you?'

Cary nodded. 'Yeah, with me.'

Don't overstep, mate.

'Well, what I mean is, I could sleep on the couch in the sitting room and you could have the bedroom to yourself.'

She hesitated for what was only a few seconds but seemed to Cary an eternity.

You blew it, mate.

Finally, she looked into his eyes. 'Gee, Car, I was almost gonna say yes–until you got round to the sleeping arrangements.'

He could feel his body temperature rising. 'Well, how about you sleep wherever you want–lady's choice.'

'Fair play, lad, fair play to you.'

They made their way up the narrow staircase and stood in the sitting room embracing, then kissing again. Rosie took his hand in hers and led him into the bedroom.

Cary took off his slacks and collared shirt, then pulled on a pair of pyjama bottoms while Rosie was in the loo. He was lying on the bed when she emerged. She was still wearing her blouse but had donned an extra pair of pyjama bottoms he had set out for her. They were of course sizes too big for her and she pulled them up high above her waist and cinched them there, then strutted in front of the window like a model on a catwalk.

'Now the neighbours are gonna think I got some dude stayin' over, Rose.'

She chuckled. 'Yeah, some dude dressed like a carnival clown.'

Then she peered into his closet and removed one of his shirts. With her back to him, she took off her blouse and bra, then pulled on the shirt. She could almost wrap it twice around her thin frame.

Cary was watching her. 'I guess I shoulda thought this through better, eh? Maybe suggested you bring a nightgown or something?'

Rosie shook her head. 'That wouldn't do, now, would it?' she began with an ironic smile. 'It would send the wrong message, yeh know? Like you were planning to seduce me. Some girls might be offended, yeah?'

She let the shirt hang with the front unbuttoned, then lay down next to Cary, rolled over and snuggled up to him. He wrapped his arms around her.

'Wow, it took us a lotta years to get here, eh, mate?' she said.

His arms encircled her. 'Yeah, I guess. But it's been worth the wait, ain't it?'

'Yes, it has,' she replied.

'A fella could get used to this real easy, yeh know.'

She touched a finger to his lips. 'Let's take it one day at a time, right?'

He slid his hands down her back to her waist.

'But Car,' she whispered into his ear.

'Yeah?'

'I think–I think we oughta talk first.'

Danger, danger, steady on, mate.

'I–what I mean is we gotta take it easy. Yeh see, I'm a little, well, yeh know, inexperienced.'

Cary understood what she was saying. He was a bit surprised– she was twenty, after all–but he understood. 'No worries.' He touched the tip of his nose to hers. 'And for your information, I am probably the closest thing to a virgin that ever graduated from DCU.'

This intrigued Rosie and she wanted to ask him just what he meant by 'the closest thing to a virgin.' But just as she was about to ask, she got distracted and everything got blurry.

Now his hands slid still farther down, stroking her buttocks.

'I'm sorry, Car, but there's one thing more.'

Bright sunlight was streaming into the bedroom the next morning when Rosie awoke. Her head was aching a bit, probably from the champers, she thought.

Cary had been up a while and she could smell coffee brewing. She pulled on the shirt and pyjama bottoms that lay on the floor, then stepped barefoot into the kitchen. Cary was standing over the tiny stove, spatula in hand.

'Good morning, sunshine,' he said with a smile.

Rosie nestled up next to him, wrapped both arms around him, and kissed his neck.

'Sleep well?' he asked.

'M-hmm,' she replied. 'Nothin' like champers and a warm bed mate, yeh know? How're you doing?' she asked, stroking his cheek with one finger. 'Good night?'

'The best.'

She leaned back so that she could look into both eyes. 'You okay, with–*everything*?'

'Couldn't be better,' he said breezily. But then he set the spatula down, turned and wrapped his arms around her. He kissed her long and firmly, as if to emphasise the point, then repeated it: 'With *everything*.'

For last night, at long last, the full mystery of Rose of Glenkerry had been revealed.

'But why didn't you tell me before? Did you think it would matter?' asked Cary, holding her close to him, his lips on her ear.

'Of course I did. How could I not think that? How could anyone? And anyway, it's not something you just blurt out to someone, even a good friend, do you? Not unless that someone needs to know.'

He handed her a cup of tea, then poured himself some coffee. They sat at his small kitchen table.

'So, when did this all start?' he asked.

'You really want to know?'

He nodded. 'A course.'

She sat at the kitchen table and Cary sat opposite her, watching her intently.

'Well, I think when I was eight or nine, maybe. I started havin' these cramps and painful bowel movements.' She paused and chuckled. 'Are you *sure* you want to know?'

'Yes, Rosie. I want to know. And I ought to know, especially, you know, if we're together–which I totally hope we are.'

'Well, Ma and Pa took me to the doc–the quack as my da called 'im. He said it was probably just anxiety. "Nervous colitis," he called it. And it's true, I was anxious. But it wasn't nerves that caused the problem, it was mostly the other way around, I really believe that.'

Again Cary was remembering Rosie from primary school. She had always been shy and standoffish, he recalled, and she had missed a lot of school, for reasons he had never understood.

'Then when I was ten or eleven, it flared up really bad. Scours almost every day, and pain, and bleeding.' Again she paused. 'You want me to stop now?'

He shook his head and smiled. 'Don't worry 'bout me, Rose. I'm not gonna run away. This is my place, remember?'

She laughed. 'Finally, my da agreed to take me to a specialist in Wicklow Town. That guy did some tests and faffed about for the longest time over what it was and what to do. Then he sent us up to Dublin, to a clinic that specialised in these things. Well, you might as well a asked my da to walk through the gates of hell, that's how much he hated the idea of more doctors, more tests, more blather.'

'Did the clinic figure it out finally?'

'Well, the doc there was really nice. I was afraid and Ma was too that those high-falootin' specialists 'd be cold as fish. But he was just the opposite, Car. And after weeks of tests he got very serious one day, he said he thought I might have Crohn's disease. Do you know anything about that?'

Cary shook his head.

'Well, it's what they call an autoimmune disorder. It's where your immune system sort of attacks your intestines, rejects them I guess you could say. And the lining of your whole digestive tract becomes inflamed and ulcerated.'

'It sounds awful.'

'Well, it is, or so I've heard. Fortunately we didn't even have a computer in the house, so I didn't try to find out about it. If I had, it would've scared the hell out of me–even more. Thankfully, as it turned out, I didn't have Crohn's. I had what they call ulcerative colitis.'

'I was feeling really awful by this time. I was out a school for months and I was home feeling miserable. The only thing that made me feel better was not eating. Which I tried more than once. But after a day or two I'd feel so ghastly that I'd have ta start eating again. So it was either eat and feel like crap–or don't eat and feel like crap.'

She reached across the table and held his hands in hers.

'I remember back then you sent me get well cards you'd made. I don't suppose you had any idea what was goin' on, we kept it pretty much in the family. But those cards were so sweet. They really helped me, yeh know? Kept my spirits up.'

She sighed.

'Finally, in February or March, after months of bein' sick in bed at home, they admitted me to Mercy Hospital in Dublin. I was there for almost a month. I was bleeding so much they had to give me transfusions, again and again. And a few times my blood pressure got dangerously low.'

Tears were welling in Cary's eyes as he watched and listened to Rosie's harrowing tale that she delivered so clinically, so matter-of-factly.

'I'm sorry to put you through this, Rose. You don't hafta.'

She shook her head. 'I'm okay. Anyway, I nearly died a couple times in there. One day when I had enough strength, I asked that nice doc if there wasn't a fix, a solution. I asked him when my parents weren't around–I didn't want them to know what I was thinkin', that I was gonna die. That's when he told me about the surgery.'

'I had no idea they could do that, yeh know what I mean, Car? Take out your intestines? How was that even possible? He explained it all very carefully–in words I could understand. He made it sound like it wasn't too big a deal. It's called an ostomy. They remove the diseased parts, stitch up your butt, and make a hole, a stoma, in your belly. And that's where the pouch goes.'

Last night she had showed him. She had lowered her pyjama bottoms, then her knickers just enough to reveal a flat plastic pouch, maybe four inches across, pale brown against her white skin. She had joked about it. 'See, I'm a kangaroo, with a pouch.'

Cary was stunned, not so much at the revelation as at Rosie's frankness and good humour about it.

'Ma and Pa freaked out when I told them, but I had already made up my mind. If it was this or die, I was okay with this.

Remember, I'd just turned twelve. All I wanted was to feel better and be out playin' and goin' to school with the rest of the kids. I didn't think of the future. Heck, at that age, who does?'

'But it wasn't till my periods started and my ma told me a little about all that that it finally dawned on me.'

Now Rosie's air of detachment began to crumble and tears trickled down her cheeks. 'Cause I started wonderin', what boy…' Her face, that sweet, innocent face, contorted. 'What boy would ever want me, the way I am–ya know?'

Cary stood up, walked around behind her as she sat in her chair, and wrapped his arms around her.

'Well, this boy wants you, Rosie,' he said as their eyes met. 'And he wants you more than he's ever wanted anything in the world.'

'Pouch and all?'

'Pouch and all.'

'Thanks, Car. You have no idea how much that means.' She turned and looked out the window, her chin quivering. 'Jimmy, he used to tease me about it, call me names. And not in like a playful way, but hurtful. Like I was some kind of I don't know what, a…' She paused. Her breathing became laboured.

'What, Rosie, what did he call you?'

'A freak of nature,' she replied, the words bursting forth with a torrent of tears. 'Just the other day, at the hospital, he said it again.'

Now she cried and cried hard. Cary held her, stroked her back, and tried his best to comfort her.

'He's gone, Rosie. For a long, long time. And you are nothing like that–you are the loveliest lass I've ever known, outside and in. And I'm sorry it took so many years for me to say it, okay?'

Rosie calmed down, then looked up at him and smiled.

'Thanks, love.'

'And remember when I said last night how impressed I was with the way you'd handled all the family business you been through?' Rosie nodded. 'Now, my God, Rosie, you seem like some kind of Wonder Woman to me.'

She laughed through her tears. 'I'm no Wonder Woman, Car. I'm just, as you say, Rose of Glenkerry. And I got the most wonderful lad in the world tellin' me he cares for me–imagine that.'

'So, do you still have problems, I mean, with–digestion or whatever?'

She shook her head. 'Not much really. I have to watch my diet, change things regularly, yeh know, and always have supplies on hand. And once in a while I have pains, and very, very rarely I get a temporary blockage in my small intestine. When I do, I have to go to hospital. One time a couple years ago Ma bundled me in the car and drove me to Wicklow when I was having some especially painful abdominal cramps and we thought it might be a blockage. The road along the river was very bumpy and she was drivin' too fast, I suppose. And suddenly I said, "Stop, Ma, turn around. We can go home now." The blockage had cleared–thanks to those bumpy roads.'

They both laughed.

'Except for those things, you can carry on pretty much as normal then?'

'Yeah, couple years ago I took scuba lessons in Wicklow. When I told my doc about that he was so impressed he said he wanted me to talk to other young ostomy patients, that my story would inspire them, maybe encourage some kids who were reluctant to have the surgery. So I went to a couple of group sessions at that clinic. It was such a good feeling, Car, bein' able to help those kids face this.'

'Wow, that is so great, Rosie. Yeh're a model.'

'But the one thing that I always feared was, yeh know, sex. And I bet that's on the mind of every one of those kids, at least once they're of an age to think about such things.'

'That's why, back then, I sorta held back. Do you remember? I knew I could never trust any of the boys in secondary school to keep it a secret. All I could think of was how it would feel if I slept with a boy, he told his friends, and pretty soon everyone knew. Not that it's shameful, but it's personal, and I could imagine kids lookin' at me, makin' crude jokes, yeh know?'

'I would never…'

'I know, I never thought you would. But I was still nervous about how you would react. Even last night, when you said how I never stopped surprisin' you, all I could think of was what this might do to us. For a while there it felt like we, like you and me, were heading for a cliff.'

'And now?'

'No fears, thanks to you, mate. No fears.'

'Rosie, you oughta write a book.'

There had always been a special bond between them, thought Cary. But now, now it felt different, like their souls were bound together forever.

You and Rosie, yeh've crossed the Rubicon together. Congratulations. But about that Rubicon thing, remember. Once you're on the other side, mate, there's no goin' back.

21

GLENKERRY FOREVER

After breakfast Cary and Rosie stepped out of the front door of 1 Upton Road. Just then Cary's mother drove by and waved at them both. She now knew the truth about her son and Rosie.

'Oh, well, the old Glenkerry fishbowl, right?' said Rosie.

They started walking up the lane. 'She's known for a while—about us, I mean,' began Cary. 'She was smitten with Siobhan, of course, and hellbent on marryin' us off, even though I said a thousand times Shiv and I were just mates. And then when we decided on the London move, Ma was convinced that we were getting serious. I had to start all over with the "We're just mates, Ma, and we're just gonna be flatmates in London is all." She wasn't buyin' it, I suppose. Until you and I got—well, involved.'

'Are you sayin' you never saw you and Siobhan as anything more than friends? Not even *flatmates with benefits*?' she asked, crooking her fingers to form air quotes. They both laughed.

'Well, Rosie, every fella has his dreams, yeh know, his fantasies.'

'And this fella?'

'He had a few, I'll admit.' Cary repeated Del's comment about those pillow fights in knickers. Rosie found that hilarious. 'But Siobhan never gave so much as an inkling that she had any of those kinda feelings for me.'

'Maybe that was because you never fessed up yourself, yeh think?'

Now they were standing in the lane in front of Cary's mother's house, looking back on the village below, both in a reflective mood.

'We're complicated creatures, yeh know, *Homo sapiens*?' said Cary. 'Don't know what we want–or who we want–or how the hell to get it when we do.'

'Well, if you want this *Homo sapiens*, Car, I'd say you got 'er.'

'So it's true, eh, just like the poem says: you 'built a bower in your breast'–for me.'

Rosie threw him a threatening look. 'Hey, lad, remember I'm trained in Taekwondo–one well-placed kick and you could be outta commission for a long time.'

They both laughed, then embraced, then had to stand apart for a moment as a big yellow manure spreader came rumbling down the hill. They watched it–and smelled it–as it passed. Rosie recognised the driver and gave him a wave.

'Well, ain't that romantic, eh?' observed Rosie sardonically.

Cary nodded. 'True Irish romance is what that is, kissin', huggin', and spreadin' clap.' He paused for a moment, thinking about what he'd just said. 'Gee, maybe I should write a poem about love and manure.'

Rosie chuckled. 'William Butler Yeats and James Joyce got nothin' on you, mate.'

They kissed once more. Just then a late model Volvo came up the hill and drew to a halt beside them. The driver lowered his window. He was a tall, strapping blonde fellow who didn't look familiar. But then the passenger door opened and a young woman stepped out.

'Siobhan? Oh my God,' said Cary. She came right up to him and gave him a hug. 'What the heck you doin' in Glenkerry–in Ireland, for that matter?'

'Well, I wanted to surprise you. And by the looks of it...' Her eye shifted from Cary to Rosie, then back. 'By the looks of it, I succeeded.'

Cary blushed. 'You remember Rosie? Rosie O'Malley?'

'Yeah, a course. Hi Rosie. This is Anders, from Stockholm.'

The young man turned off the engine and stepped out of the car, shaking hands first with Cary, then with Rosie.

'We work together at Greater London Software Systems,' explained Siobhan.

'Shiv's told me all about Glenkerry,' said Anders. 'And you lot. It's good to meet you at last.' He gestured toward the town centre. 'This place, the way Shiv talks about it, is like–legend.'

Cary urged them to pull the car into his mother's drive and visit for a while, which they did.

'So Rosie, I hear you and your mother have reconnected,' said Siobhan as they settled in the sitting room.

Rosie smiled. 'Yep. Thanks a good bit to this fella,' she added, looking appreciatively at Cary.

Then Cary spoke up. 'And as you've already heard, the *Glenkerry Gazette* is back in business. Or it will be soon. And Rosie's gonna be our staff artist and photographer.'

When Catherine returned from her errands, she was beside herself at the sight of Siobhan and wanted to know all about London, her life, her work, etc. As Cary showed Anders around the gardens, Catherine and Rosie fixed tea. Catherine took the opportunity to quiz Siobhan further.

'Fine lookin' young man, that one. So, you been seein' each other long?'

'Oh, no, Anders and me, we're just friends.' Catherine nodded. 'And co-workers.' Catherine nodded again. 'And flatmates.'

At that Catherine rolled her eyes. 'It's all *mate* this, *mate* that. Too many mates, not enough mating, that's what I say.'

The three women laughed together, although Rosie thought Catherine tossed a special glance her way, one that said, 'but once in a while, miracles do happen.'

Tea and biscuits were served in the garden.

Finally, Siobhan and Anders departed, off to Dublin to visit with some of Siobhan's friends from university.

'Oh, I am chuffed to see Siobhan again,' said Catherine as they watched the Volvo pull out of the drive.

'Such a sweet colleen, is that it, Ma?' asked Cary with a wry smile.

She nodded.

'Yeah, well, I got me a pretty sweet gal now, Ma, and she's a *proper* colleen–born and bred right here in Glenkerry.'

'She is that, Car, she is that.' Then Catherine hugged Rosie till the lass thought she would burst.

'Well, I'll leave you two alone,' Catherine added, and went into the house balancing a tray full of empty cups, saucers, and leftover sweets.

Cary and Rosie walked out to the lane. 'I suppose I better get to work, then, Rose.'

'Yeah, you better get crackin' if yeh're gonna start sellin' papers.'

'But I'll see you later, maybe?'

'Yes, Ciaran McGurk, you will see me later, you will indeed.'

Cary watched as Rosie walked up the lane toward her house. Then he turned and his eyes scanned the cluster of stone buildings in the village below and the patchwork of green pastures beyond. Glenkerry, this place where he was born and raised, it would remain peaceful and unspoiled. And he would continue to be a part of it, though his life, it seemed, had changed forever.

AN DEIREADH

GLOSSARY

An Dílis –The faithful

Bairn – Child

Beaker – Nose, or a cup

Bewley's – A popular Irish tea

Boke – Vomit

Bollocks – Testicles, or an expression of contempt or annoyance

Boot – The trunk or storage area of a car

Brolly – Umbrella

Bus Éireann – The state-owned bus and coach operator in Ireland

Camogie – A women's team sport with stick and ball played in Ireland

Champ – Popular dish of mashed potatoes and scallions

Champers – A slang expression for Champagne

Chissler – Child

Chipper – Fish and chips shop

Colleen – A girl or young woman

Creche – A nursery for young children

Coláiste – College, secondary school

Comhairleoir – Councillor

Craic – Good times, friendly social activity

Demesne – Land associated with a manor or other large estate

Doss – Sleep rough, bed down, crash

Eejit – Idiot

Flex – An electrical cord

Footpath – Sidewalk

GAA – Gaelic Athletic Association, a sporting association in Ireland that supports Gaelic games

Gaeilge – Gaelic, Irish

Garda (pl. gardaí) – The Irish police, also the title of an Irish police officer

Garda Síochána, An – The national police service of the Republic of

Ireland
Heart of corn – Good-hearted
In donkey's years – A very long time
Jumper – A sweater
Kit – A uniform, outfit, gear
Knackered – Tired, exhausted
Knickers – Women's underpants
Leaving Certificate – The final exam in the Irish secondary school
    system
Loo – Toilet
Lorry – Truck
Lough – Lake
Murder (a pint) – Eat or drink with gusto
Machnaimh – Reflections
Pew – A bench
Press-gang – Forcibly enlist in service
Quid – Old term for a pound (currency)
Scuttered – Drunk
Shandy – A drink made of beer mixed with fruit juice
Shemozzle – Argument
Sláinte – To your health
Slán agat – Goodbye, said by the departing person
Slán leat – Goodbye, said by the person staying
Spanner – Jerk; hindrance
Stirk – A yearling bull or heifer
Tarmac – Asphalt, macadam (a trade name)
Tick yes – Agree, say yes
Torch – Flashlight
Townland – A small geographical division within an Irish town
Trainers – Running shoes, sneakers
Uilleann pipes – An Irish bagpipe
Up the spout – Pregnant
Whitsunday – A religious holiday, the seventh week after Easter

ACKNOWLEDGEMENTS

In June 2022 I visited County Wicklow, spending time in Bray, Enniskerry, and Wicklow Town. I hiked a magnificent section of the Wicklow Way, waded in the cool waters of the Glencree River, toured the lush gardens of Killruddery House, and trod the hallowed grounds of St. Kevin's Monastic City at Glendalough. I was favoured at every turn by the smiles, the laughter, the friendliness of Wicklow's people. I hope that experience along with a good deal of reading and research have made my book an accurate reflection of Wicklow and Wicklovians.

American readers will have no trouble imagining the Glenkerry Mall proposal. It is a scenario that has played out again and again all over the United States since World War II. Who can say how many acres, how many square miles, of rich farmland have been converted to vast shopping centres and endless parking lots, often leaving once vibrant town centres little more than ghost towns? Many Irish towns and counties, including County Wicklow, have had the good sense to restrict such 'out-of-town shopping centres,' striving to preserve the rural character of those communities by limiting large-scale commercial developments to major urban areas. Thankfully, projects such as the 'Monster Mall' described in this book are not likely to gain approval in Ireland today.

The major plotlines and characters of *Rose of Glenkerry* are products of my imagination, with one exception. In Chapter 4 when Cary and his mother visit the cemetery in Glenkerry, Catherine tells her son about one of his ancestors, Hannah McGurk, who emigrated to America in 1849. Hannah McGurk was a real person, and her transatlantic voyage with four children while her husband was in a Tasmanian prison comes right out of my own family history–Hannah McGurk was my great-great-grandmother. So when Cary muses that he might have a distant cousin in America, that distant cousin could be me.

As always, I am indebted to my wife, Susan D. Milsom, for her careful reading, editing, and comments on early versions of the book.

Credits

Page 60. Glendalough, from Milburg F. and Blanche McM. Mansfield, *Romantic Ireland Vol. 1*. Boston: Page and Co., 1905. Illustrator Blanche McM. Mansfield.

Page 108. Dublin, from Thomas Walford, *The Scientific Tourist Through Ireland*. London: John Booth, 1818.

Page 156. Cork City, from Mansfield and Mansfield, *Vol. 2*.

Page 186. Fitzwilliam Square, Wicklow. Wrench Postcards, Ltd., ca. 1905.

Page 194. Claddagh, Galway, from Mansfield and Mansfield, *Vol. 2*.

Page 206. The Wicklow Mountains, from Elisée Reclus, *The Earth and Its Inhabitants*, Vol. IV. New York: D. Appleton and Co., 1881.

Page 214. Vale of Avoca, from Mansfield and Mansfield, *Vol. 1*.

Page 232. The Bridge, Shillelagh. Wrench Postcards, Ltd., ca. 1905.

Page 254. The Black Castle, from Robert O. Newenham, *Picturesque Views of the Antiquities of Ireland Vol. 1*. London: Thomas and William Boone, 1830.

Page 262. Bray Postcard, Detroit Publishing Company, 1905.

ABOUT THE AUTHOR

Robert T. McMaster grew up in Southbridge, Massachusetts. He holds a B.A. from Clark University and graduate degrees from Boston College, Smith College, and the University of Massachusetts. He taught biology at Holyoke Community College in Massachusetts from 1994 to 2014. His parents' reminiscences of growing up in early 20th century America were the inspiration for four novels, *Trolley Days* (2012), *The Dyeing Room* (2014), *Noah's Raven* (2017), and *Darkest Before Dawn* (2022). He is also author of a biography, *All the Light Here Comes from Above: The Life and Legacy of Edward Hitchcock* (2021). He has at least two ancestral ties to Ireland: John and Katharine McMasters emigrated to America from County Antrim in about 1713; Hannah McGurk and her children lived in County Tyrone before making their journey to America in 1849.

COMING SOON

Book 2 of

The County Wicklow Mystery Series

by Robert T. McMaster

With its tidy villages and green pastures dotted with grazing sheep, County Wicklow might seem an unlikely setting for mystery and intrigue. But when the timeless beauty and tranquillity of the 'Garden of Ireland' are shattered by a suspicious death, Cary McGurk, Rosie O'Malley, and their Glenkerry friends find themselves embroiled in another spell-binding adventure. Watch for Book 2 of the County Wicklow Mystery Series, the exciting sequel to *Rose of Glenkerry*.

Anticipated Release Date: Fall, 2023

For additional information please visit

www.WicklowMysteries.com

THE TROLLEY DAYS BOOK SERIES
Novels of early 20th century America

by Robert T. McMaster

The nineteen-teens was a tumultuous era in American history. The pace of social change was dizzying: the rising tide of worker unrest, the battle for women's suffrage, the scourge of discrimination against minorities. New technologies–electricity, the telephone, the automobile–were transforming life. Meanwhile the war in Europe was drawing America inexorably into its vortex.

Author Robert T. McMaster transports his readers back in time to early 20th century America in the Trolley Days Series of historical novels. Set in a bustling New England industrial city, these books follow the lives of teenagers Jack Bernard and Tom Wellington through good times and bad, hope and despair, love and loss. Readers young and old will be captivated by the world of their grandparents and great-grandparents, an era seemingly remote that nonetheless speaks to us across the generations.

Trolley Days, *The Dyeing Room*, *Noah's Raven*, and *Darkest Before Dawn* are currently available in paperback and in several eBook formats. For additional information please visit

www.TrolleyDays.net

ALL THE LIGHT HERE
COMES FROM ABOVE:
The Life and Legacy of
Edward Hitchcock

by Robert T. McMaster

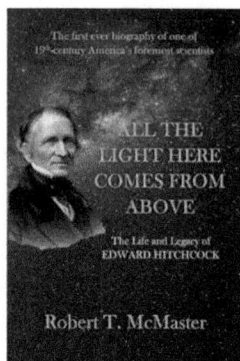

EDWARD HITCHCOCK (1793-1864) was one of nineteenth-century America's foremost scientists. Best known for his pioneering research on the fossilized tracks of dinosaurs, he was also a geologist of international reputation, one of the first American scientists to embrace the theory of continental glaciation. A professor at Amherst College for nearly four decades, he took over the presidency in 1845 and saved that venerable institution from dissolution.

In *All the Light Here Comes from Above: The Life and Legacy of Edward Hitchcock*, Massachusetts author Robert T. McMaster brings Edward Hitchcock to life, revealing the humanity of the man with dignity, charm, and humour. Relying largely on Hitchcock's own words from his letters, notes, and other unpublished manuscripts, McMaster presents an intimate view of Edward Hitchcock, his scientific achievements, his theological writings, as well as his battles with powerful personal demons that threatened him at every turn.

For additional information please visit

www.EdwardHitchcock.com

Lightning Source UK Ltd.
Milton Keynes UK
UKHW050810100223
416610UK00019B/1795

9 781087 966793